Visible Ripples

Visible Ripples

M.E. Strautmanis

PURPLE PORCUPINE
PUBLISHING

Purple Porcupine Publishing
P.O. Box 555, Stewiacke, NS B0N 2J0
Purpleporcupine.ca

Editor: Penelope Jackson

Library and Archives Canada Cataloguing in Publication

Title: Visible ripples / M.E. Strautmanis.
Names: Strautmanis, M. E., author.
Description: Series statement: Reverse ripples ; 2
Identifiers: Canadiana (print) 20250170272 | Canadiana (ebook) 20250173964 | ISBN 9781738899593
  (softcover) | ISBN 9781069392107 (EPUB)
Subjects: LCGFT: Novels.
Classification: LCC PS8637.T735 V57 2025 | DDC C813/.6—dc23

For KH.
Thank you for listening to my stories and sharing my dreams.

TABLE OF CONTENTS

Prologue

I looked down at our fingers entwined. His skin so dark and my fingers so pale in comparison, despite my tan from the past week, spent in the sun. I stared at them, willing the slight blue tinge on my fingertips to vanish. The harder I stared, the more I could see the blue light almost vibrate in waves from my fingernails. I felt dizzy.

Not now, not here, I said to myself, feeling the tightening in my stomach and the pounding inside my head signal what was going to happen with me. I could not prevent it, I could not avoid it, and I sometimes had no warning that something was about to happen. I had spent the last eighteen months coming to terms with this anomaly, but I was still not used to having this…let's call it my ability. Maybe I never would be.

I looked up and Jarad smiled at me, innocent, unknowing, and unaware of the chaos I felt at this perfect moment on the beach. I smiled back, liar, actor, deceiver that I am, and gently separated my fingers from his.

I made my way across the sand to the bride and groom, my two dearest friends, and mouthed that I would catch up with them at the reception. As maid of honour I could legitimately invent the need to check the venue and coordinate with the caterers. They hugged me, grateful for all the wedding preparations I had put in place, and then went back to their champagne toasts and their families' rapt attention.

I made my way up the sandy beach to the jeep. I looked over my shoulder and saw my father staring at me. His intense green eyes were like those of a predator, laser sharp on my retreating back. His eyes met mine. His face held a question, and I smiled at him reassuringly and gave a little wave. He continued to stare into my eyes and he could see that something was amiss, despite my smile of reassurance. He'd been my father for twenty-seven years and my dad for barely over a year. It was still a surprise to me that I had two parents, two parents who were a couple. Two parents who had bridged the gap of time and years and come together again.

The pounding in my head intensified. I made my way carefully to the jeep. I felt as if I would stumble on the flat ground if I wasn't careful. It was like playing "the floor is lava," as I felt unbalanced, but not on purpose. The door handle felt cool to my touch, despite the fact that the jeep had been parked at the beach all afternoon. I turned the ignition key and blasted the air conditioning. As I slowly backed out and turned to exit the sandy parking area, I felt a tremor shake me. My body was suddenly freezing and I turned off the AC. I pushed the button to roll down the front windows, but the coldness didn't leave me.

I hadn't felt this cold since I was in New York and a freak storm blanketed the city a year before in November. I had slogged home that day through sidewalks covered in slush with blowing snow buffeting me, in sneakers and a blazer, thawing out only after a long hot shower, a hot water bottle on my feet, and two bowls of hot-and-sour soup.

Now I was in the 85 degree Caribbean heat and my body was shivering and my teeth were chattering despite the warm air wafting in the windows. My fingers gripped the steering wheel and I could see the telltale blue glow that signifies death to me. But whose death? *Please not now*, I silently prayed to myself. Everyone I cared about in the entire world was alive and well on that beach. *Why here? Why now? Who? Who has died?*

I drove with no idea where I was going. The reception venue, the Upstairs at Papayas Restaurant, was all set. The wedding planner had done a perfect job. Everything was coordinated, confirmed, finalized, and ready for the reception for the intimate wedding party of twenty people.

What was I doing? Running? Running away from myself? I *have finally come to terms with what I am. What I can do. I've accepted the time ripples that hide inside me. Now what?* My fingertips tingled with the bluish glow. I gripped the wheel praying the threatening headache wouldn't manifest and I drove on autopilot around the tiny island that can be entirely circumnavigated in thirty minutes.

Images blurred as the miles whizzed past. Ever mindful of the wild horses that have lived on the small island since the time of the conquistadors, I slowed at blind turns and on the hills, but I was driving on mental autopilot while I replayed what I saw during the wedding. Images of the wolf dog, the two young people in tunics, melded into images of my friends. Shadows or mirages? Was I suffering from heat exhaustion? My dear friends, my longtime best friend and my dearest new New York friend. The image before my eyes, blurry, ethereal, but real. I saw what I saw. Down to the tiniest detail on the hem of her tunic. Embroidered lotus flowers in an elaborate swirling design. Can the mind make up such details? Was it a hallucination? I was questioning myself the same way I did when the time ripples first started. All these months later, I knew I was not crazy, yet I felt crazy for what I'd seen on the beach.

There had been so much going on with me in the past year, ever since my fall into the bioluminescent bay, that nothing surprised me anymore. Still, I was mystified. What had I seen? Did I see the two people? Did I see that dog? Everything looked so real. I could see the dog's fur quivering when he walked. His silver eyes flashed like sparks.

There were no answers, and the longer I drove the more certain I was that there was a very specific reason I'd seen what I saw.

Chapter 1

After the Wedding

My father approached me the minute I arrived late to my best friend's wedding reception. I was the last to arrive, and the party was in full swing. A steel-drum trio was playing a mix of calypso and reggae and everyone was up on the small circular dance floor.

"Pia." He leaned close to my ear. "Are you all right? What's going on with you?"

Good question. What is *going on with me?* The drive helped calm my nerves, my fingers were back to their regular colour, I had stopped shivering, but in the far recesses of my mind lurked dread. I could feel its tentacles take hold and squeeze tight. I was very adept at compartmentalizing the feeling. I had learned that trick over the last year, but the weight of it still pressed on me.

I dreaded finding out who had died, or who was about to die.

"I don't know," I answered honestly. "I felt unwell, probably heat stroke and nerves, and needed to clear my head." I hoped that would appease his curiosity and I could make myself get into the party spirit. My two best friends were now married. This was a celebration, not a time for me to become self-absorbed about something that may or may not happen. I added, "It's been so busy, I've barely sat down." I forced a laugh, but even to my ears, it sounded fake.

He stepped back from me, cupped his hands on either side of my face, ensuring he had my full attention, and whispered, "I saw that dog." He dropped his hands, but remained staring at me to gauge my reaction.

"What?" I was stalling.

"You heard me," he said matter-of-factly. "What was it doing there?"

He saw the wolf dog. The huge animal standing watch over the wedding and then waiting as two people who do not exist made their way with him into…into what? An invisible realm? The past? The future? Insane. That's what this whole conversation is.

If he saw the dog, then maybe the dog was real. But it couldn't have been real, the logical side of my brain screamed, *because it vanished, literally into thin air. Did he see my two friends meld into the two tunic-clothed teenagers, or vice versa?*

"I wish I knew." Another honest reply. I was too mentally exhausted to lie. He saw the dog. I saw the dog. The dog did not exist. Now what?

At that moment Sam rushed up and hugged me. Her dress swirled around her. Her beautiful long hair was loose and blowing in the breeze. She had never looked so beautiful or happy.

"It's perfect. Everything is perfect. Thank you for everything, Pia." Her enthusiasm and excitement were contagious.

It was perfect, there was no other way to describe the wedding week. Even the weather had been phenomenal. It's always iffy during hurricane season, but the good weather prevailed, just as Sam predicted. *So what if there was a real or unreal dog and vision on the beach? My real friends are celebrating their union and I need to get my head in the game.*

I hugged her back and said, "I want to dance with your husband tonight."

"Oh my god, my husband! I have a husband. Yes, dance with Kash. Dance with my husband Kash. Pia, you made all of this possible." She opened her arms wide and did a 360 degree spin. Her dress whooshed and flared and she could not have looked more exotic and stunning.

I knew she didn't mean the party. She meant them meeting and falling in love. I didn't set out to matchmake, it just seemed to happen on its own. Destiny, I often thought when I pictured the two of them. There had been something very old about their new relationship from the very beginning. Almost as if they were just waiting for the right time in their lives to meet. Perhaps none of it was by chance. Maybe everything was predestined. *Me cutting my skin on lava rocks and then falling into the bio bay. Why did I even fall? You'd think all those years of parkour would've given me better balance. Oh, my aching head.*

Kash came over, took my hand, bent down and kissed his new wife on the forehead, and led me to the centre of the small dance floor. We danced to a saucy salsa number, which cleared my head, made me feel alive, and had us both sweating and laughing. When the song ended, everyone clapped. Kash said he was Puerto Rican after all, of course he could move his hips like that. I took a bow and said that I learned my moves from watching *Dirty Dancing* a thousand times and Sam piped in that it was true. The entire wedding party flocked to the dance floor for another spicy salsa number.

I sipped from a bottle of water and did my best to shake the feeling of dread from me, and it almost worked.

The island was empty of tourists, and many places had closed for a month before tourist season ramped up again. We were lucky, or I should say Desiree was lucky, to connect with the owners of Papayas and to be able to book it, catered and staffed, for the wedding. Date palms formed a wind barrier around the open patio area, and the pendant lights made from thatched palm leaves cast shadows that rivalled a disco ball. It was a magical place at night.

Desiree had hung fairy lights around the perimeter and used tulle ruched on table edges. Simplicity was not only cost effective but stunning as well.

I watched as my parents, together again, danced the night away. I felt a pang for the fact that Robert should have been with me, and then I cursed him for invading my mind at this perfect time.

Sam and her dad started their father-daughter dance, at which point my father looked over at me and nodded at the dance floor, hopeful. I shook my head and pointed to the bride as if I didn't want to crash her number. I wasn't sure why I wouldn't dance with my father. Pigheadedness, my mother said afterward, and I agreed. I defended the action, saying it was for the bride and her father, not for us.

Jarad and I danced a couple of numbers, and it was pleasant, but my body didn't react to him in any way other than comfortable friendship. He was so sweet and considerate, and a part of me acknowledged that I needed a take-charge kind of guy. I pictured the Marlboro Man on his horse, riding in to whisk me away to have his way with me. That thought was forbidden in this Me Too era, but nonetheless, it was kinda what did it for me. I was mostly honest with myself about loving the hint of danger and intrigue. Sam had spent countless hours psychoanalyzing my old habit of one-night stands and waffled between my abandonment issues and the fact that I was a bit of an adrenaline junkie. We always ended up laughing, with her adding sagely *be careful* to every session. I was careful. I was always careful with my body. Unfortunately, I wasn't careful enough with my heart.

The rest of the evening was much the same, eating, drinking and dancing, and I finally fell into bed at four a.m., so exhausted that even the crowing roosters couldn't disturb my sleep.

The next morning, over my third cup of coffee, my father texted. I held the phone angled away from the morning sun's glare to be able to read it.

Keep tonight open. Not a question.

Okay, I thought. *Tonight is wide open.* The wedding was over and I had no concrete plans for the rest of the week. Jarad and I talked about taking the ferry over to Culebra before the week was over, but other than that, I planned on swimming and some snorkelling at Orchid Beach. If I was lucky, the leatherback turtles might even swim around me.

My fingers tingled. I held them up in front of my face—no blue tinge, but I could feel it building inside me, invisible pinpoints of electricity. My stomach felt heavy as I contemplated death lingering in my life now, on this very happy week. Death was my day job, but now it had become my constant invisible companion, waiting in the wings to make an entrance.

I went for a run to clear my head. I worked up a good sweat, picked up the *San Juan Star*—the only English newspaper on the island—and walked back to the house, dread still holding me hostage.

Chapter 2

The Decision

I unwrapped a packet of green tea and poured the contents into a tea ball. I knew I had been drinking too much coffee, and somewhere in the recesses of my mind, there was a memory of green tea once helping me with a hangover. Was I hung over? I felt like I was walking through a fugue, so I must be. The water boiled and my phone chirped a text again.

"Jeez, Juris," I said, rolling my eyes. I was still not comfortable calling my father *Dad*. "I said I would go with you."

But it wasn't Juris, it was Carlos, my grandmother's boyfriend. Companion. Partner. What do you call a couple in their seventies who aren't married? *Boyfriend* sounded too juvenile.

It's early for him to be calling or even awake, I thought as I picked up the phone and walked back outside with it.

Call me right away was the text.

"Good morning, Carlos, is everything okay with Nona?" I hoped that wasn't causing my feeling of impending doom. Not my beloved grandmother. I pictured her at the wedding dancing up a storm with the groom putting my moves to shame. *Please let her be all right*, I prayed.

"Si, yes, she is well. That is not why I reached out. It is a matter of some urgency. Can you meet me at Mosquito Pier?"

"Now? The pier? Sure, I guess. I'll grab a quick shower and head over." I started back towards the house.

"No time for that. Come right away." He disconnected.

I stood still for a second, pondering what could be so important that I couldn't spend a few minutes in the shower. Nothing, and I mean *nothing,* moved quickly on Vieques. It was like living in slow motion on the island, and you either accepted that or were frustrated the entire time you were there.

I traded tea for keys, grabbed my bag, and clipped my watch on my wrist, marvelling at the beautiful face of the gold Piaget my mother had gifted me, wondering for a second if my father, the original owner, had noticed me wearing it at the wedding. Then I went out to the jeep.

Mosquito Pier is a sight at any time of the day or night. This huge white concrete appendage juts out into the Atlantic side of Vieques. It is ideal for fishing off or snorkelling underneath. It is visible from the air, and in my mind signals that our island hopper plane is ready to descend to the small airport just north of the pier.

As I drove up the gravel causeway leading to the pier, which was perpendicular on the left at the far end, I could see flashing lights and too many vehicles for this time of the morning. My mind raced with too many possibilities. Did a fishing boat sink? Had someone fallen to their death? What was going on here? But mostly, *Why am I here?* I put the car in park, turned off the ignition, and reached for my purse on the passenger seat. As I reached over, I could see my fingers were tinged blue and glowing. Not just my fingertips anymore; the whole length of my fingers. I shook my head to clear my vision. It was faint, but it was there. Why? My heart was racing, and I swore as I realized I hadn't brought a bottle of water. I used my hand to wipe the sweat beading at my hairline and wished I had at least rinsed off in the shower.

I was jolted by Carlos opening my door. "Pia, thank you for coming. You will be acting in an official capacity," he said sharply as he guided me over to the pier. He was always dressed in linen pants and shirts, and although it was a fabric that wrinkled, he always looked freshly pressed and very dapper.

"Official capacity? I have no credentials here. What are you talking about? What happened?" I was looking around, scanning past the cars and vehicles as we headed up onto the large structure, which looked like a group of outdoor kiosks. There was a makeshift tent erected to one side and he led me there.

"You know there is no doctor on the island?" he said as we walked.

"Carlos, you know I'm a pathologist. Is someone hurt?" Still walking, almost to the tent now.

"Yes, but they are too late for medical attention. Pia, a small plane crashed sometime in the night or the early morning."

My first thoughts were of Sam and Kash. They were flying over to Culebra for their honeymoon. *Oh no!* My mind screamed and my fingers tingled. *Not my best friends in the world. Please no! Don't let it be them!*

"This is very unusual, Pia. There hasn't been a small-plane crash since 1984."

"What happened then?" I asked him.

"A small aircraft took off from here, heading to St. Croix. It came down right after takeoff. Very sad. It was deemed to be pilot error. I knew the pilot, and it was very surprising to me."

"Wow. So was he killed?"

"Yes, he and his passengers died. It was a tragedy, for sure. He was an excellent pilot. Very troubling for the rest of us. I had flown with him many times. He was very exacting and no amateur."

Carlos had recently retired from flying. He sounded like he missed it, the excitement, the adventure. He said he was happy in retirement and stayed busy, but I watched him watching planes go by in the sky.

Carlos waited while a uniformed man finished speaking to two uniformed officers and then turned to us. They shook hands and Carlos introduced us. "Thank you for coming, Doctor," he said as he shook my hand as well. "If you would be so kind as to verify their deaths and sign some paperwork, we will arrange to transport them to San Juan." His English was perfect. I was relieved Carlos didn't have to interpret for me.

As the captain turned to lead us to the tent, I grabbed his arm. "Can you fill me in as to what happened?"

He seemed surprised by my almost desperate tone. "Oh, certainly. Around ten last evening, that small plane"—he pointed to his right, and I saw the small white plane on its side, bobbing in the waves—"went down on its way over to Ceiba. A five-minute flight. Somehow no one knew until a fisherman saw the plane this morning."

"No one knew? Didn't he file a flight plan?" *Assuming it's a he.* Sam and Kash were not flying to Ceiba. Relief flooded my body and my heart left my throat and resumed its position in my chest.

"No, not required for a personal plane. Pilot plus one passenger. The plane was towed, their bodies were retrieved and are inside." He led us to the white tent and pulled back the Velcro flaps.

He stepped in and I followed. Two bodies lay on blue tarps on the concrete ground. They were covered by white sheets that clung to their bodies. It was hot inside the tent and it smelled of death and seawater. The light, diffused by the white tent, was somewhat hazy; however, my eyes adjusted. I was looking at a bigger male and a smaller female form.

I knelt down on the tarp and pulled back the sheet.

The female had very long dark hair, now a tangled mess. Her skin was gray and mottled and she was bloated. Her eyes were closed and somewhat sunken. Her lashes were spiky and separated and looked cemented to her face. Her mouth was twisted in a grimace, as if she had eaten something distasteful. Definitely dead and more than likely drowned. That assertion would require further tests. But there was no blood, no apparent trauma. She might have been beautiful in life, but death is not a good look for anyone.

I stood up and moved over to the male. My hands were shaking and my fingers were tingling as if I had stuck them in an electrical socket. I reached for the sheet and stopped before I pulled it down.

I asked the constable, standing at the tent entrance, if he could find some agua for me. Carlos was behind him and volunteered to go. The captain left with them, telling Carlos there was a cooler in his vehicle. Their conversation grew dimmer as I became aware of a ringing in my ears and white dots were dancing in my peripheral vision as I pulled down the sheet.

Before I even looked, I knew it was Robert. Captain Robert. The pilot. For a brief, wonderful time, my pilot. My lover. My fantasy come true. The best relationship I had ever had. I knew and had loved every inch of him. He had deceived me and outright lied to me, led me on and then moved on. He had hurt me. And now he was lying dead in front of me. My heart raced, my breathing was unsteady, and my fingers were still tingling. I balled my hands into fists and watched as bluish waves almost danced from my hands. Taunting me.

I calmed my breathing and weighed my options.

I knew that right there and then, in this tent on this pier, I had the power in my tingling, pulsing fingers to reverse this final outcome and Robert could be alive. The ripples that had become part of me ached to reach this man. My fingers longed to touch the face I had held in my hands many times and kissed every inch of. I loved to run my fingers through his graying hair. Brush it back off his forehead. His strong shoulders, his tapered waist, and his…*Oh my god, what am I doing? Fantasizing over a dead man. Get a grip*, I told myself. *Be professional.* I could feel sweat running down my neck.

When we were together, it was as if we had always known that we were meant to be, that we'd waited for each other. We were so matched. It was—well, the best sex I had ever had. I'd had many encounters before him, and all of the others paled in comparison. Robert and I together were electric. Visceral, feral. Hungry for each other, grabbing, pulling, kissing, squeezing, stroking, pounding…and then he disappeared from my life. No explanation. Well, to be truthful, he tried to explain with vague answers and lies. I would rather know nothing.

And here he was. Very, very dead. I never wished him happiness after he vanished from my life, but I definitely did not wish him dead. Sam was the only one who knew the details of what had happened and helped me work out the feelings of abandonment Robert triggered. My father walked away before I was born, and then Robert, who said he loved me, walked away from our relationship. It was a difficult time for me, and Sam was my lifeline. She listened for hours, never judged, and I vented until I had nothing left to say. *I'll have something to say now. Wait till Sam hears about this.*

I pulled back the sheet to his waist. He was wearing a white or off-white Cubavera shirt, the kind he, Carlos, and many other men on the island favoured. Linen with embroidered plackets running down the front, lightweight, patch pockets and side vents. His face looked serene. Dead, but serene. He was gray and bloated and had a gash along the hairline on the left side of his head. The deep tear in his skin gaped and was about six inches long. The edges were ragged and for a second it reminded me of the stick-on scars I wore once with a zombie costume. I squelched the laughter bubbling up inside me. Completely inappropriate and unprofessional. I was frozen for what seemed like minutes, but must have been seconds. My whole body was tense, poised, waiting.

The air around us got heavy; I could almost hear a clock ticking inside my skull. *Do it, do it, do it* rang out inside me. *Touch him. Reverse this finality. Do it.* I was afraid to move. I was afraid to touch him. I was holding my breath.

I felt a black cloud descend over me as the realization truly sunk in that I could literally change this event. I could make this go away as if it never happened. I could lay my tingling blue hands on this man, my ex-lover, and he would not be lying here dead. *Do it,* my heart beat the cadence, *do it, do it. Just reach out and touch him. You know you want to.*

Seconds were ticking by as I contemplated this feeling of power in my hands, in my grip, in my touch, as all the hurt and uncertainty I had felt the previous year came rushing back into my mind.

How he stood me up at Thanksgiving, didn't respond to texts or answer calls, and fabricated excuses. I didn't ask for a lifetime commitment from the man, but I did ask that we not lie to each other. He had promised he would never hurt me. And he had done just that. *Do it, you know you want to. Save him. Save him. Make him yours again. Make this all disappear.*

My heart longed to feel the love we had shared—and then suddenly, a wall came up and my mind said *No, don't do this. Step away and do not touch him. Get up, Pia, and walk away, just like he walked away from you.* This cold, calculating part of me took over. *Damn him. Damn him for ruining a perfect long-distance relationship.*

I stood up.

I heard voices and Carlos came into the tent and handed me the bottle of water. It was ice cold and exactly what I needed. I downed the entire bottle and handed it back to him. His eyes widened in surprise.

"Are you all right, Pia?" He glanced down at the body and back up to me. "Is that…?" He gestured at Robert.

"Yes, Captain Robert," I whispered to Carlos. My voice was low, reverent. He nodded solemnly. The moment had passed. My hands no longer tingled. I felt the cloud lift and my body felt light and hydrated.

"Do you know this man?" the police chief asked me, handing me paperwork to sign.

"Yes, I do. This is Robert Rivera and that is his wife, Sofia."

Chapter 3

Feeling Guilty

Carlos followed me back to my grandmother's house, Casa Pia. It was named after me, Cassiopeia, her idea of a play on words. I waved goodbye to him and I went straight to the shower.

Feeling clean but on edge, I made myself a shake with fresh fruit and the cold green tea from earlier and walked down to the water's edge to process my morning and my churned-up emotions.

Robert. How I had loved that man, since I was a teenager who didn't even know what love was. How I had practically vibrated with excitement when we were near each other. How I had counted the minutes until lunchtime when I could text him, send him a funny meme or an emoji blowing a kiss. I had loved our long-distance relationship, me in New York and him based out of San Juan, Puerto Rico, flying to the east coast most weeks. Long distance suited my life at the time. He said it suited him too. As a pilot, he was often in New York and would surprise me. He had flown me to Boston to meet him and I had been twice to his home in Vieques. He had secrets, as we all do. But his secrets ruined us. Now I know why it suited him to have me two thousand miles away.

Last year I had started a new job, was busy learning and dealing with my newfound powers, and seeing him on weekends was my way to blow off steam or stress or angst. Back then I was missing my best friend, Sam, who had moved to Los Angeles, and was confronted at that time with my absentee father wanting back into my life.

What fun Robert and I had, in and out of bed. We took walks in Central Park, ran along the Hudson, and had breakfasts at Teacher's. Never an argument, never a moment of discord. Idyllic. But it ended abruptly and I never really understood why. Now his life was over. I wished I could call Sam, but she was on her honeymoon and this was not a honeymoon topic.

I walked over to the chaise longue, sat down, stretched out, and promptly fell asleep.

"Pia, Pia, wake up, are you okay?" I looked up into Jarad's aviator sunglasses. "You're baking out here."

Jarad, Sam's older brother and my current almost-relationship. We were close to becoming something, but we were both cautious and taking things slow. Neither of us wanted to be only a wedding hookup, despite the fact that something had been building between us over the past year. Jarad had been more of the pursuer. I was numb after Robert and I broke up. Disappointed, discouraged, more than a little hurt. I was numb to wanting to start anything or even to put myself out there. But Jarad persisted. He was funny, kind, and non-demanding.

I could feel the sun's heat had toasted me a bit, but I was already tanned from a week in Vieques and wasn't too concerned.

"What time is it?" I asked, sitting up and rubbing my eyes.

"Noon," he replied and moved to block the sun from my eyes. "Want to go down to Duff's for lunch? My brothers are already there."

He reached his hand out to me to pull me up and we went into the house. I grabbed my bag, glasses, and phone. No texts from anyone. I felt a tiny bit of guilt creep into my psyche. *Guilt? Over what?* And then the entire thing came flooding back to me. *Robert, dead. I didn't do anything when I absolutely could have saved him.* I staggered.

"Pia!" Jarad caught me and led me to the sofa. "You must have sunstroke." He quickly went to the bathroom, returning with a cold cloth. He held it out to me.

"Put this on your forehead for a few minutes." His concern should have warmed me, but it was annoying. *He's too nice.* I immediately banished the thought.

I lay down and did as directed, but knew I didn't have sun stroke. I had massive guilt over leaving Robert and his wife dead on the pier. I could have reversed that final outcome and I chose not to. I knew what I was doing when I opted to not touch him.

Why did I not do anything? Was I that petty? Jealous? Vengeful? Spiteful. Yes to all of those. I chose not to save this man who thwarted me. Dismissed me from his life. What kind of person was I? He didn't deserve to die because my ego got the best of me. Once more I wished I could unload on Sam, that she would listen and offer sage advice. I took a deep breath, pushed thoughts of guilt and Robert out of my mind, and went with Jarad to lunch.

Chapter 4

Plans with Juris

I spent the day with Jarad, so easygoing and so like Sam in his gestures and sense of fun. Fortunately he is taller than Sam's five feet, no inches.

It has been my experience that tall women—and I am six feet tall—intimidate men. Jarad is taller than me. Sam's three brothers are all tall. The mystery of genetics; their parents are on the short side. Sam constantly complains about her size and gets no argument from me. I have never wished to be shorter, and I have spent years listening to Sam envy my height and tell me she would do anything to be a few inches taller.

We both ate too much, drank way too much rum, jumped off the small pier in our clothes, whooping like little kids, took a long walk around Esperanza, and then went back to the house for more cocktails. In the heat, I was sweating out the alcohol, so refuelling didn't affect me as much as it would back in New York. But still, I knew I was numbing myself a bit. I needed a day like this to take my mind off what a terrible person I was.

I had a choice. Had I made the wrong one? Flashes of Claudia Baskin, barely a teen, whom I could not save, flashed in my overactive imagination. I had compartmentalized that episode and rarely thought about it. Now it came flooding back to me. Claudia, a bullied and troubled thirteen-year-old who decided taking her own life was better than living with the daily barrage of teenage social media tormentors and school bullies. The school and the board of education had been sued by her parents and the case was being settled out of court. Beyond sad, and more common than I'd realized.

I was blissfully, maybe naively, unaware of cyberbullying in my own schooldays. Currently the country is in crisis and social media plays a huge part in what is happening in classrooms and behind closed doors at home. I had volunteered for a conference on just that topic and was very much looking forward to it. Jarad was planning to meet me there in Binghamton, New York, next month. We would try a weekend together and see if this was something we wanted to pursue. Another long-distance relationship for me to navigate. Truth be told, I was scared to death of doing this again, but I was really looking forward to the conference. Life is just beginning for teenagers. Death is so final. No one should die because of social media.

With suicide and the plane crash on my mind and too much alcohol in my system, it was no wonder I had completely forgotten about my father and our plans for the evening. The day felt as if it had already been twenty-four hours long when he arrived.

I was sitting on the shaded porch drinking yet another rum and parcha, a delicious frozen concoction Jarad had whipped up. It had been the signature cocktail at Sam and Kash's wedding—a "Kashin Fruit," they had named it, because *parcha* is the Spanish word for "passion fruit juice."

I was feeling no pain as my father walked onto the porch and asked if I was ready to go. I caught a flash of annoyance on his face as he looked from me to Jarad.

Jarad stepped forward and shook my father's hand. "How are you, sir?" he asked. Ever polite.

"Fine, and you? And please, call me George."

George? I was surprised. I had thought of him as Juris my entire life. Even though I never knew him, I'd heard my mother talk about Juris thousands of times. Now he was George, the American translation.

"Pia? Are we still on?" He looked at me with what seemed like hope.

He stood there, so impossibly handsome, this stranger, this man, this father, dressed casually in dark green shorts and white polo shirt, his sunglasses in his hand. Having no idea what he had planned, I suggested Jarad join us. "Is that okay?"

He seemed uncomfortable, as if he didn't want to say no, but he didn't say yes either.

Jarad sensed his pause and jumped in. "No, hey, you two go. I'll meet up with the guys. They're going fishing with Trez." Trez, Kash's best man and best friend.

I threw Jarad a grateful smile and kissed him lightly on the cheek, whispering "Thank you" as he took his leave.

I turned to my father. "What the hell? That was incredibly rude of you. What could you possibly want to do that Jarad can't join us for? And where's Mom?"

He held up his hands. "Whoa, Pia, calm down."

"I'm calm. I don't understand what you and I have to do that he can't join us for."

"I want to go to the bio bay with you. I need to go there." His eyes looked worried. "Your mother is with Nona and Carlos. She'll meet us afterwards."

That revelation stopped me in my tracks. The bio bay. Where it all began for him, and for me. I hadn't told my father about what happened to me as a result of my time in the bay. He had no idea that what happened to him also happened to me. It changed my life.

He'd revealed what had happened to him to my mother, but she didn't fully understand what he told her. What he told me. I got it right away, because I was living it. Our shared magical ability to transport back to a time that has already passed. The reverse ripples, he called it. The ripples of time, backwards. Yes, I got it. I lived it. I felt powerful at times and other times I was shaken to my core. This power couldn't be real. And yet it very much was. He shared his secret with me, but I hadn't shared mine with him.

Again my mind went back to that morning on the pier, and I felt the waves of guilt wash over me. *Should I have done something? Robert is gone. I missed that chance.* Again, I started to beat myself up. Recriminations for not doing what my hands longed and ached to do.

I knew something was going to happen when I was at the wedding on the beach. I felt it then. I knew it was building inside me. Now all that was left inside me was the pent-up feeling of guilt that I did nothing. Should I confess to my father? What would he think of me? It certainly couldn't be worse than what I was thinking of myself. I felt like a total shit.

And now he wants some kind of bonding moment, father and daughter at the bio bay?

I cleared my throat and asked him to sit.

"Do you remember last year, I told you about the man I was seeing? The pilot?"

"Yes, of course I do. He didn't show up for Thanksgiving, right?"

"Yes, well, he didn't do a lot of things, but we ended up— well, he kind of ghosted me."

"Yes, your mother filled me in. I am so sorry he did that to you. It was awful of him, but I am not without guilt too, Pia, for what I did to you and your mother. If I could do it over again, I would never have left her. You. Both of you. I should have stayed."

He put his head in his hands.

I waited, knowing he was not done.

He looked up. "Is he here on the island? Are you okay? Are you seeing him again? He was from here, if I remember correctly." He stared intently at me. He crossed his long legs, and even in the fading light, I could see the deep tan of his ankles. He gave me my long legs. Long limbs. Blond hair. I physically resembled him so much it made me gasp whenever I saw him.

"No, god no. That was completely over last year, but his plane crashed last night. He's dead. I was at the scene this morning." I finished my drink, wishing I had another.

"Oh, Pia, I am so sorry to hear that. Your mother told me about the crush you had all those many years. And how much you enjoyed when he would visit New York. Wait, why were you there?" He sat up tall and leaned towards me, elbows on his knees and his long fingers clasped together.

"I was there in an official capacity. There is no doctor or medical examiner on this island. I signed the report, and the bodies are going to be transported to the big island."

He was quiet for a moment, and then asked, "The bodies?"

"His wife was with him."

"Oh, his wife." The words hung heavy in the still air. The coquis hadn't started up their nightly chatter and chirping.

I said nothing. I was thinking about Sofia. She worked for the airline. I had actually seen her before in San Juan airport. In fact, she had winked at me once and I couldn't figure out why. Now I know that she winked because her husband, the pilot, Robert, was late for his flight. Her husband. The man I had slept with the previous night. The thought still made me boil with anger. That lying prick.

I rolled my eyes, remembering how excited I was to see he was flying my plane to New York City after my blissful summer in Vieques. I had fantasized about him for years, had reconnected for one night and began a torrid, three-month, long-distance relationship with what I know now was a married man, a liar, a cheater, and a heartbreaker. My rage bubbled up. *Liar, liar, liar!*

"How did you end up on the pier?" He reached forward and put one hand on my arm. On my watch. His watch. I jolted. I felt a zap of static from his hand and the hairs on my arm stood on end. I shivered. He felt it too and withdrew his hand, holding it up in front of his face, looking at it as if it was a foreign entity.

I pretended I didn't notice, and told him about Carlos calling me.

Neither of us spoke for what seemed like an eternity, then he quickly stood up and said brusquely, "You've had a long day. Pia, you look exhausted. Let's do this another night."

"When do you and Mom fly out?" I asked him as I stood up and rubbed the back of my neck. I could feel a headache coming on. I was glad to be let off the hook as I wasn't feeling up to being with anyone, let alone him and the bio bay. I was suddenly afraid of what might happen if I went there. Irrational, as what had already happened to me was unbelievable and impossible. *What else can happen that hasn't already?*

"We're here for another week, then New York for a week." He hugged me tight and then turned and started down the path. The coquis started to chirp loudly, and my head was killing me.

"Rest up, Pia. I'll call you tomorrow, okay?"

He was waiting for an answer, so I nodded.

"I want to go there while there is the least amount of moon."

I nodded. The bioluminescence is the brightest with no moon. I felt excitement at the thought of slipping into that cocoon of bioluminescent water. To feel it welcome me, energize me, remember me. *Yes*, I thought, *the bay wants me to come back.*

Chapter 5

The Reverse Ripples

No moon. When the sky is moonless with trillions of faraway stars, the bio bay shines its magic light underwater. The amazing microorganisms, called dinoflagellates, light up when agitated in their saltwater home. The mangroves all around the perimeter provide the perfect nutrition for the organisms. Especially the red mangroves. They give the food these organisms require to thrive. And thrive they do. The bay is the brightest it has ever been, measured by counting how many organisms there are in a gallon of water.

With any surface or underwater disturbance, the waters of the bay glow as if floodlights have been flipped on. It is magic, pure and simple. Bioluminescence is otherworldly, visually unbelievable, and as you feast your eyes, your brain cannot believe it's actually happening. It is the stuff of dreams, psychedelic trips, fantasies—and it's very much a reality.

I first experienced the bay as a teenager. When I took Sam last summer, what happened to me changed me, shaped me into a different person, although I didn't know exactly what it changed. I had no idea if this time-ripple ability inside me would be with me forever, or if somehow, someday, it would fade away and I would no longer be able to reverse time. No, that wasn't what I did. I altered time to make the dead not die. Not every time I was in contact with a dead body, which was mostly every day in my line of work, but sometimes. Randomly, with no warning, sometimes the ability telegraphed itself and I felt it coming.

I couldn't go back in time and fix heartbreak or get the winning lottery numbers. I couldn't prevent natural disasters or predict election results. I could simply interact with a deceased person. I never knew who would trigger this response in me. I could go weeks with no ripples, then experience three in one week.

If I had chosen a different profession, one where I was not face-to-face with death every day, would I be experiencing the reverse ripples?

My father manifested them just one time. One time that changed him forever. That time he should have died, and yet he did not. Obviously death had to be present, water had to be present, but what else? What made it happen? And why not every time?

I was confronted with death every single day at work and yet I didn't feel the ripple every day. But when I felt it, I acted on it, every time…until the time with Robert on the pier. It all came back to Robert. Was that a mistake? Was I going to obsess about it forever?

Working in a morgue, being around dead bodies all of the time, it would be beyond exhausting to see the ripples with every person I encountered. It happened once in a while, randomly. Sometimes I could manifest it at will, and other times, I could push the feeling away. If I thought about it too much, I felt like I was insane. Logically this could not be happening, and yet it was. Over and over and there were people out there that I didn't even know in real life, who were alive because of my intervening after they died. They had no idea they were in the morgue and then not. Crazy. It could not possibly be real.

Living with this ability to hold people's actual lives in my hands had become a monumental task of trying to stay sane, compartmentalizing the ability, talking it out with Kash and Sam to prove to myself that I was not, in fact, insane, and moving forward into each new day, secretly hoping it didn't happen and secretly hoping it did.

I had consciously suppressed this ability to ripple time while I knelt by Robert's lifeless body on the pier. Although I ached to touch him, I didn't put my hand anywhere near him, afraid that if my fingers were even inches from his skin, we would be transported to the previous day and his plane would not have crashed. Possibly he might not have even boarded the flight. But he had boarded his precious little Cessna with his beautiful wife, and their plane had gone down in the Caribbean Sea. And their lives were over.

I had saved people I didn't even know, and then chosen not to save the man I loved.

The burning question, besides the obvious "How is this possible?" was: *Why? Why me? Why my father? Are we the only ones? Thousands of people have visited this bio bay over the last forty-odd years. What makes us so special? Are we the only ones?*

It was a heavy secret to carry, more like a burden. If anyone other than Kash and Sam knew about it, my life would change, and not for the better. It had to remain our secret, and yet I found myself longing to tell my father.

After all, he confessed his secret to me. I understood at the time that his confession was also his justification for abandoning me and my mother. As much as I longed to talk about it, to try to get some clarity or a different perspective, so far, I had resisted the urge to confide our shared secret. Father and daughter, both able to transport back to a time before a death occurs. Randomly, and twenty-six years apart, this phenomenon took hold of both of us. And he'd seen the phantom dog. We were more alike than I'd ever realized, my father and I.

One more drink, a small Kashin Fruit, to anesthetize myself into a much-needed full night's sleep.

Chapter 6

Crash Talk

The next morning my phone chirped a text and I opened my eyes to a rainy, gray day. I was used to sunny Vieques. It doesn't usually rain in the morning. Rain makes an afternoon appearance, appearing swift and sudden around four. Fifteen minutes of powerful downpour, then fifteen minutes later everything is dry like the rain never happened.

We had fun last summer with Sam posting videos on social media during the deluges. Rainforest Showers were a viral hit. Sam's waist-length hair and bikini-clad body certainly helped. All in good fun, but she doesn't mention them anymore. Her hundred-thousand-plus subscribers might be missing her vids, but she jokes that was the extent of sowing her wild oats.

This morning as the rain beat against the shutters and palm fronds and the wind whistled, it sounded almost like a hurricane. *Could be*, I thought. Hurricane season is June through November. It was risky to plan a wedding during hurricane season, but it worked out well. A little rain hurts nothing, and the sound is pretty amazing.

I picked up the annoying device and saw a text from Sam. Weird that I had been just thinking about her. The bride, my beautiful best friend, was texting me while on her honeymoon.

I touched the screen and read, *Have you heard? Everyone is talking about the crash. That's your Robert, right?*

My Robert. What would Sam say if she knew I was called to the scene? I would not open that can of worms while she was honeymooning. Maybe not ever.

I answered *Yes*, inserting a sad-face emoji. *I heard. It's terrible. Now go back to your honeymoon.* I clicked the phone off.

I made a pot of coffee thinking that the power might go out at any minute and I had better brew it while I could. I pulled some fruit out of the fridge and started dicing it up. This weather lent itself to hanging out on the covered porch, playing Bananagrams or Cards against Humanity or doing a jigsaw puzzle. I fully expected the troops to arrive, and I wasn't disappointed. Mik and his wife came, along with Nona and my parents.

Trez walked in soaking wet, Juan right behind him.

"How was the fishing?" I asked.

"Not good," Trez answered, with a serious face. "Juan caught all the fish." He mock-punched his new friend, or love interest if I was reading things correctly. "He didn't leave any fish for us."

Juan laughed. "Mad skills, man. So sorry the city boy can't fish."

"Hey, I caught the dorado," Trez said proudly.

We all laughed as he showed his screensaver to everyone again. There was the famous fish that had garnered ten thousand likes on social media. It had truly been delicious. Then the video of us digging into that whole fish eclipsed the photo likes. Crazy what people want to see on social media.

Trez went into the bathroom and came out drying his hair with a beach towel. He threw it to Juan, who gently dried his face and dreadlocks.

They all accepted coffee and we went outside. The wind was still whipping and the leaves beat against the railings on the covered front porch. It was deafening.

"Did you hear about the crash?" Juan asked me, raising his voice to be heard over the din. Juan knew about my fling with Robert.

I avoided looking at him. "Yes, terrible. Really sad. Even Sam heard."

Trez said, "Does that crash have anything to do with the tip of the Bermuda Triangle being here?"

Juan and I answered at the same time. "No!" I said emphatically, while Juan replied, "Si, I bet it did!"

We all laughed, but I felt uneasy. *Did* it have anything to do with the mysteries around the Bermuda Triangle? I decided to ask Carlos when I saw him. He was researching the oddities surrounding the Triangle. After all, Robert was a seasoned pilot and the weather had been absolutely fine the evening the plane went down. Why had his plane crashed? He couldn't have been higher than two or three thousand feet. I forced myself to stop thinking about it.

Soon Jarad and his other brother arrived and mimosas were swapped out for the coffee.

Jarad was a good sport when I beat him at three games of Bananagrams, and then no one else would play me. I zipped the tiles into the banana-shaped pouch and turned to my grandmother.

"Where is Carlos?" I asked, hoping to bring up the Bermuda Triangle angle to him.

"He had a morning meeting. Something about his article." She accepted a mimosa from Juan and continued, "He will be here as soon as he can."

My parents, today in matching navy Bermuda shorts and white tanks, went inside, and my mother started making sandwiches and a fruit salad for a buffet brunch. The power in the house had flickered a couple times, but stayed on. The buffet would be gourmet all the way. My mother came to Vieques with a suitcase full of foods she couldn't buy on the island—truffle butter, watercress, sourdough bread, fresh cheeses, and herbs.

An only child who raised an only child, my mother could whip up a smorgasbord of food delights for a party of twelve in the blink of an eye. She says she loves giving her "inner Julia Child" a chance to create.

I went into the kitchen and asked if I could help. My skills were not as extensive as her creativity, but I would be happy to be relegated to chopping and mixing.

"We've got this," my father replied and popped a cornichon into his mouth. My mother swatted him with a dish towel. The perfect picture of domestic bliss, and I felt like I was in *The Twilight Zone*.

My mother raised me solo for twenty-six years, pining after my absentee father. Now here they were, together as if those lost years didn't even matter. And maybe they didn't. They couldn't get them back, so why mourn them?

My mother had forgiven his absence and allowed him back into her life. Our lives.

Would I be so forgiving? I'd been dismissed by a man I had a three-month relationship with, and with the chance to give him back his life, I'd chosen not to. I was a terrible person. What would my mother say if she knew? Why had I made that choice?

Snapping me out of my self-recriminations, my mother said, "Have you heard from Sam?"

Glad to have a neutral topic, I answered, "Yes, she texted about that plane crash. Robert was killed."

"Carlos told us. I am so sorry. How awful." She walked over to the counter stool I was sitting on, stood behind me, and put her arms around my shoulders. I could feel the warmth of her body, her heart beating. She sighed. "You never know when someone's time is up." I knew she was saying more in that one statement than it appeared. She just described, in a nutshell, her reasons for forgiving my father's absence and choosing to be with him now.

I do, I thought. I knew when someone's time was up. I knew at the wedding on the beach that something was happening to someone near me. I looked at my hands now, tanned and strong. No blue tint. Not shaking. The hands that could have saved Robert and did not.

The weather cleared and we all walked down to the beach to eat at the shore. It was a wonderful afternoon, and I was able to forget about the crash. Carlos arrived and regaled us with Bermuda Triangle myths and stories. A born storyteller. My grandmother was lucky to find love a second time.

I wanted to get him alone and ask him if he thought there was any real possibility that Robert's plane had gone down because of the Bermuda Triangle, but everyone stuck together. I would never have given credence to the fantastical Bermuda Triangle legends, but now, after bioluminescence had changed me, I had no choice but to believe anything was possible. Robert had been an excellent pilot. He had worked for a major airline for over a decade. What could possibly have caused the crash?

Other than me obsessing, the day was perfect, and when the sun went down my father cornered me and suggested we head to the bio bay.

"Juan said we can use his electric Seahawk inflatable." He seemed to think that using the inflatable boat rather than kayaking would make me acquiesce.

"Okay, sure, why not?" I said, summoning the energy to go change into a swimsuit, shorts, and a long-sleeved tee. The winds whipped on the bay at night, and I could already feel a chill in the October air. I hoped the morning's rain had not cooled off the water too much. I didn't know if we were going to swim, but I definitely didn't want to be on or in cold water. At the lowest it would be in the seventies, which wasn't really cold, but wasn't as warm as the eighty degrees it reached in the summer. I shuddered at the thought of being cold, and then scolded myself for being such a wimp. *I'm in the Caribbean, for god's sake, how cold can it be?*

Chapter 7

The Bioluminescent Bay

It was absolutely pitch dark on the bumpy road to the bioluminescent bay. I marvelled at my father's driving skills, then remembered he'd spent my entire lifetime in the wilds of Alaska; no wonder he drove competently over rough terrain. I could barely see the road as we navigated into the jungle for the five-mile trek, and it was an otherworldly feeling of bumping through the blackest of nights to the bay. The jeep handled great, but I still felt my bones rattle and my teeth bang together for the entire journey. Finally, we arrived with an abrupt stop at a clearing.

"Juan said the boat is tied to a tree on the left of the water with a green-and-yellow rope." He got out and went to the back of the jeep to get the life jackets I insisted we take along.

I got out and pitched forward in the dark, my feet not knowing where the ground began. I removed my flip-flops, grabbed the towel I had dropped, and straightened up. I headed over to my left, my arms out in front of me, groping.

I couldn't distinguish colours in the dark, but then suddenly remembered my phone's flashlight and tapped it on. There were half a dozen dinghies tied up and bobbing in a few inches of muddy silt at the water's edge. I felt my feet sink, squelching mud up between my toes. Not a completely unpleasant feeling or sound as the mud sucked my feet at every step. *Squelch, squelch, squelch.* There was a rotten smell of decayed vegetation here near the mangroves, and my stomach started to roil. I felt as though I might vomit at any moment, but as I looked up, I saw the bright yellow-and-green rope and swallowed hard.

"I found it," I yelled over to my father. The coquis were deafening now, *coqui coqui*, their chirping echoing around the mangroves and exacerbating my too-quickly beating heart, upset stomach, and sweating forehead. I used my towel to wipe off the sweat and wondered what in the hell was wrong with me. I used to get migraines and I prayed that this wasn't the beginning of one as I heard the jeep door close.

I untied the rope and pushed the small boat out until I was in water up to my thighs. I threw one leg over and then the other as my father tossed the two life jackets in. He pushed the boat out deeper and then jumped in.

He started the electric motor and we buckled into the life jackets. I could barely tell it was running over the night noises. We were purring slowly but steadily towards the middle of the bay. Fish skittered and flitted as the boat moved. Their glow mesmerized me even though I had seen it many times. It was magic. My magic. The magic that changed me.

I closed my eyes and pictured falling out of the kayak when I came with Sam. Falling into the bay had been the catalyst to everything magical, paranormal, unfathomable, that had happened to me since then. I wondered if I should tell my father. *No*, my inner voice said, *this is not the time. Sit back and enjoy the ride.*

I stared into the water, looking for…what? For answers, for something, but I did not know what. I felt a pull, a pressure to slide into that pitch-black water. Even the shapes of the fish, the jellyfish, and a huge manta ray under the water did not deter me from wanting to be one with them in the water. I dipped my hand into the water and felt its warmth. I lifted my fingers to my mouth and tasted its saltiness. I rubbed the saltwater all over my face and felt my skin tingle. I felt alive, vibrations racking my body. I felt the night sounds and the lapping water and the heaviness within me converge into an out-of-body sensation. I was floating almost on the surface of the very salty water and turned around to see if my father noticed.

I couldn't see my father at the back of the boat. The darkness was absolute. I put my hand in front of my face and could not see it. It felt so strange to be in this blanket of night floating above the boat somewhere between sky and water. There were no stars now as clouds covered the heavens, no moon, no ambient light. The local Historical Trust had done a fantastic job of eliminating all light sources around the bay. Growing up in New York City I never saw real darkness like this. Even as a child when I closed my bedroom blinds, street lights peeked in the sides. It was comforting. My night lights.

"Here we are," my father said too loudly.

I opened my eyes expecting to look down from above at the boat, but I was sitting normally. *Had* I floated? And if not, what was going on with my mind?

"Yes, here we are." My voice sounded foreign to me, as if it was coming from someone else. Did he not see or sense anything strange going on with me?

He hesitated and then began. "Pia, I told you about what happened to me all those years ago. I believe it was because of my swim in the bio bay. Something changed me. Something magic. I haven't been back since, and somehow I just wanted to see. All of these years away from this, from you, from your mother. My self-imposed exile. I wanted to see it, to touch it. I need to see it."

I felt the exact same way. The hypnotic pull of the bay called me. It was all I could do to refrain from sliding into the water.

"See what?" I asked, biting my tongue to keep from telling him that I'd experienced something similar.

"I don't know. See if it felt the same. See if the magic was still here. I thought I had gone crazy, kept telling myself that there was something wrong with me. But there wasn't. Something happened to change me, but I wasn't crazy."

The boat rocked slightly as the anchor dropped about fourteen feet and hit bottom. I grabbed the seat to steady myself. There was rustling at the back of the boat as he moved around.

"What are you doing?" I asked, but I knew. He was going in.

"You coming?" he asked as he slipped into the water. The rays of blue-and-white light shone all around him as he agitated the water. Fish dashed away as he treaded water.

I wanted to go in. I needed to go in. I was afraid if I went into the water, I wouldn't want to come out. It had such a hypnotic pull on me. I felt I could submerge myself in this magical bay and stay there forever. Nothing mattered but being in the water. Not the darkness, the large fish, the possibility that the water was cold, the cool breeze. Nothing mattered but being in the bay.

"Yes," I said as I toppled in. The splash I created sent underwater life shooting off in every direction. I laughed and ended up with a mouthful of very salty water. I sputtered and my father laughed with me.

Just as I remember it, I thought. I treaded water about six feet from him with the inflatable bobbing a few feet further away. We were buoyant because of the life jackets, although the high salinity of the water would have kept us afloat. We moved our arms at the same time and created enough bioluminescence to fill the space between us. The water was lit blue with bioluminescence and felt heavenly. I had heard from Maritza at the Trust that the level of dinoflagellates had more than recovered after Hurricane Maria devastated the red mangroves in 2017. The level of microorganisms was at an unprecedented high of three million per gallon of water.

"This is magic," I sighed, grateful he'd brought me. The night was even darker and the water ten times brighter than when Sam and I had gone with Juan.

"Pia, I am glad you came tonight. I felt so strongly about you coming with me, and I don't even know why. Your mother thinks we are having a bonding evening and I didn't tell her the difference. I am so glad to be here with you, but it isn't about bonding, it's more about sharing the experience with you. I don't even know what I was expecting to happen, but thank you."

I said nothing. His thanks had weight; he was thanking me for more than just coming out with him. Maybe for accepting his presence in my life. For allowing him back with no judgements or reservations. He was thanking me for sharing his need to feel the bay again after so many years. He had confided in me his deep secret about the bay, sensing that I would understand his need to be back.

I wished I could unload my secret, my fears, my nightmares, but I wasn't ready. Not now, not while treading water in the middle of the bay.

"How do you feel?" he asked me.

I felt so light I could fly away at any moment. "Amazing. Like I'm on fire from within." I felt as if my core was charged, lighting up the water without even moving or agitating it; the glow came from within me.

I looked down at the halo my body was creating in the water. The water glowed blue all around me. Could he see that? Could he tell I wasn't moving, yet the water was glowing?

"How do you feel?" I asked him.

"I feel renewed. Reborn. I have been waiting to feel this. It is brighter than I remember. And saltier. I just wish I had an injury to see if it healed up as fast as it did that first time I swam here. There is truly magic all around us. Can you feel it?"

I would have to be in a coma not to. I looked over at him, about five or six feet from me, with the blanket of darkness making it difficult to make out his features above the water.

However, I could clearly see the glow around his body and his arms and legs where they were moving the water.

"The bay is brighter now than ever before," I said into the night.

I couldn't wait to tell Sam how I floated, still, not moving in the water, and watched my own glow all around me, in me, be part of me. It undulated with the waves, moving but never leaving me. It was part of me, but also part of the mystery and magic of the bay. If I'd floated out of the water and levitated at that very moment, I would not have been surprised. But my body stayed anchored in the bay, bobbing in the small waves, warm and buoyant.

It felt amazing. Better than the last time, if that was even possible. *Magical. Transcendent. Ethereal.* All the words I had silently used over the last sixteen months to describe how I felt after being affected by the bioluminescent water came flooding back in a torrent. *Impossible. Abnormal. Unreal. Insane. Hallucinatory.*

Time passed. A minute. Thirty minutes. A decade. A lifetime. And we floated absorbed in our own thoughts, relishing the magical feeling.

"Ready to go? I am feeling a bit chilled." I heard him haul himself into the inflatable.

No! I want to float here forever, one with the water. I felt warm and cozy in my water world. No chills. Nothing but lightness, freedom, peace, tranquility, calmness, and oneness.

"Just another minute," I said. I could feel tears leave my eyes to mix with the very salty water. I became aware that I was crying. Tears of pure joy.

"Jesus, Pia!" he yelled loudly.

Immediately, I righted myself, "What, what is it? A shark?" I made for the boat and started to pull myself up and in.

"You are glowing blue! What did you do?"

I sat on the centre bench and looked at my body, which was indeed glowing, even out of the water. I held up my hands and was reminded of the movie *Cocoon*, where the extraterrestrial beings floated and were lit from within. I grabbed my towel and wrapped it around my shoulders, though I was far from cold. I was on fire and I wanted the feeling to never end.

He pulled up the anchor and started the engine, muttering, "Holy shit. I've never seen anything like that. Are you sure you feel okay?"

I felt great. Glowing and incandescent. The glow faded as we got to shore, but my whole body was still tingling and felt alive. Every inch of my skin was charged. I pictured lifting my arms and taking flight.

I could see the glow still between my fingers. Again, I thought of the conversation I would have with Sam.

"Are you sure you are okay? Your mother would never forgive me if anything happened to you. Nothing happened, right?" He sounded worried.

Something happened, but I didn't know what. I swallowed some water, I floated, I dreamed. Just a normal night for this New York City girl.

"Nothing happened, Juris. This was a perfect night." And it truly was. I felt reborn. More powerful than I had felt in my life. I felt as if I had been transformed for a reason, more than to randomly reverse deaths. Now I just had to find the reason, because if I didn't then I would continue to question: why me, why now, and how was this even possible?

"Don't mention that we went into the water, though. Swimming is frowned upon, especially by gringos." I laughed to lighten my cautionary words.

"Mum's the word," he replied. "I'm good at keeping secrets."

Chapter 8

The Dog

I tied up the dinghy and squelched back to the car. Juris had tossed in the life jackets and handed me a large beach towel to wrap up in. I rolled up my wet one and put it on the floor.

I looked over at him as he deftly executed a three-point turn. "Thanks," I said, my voice barely discernible as the coquis chirped like they were trying to own the night, "for tonight. For everything. For coming back." I meant it. I was thankful, especially for my mother's absolute happiness. An only child bears the entire parental burden, and I was happy that my mother now had someone special.

He nodded, his silhouette lit by the interior lights on the dash.

The ride back to the house didn't feel as bone jarring. Possibly I was still experiencing the very real feeling of floating. I was content to not converse, and as I pulled the thick towel tighter around me, I closed my eyes and pictured myself still immersed in the magical water.

"Pia." My father's loud voice broke the silence and my almost meditative trance. I resented the intrusion.

"Yes?" I replied, but didn't feel like concentrating on a conversation.

"About the dog," he began.

The dog, what dog? What is he talking about? I racked my fuzzy, still-floating brain. *Oh, THAT DOG. The dog at the wedding.* It felt like the wedding was light years ago, in another lifetime. I barely remembered yesterday, I was so tranquil and zoned out. In college I had experimented with shrooms that didn't make me feel this good. I didn't want this feeling to end and I sure as hell did not want to discuss the dog apparition.

"The dog?"

"You saw that dog at the wedding? That huge wolf hound. Didn't you?" He looked over at me briefly, but had to keep his eyes on the rutted road.

"Yes, I saw it."

"But it wasn't real. It was…" He struggled for the word. "An illusion, a ghost, right?"

"Yes. Well, maybe not a ghost." I do not see ghosts, or do I? I started to think about the people I had seen in the morgue who were dead and then not dead. No, they were not ghosts. They were people who experienced death and then did not actually die. My head began to ache.

We said nothing. My mind was racing because I'd felt the dog more than seen it. But it was very real to me at the moment. And he'd seen it also. Had anyone else?

He continued, refusing to stop talking about it. As if talking about it could answer the question. "Why? Why do you think we saw it? Why was it there on the beach with two teenagers I could see through?"

He seemed determined to get an answer from me. I had no answer.

The two teenagers melded into Sam and Kash as if they shared bodies with them. I had a sudden horrifying thought that maybe Sam and Kash were now possessed, but I pushed that thought away. Sam and Kash were exactly like they had always been. I just had to chalk it up to an inexplicable moment. Like all the other inexplicable things in my life.

"I honestly do not know. I wish I did." *Seeing something that wasn't there? Welcome to my world,* I thought. *He doesn't know the half of it.*

Thankfully he dropped it. Having a conversation about apparitions was not high on my list tonight or any night. I just wanted to feel again the way I did when I was submersed in the magical bio bay.

The rest of the ride passed in a blur. Despite wanting to close off remembering anything but what the water had felt like tonight, I could not stop thinking, overthinking, analyzing, and trying to process what I had seen on the beach the day of the wedding. Damn Juris for bringing it up. My mellow mood was gone. What had I even seen? Two teenagers who were not really there, the wolf dog, the feeling of having seen it all before, and the sense that I should know why I was seeing it all. All my emotions and feelings came to the surface and I cursed my father for breaking my peaceful trance. I breathed deep and tried to regain my calm.

Everyone was meeting back at my grandmother's house for a bonfire on our beach tonight, and their energy level would be high. I would have to fake levity and I resented that. The magic spell was gone.

Jarad jumped up at our arrival and walked over to me, wrapping his long arms around me.

"How was bio bay?" he asked, searching my face and looking over to include my father in his question.

"Perfect," we said in unison, then laughed. My father walked over and sat down with my mother. She took his hand and they whispered to each other, heads bent low.

"Do tell," Jarad continued. "We're all going tomorrow night with Trez and Juan." He meant his brothers and his two brothers' wives and him. His parents had left the day after the wedding to play golf on the big island.

My father and I regaled them with stories of the fish darting, the huge manta ray, the absolute darkness, and of course, the glow-in-the-dark bioluminescence of the water.

"I can't picture it, but I also can't wait to experience it," he said eagerly.

My father said, "Did you ever have one of those plastic glow sticks? The kind where you crack the glass vial in the middle of it and then shake it and it glows?"

"Of course," Jarad said eagerly, "every kid played with those."

His brother chimed in. "We would toss them in the backyard and our dog would bring them back to us. Well, he wasn't really our dog, just a neighbourhood stray. Always hanging around Sam. Harmless."

I could feel the hairs on the back of my neck stand up. I tried to meet my father's eye over the crowd, but he was listening to something my mother said.

"What kind of dog was it?" I asked Mik, Sam's oldest brother.

"I don't know. A mutt. Mangy. Shaggy. And huge, like a wolf. Silver eyes. Eerie. But he was harmless. I never heard him bark. Our mother would freak if she saw him in the yard. But we kids would sneak him food. Especially Sam. She loved that dog."

Strange she never told me about that dog, I thought. But then again, it was a stray. *A stray wolf-like dog, like the one I saw on the beach.* Interesting, and again, a puzzle with no solution.

"That's what the bio-bay experience is like," I said. "You jump into water filled with glow sticks that swim." Everyone laughed and voiced their excitement.

Jarad put his arm around me. "You okay?" he asked quietly, as if he sensed the undercurrent I felt rippling through me.

"Yes, I am," I answered him, and I meant it. If I didn't probe too deeply into other thoughts trespassing in my mind, the night at the bio bay had been perfect. There had been a lot of perfect moments on this destination-wedding vacation.

"Yes, you are." He squeezed my shoulder and I leaned in closer to him, feeling his solidness and warmth. *He's a good guy*, I told myself. *Maybe not exciting, but a good guy nonetheless.*

Chapter 9

Dreams

On the day of departure, Carlos and Nona drove me to the ferry. The rest of the group would be leaving on a later ferry. It's the best two dollars ever spent, to zip across the Caribbean Sea for forty-five minutes on a comfortable, high-speed boat. I've seen dolphins jump in the boat's wake. I hoped I would today. I would not think about the fact that we would be crossing where Robert's plane went down.

My grandmother gave me a tight hug and said goodbye through her tears. Carlos gave me a copy of the article he was working on. I thanked him and asked him to keep an eye on my grandmother. He hugged me tightly and reassured me that he would take care of Nona.

He stood for a moment with an arm around both of us and said that he was so lucky to have us, two amazing women, in his life. He kissed my forehead and gave my arm a squeeze.

The ferry terminal is in picturesque Isabella II, the tiny capital city of Vieques. It's the only city, really. No traffic lights, narrow streets, low, colourful, concrete buildings. People drive the wrong way up one-way streets and park haphazardly on either side. It is a very Spanish town dominated by a fortress on the hill that dates back to the time of the conquistadors, of exploration, exploitation, plantations, and exports picked by imported slaves.

Christopher Columbus landed on the main island in 1493. The name *Puerto Rico* ("rich port") comes from finding gold in the rivers. This is an old island that has seen many changes over the years.

The ferry takes you to the big island of Puerto Rico. The price is the same as when I came to visit my grandmother as a child. Children ride for free. The government subsidizes the ferry costs, and bad water and high waves often take the ferry out of commission for an indeterminate amount of time.

The ferry docks in Ceiba, once a large United States Navy base. It is then a one-hour taxi ride to San Juan International Airport. I was exhausted by the time I got into the publico and dozed off listening to Spanish talk radio, tuning out the too-rapid, excited voices blaring from tinny speakers.

My flight was on time, and I settled into an exit-row aisle seat with extra leg room, worth every penny. I managed to stay awake long enough to agree to assist in the case of an emergency and then promptly dropped off to sleep.

I woke to Robert standing in front of me. He was in his pilot's uniform for a rival airline, and although in a befuddled state, I still thought that was odd. He indicated I should follow him to the cockpit. I robotically got up from my seat and followed him. His wife was sitting in the co-pilot's seat and she looked furious. I wasn't sure if it was because I was there or if she had been mad at him before I got there. She opened her mouth to say something to him. Spitfire, rapid Spanish. I knew enough to make out my name and that she was indeed ripping him a new one. He put his hands up to get her to calm down and then said "Lo siento," I'm sorry, over and over. I watched them, looking first at her, then at him. How were they there? I knew they were dead. What was going on?

The wheels hit the tarmac and I jolted upright. The passengers clapped and I rubbed sleep from my eyes. I looked out the small window and saw the buildings of JFK airport and felt almost an apprehension at being home. *Crazy*, I thought. *Home is home, and life will get back to normal.*

I pushed aside my thoughts of Robert, the dream I'd just experienced, his crash, and warm Caribbean waters, and concentrated on calling up a ride share. My muddled brain couldn't figure out what terminal I was in or where to find the cab. Finally the fog cleared and I headed to the designated meeting point in the Terminal 5 parking garage to go back into cold, windy Manhattan.

Chapter 10

A Postcard from the Dead

New York City was a shock to my system. Two weeks in the Caribbean sun had made me a cold-weather wimp. The autumn chill in the air, the noises, the chaos of New York City, assaulted me. Luckily, turning the key in my apartment building's door switched me back into sharp New York City mode. My senses on high alert, I picked up my mail from my crammed mailbox and went to the elevator.

My plants were just barely hanging on, so I thanked them for surviving without me and drenched them. Sam makes fun of me talking to my plants. I tell her it's "only child syndrome." Growing up, I talked to plants, stuffed animals, and books, and I had imaginary phone conversations. I still talk to myself when I'm alone. I opened the kitchen window, as the place smelled stale. I longed for a trade wind to blow salty sea air through the window.

The pile of mail was relegated to the sofa; I would tackle that later. I had work in the morning, and there was no point in delaying the inevitable unpacking. I ordered Thai and dumped the large suitcase on the floor.

Once the laundry was in the washer and the food was on my lap, I picked up the mail. Bills, flyers, menus, and a postcard. I wondered when Sam had had time to write and mail a postcard on her honeymoon and smiled as I saw the pristine waters of Vieques Sun Bay on the front, and then I turned it over.

It was not from Sam. It was from Robert. My Robert, who would not be writing any more postcards to anyone, ever.

Dearest Pia,

I am so sorry for what I did and did not do.

Forgive me, R.

Forgive him for what he did and did not do? He had lied, ghosted, and hurt me. A year ago those words had been all I wanted to hear. Now…now they meant nothing, and he was no longer alive. But why would he have written for absolution? I was puzzled and more than a little angry.

My strange dream came back to my mind: Robert and Sofia arguing. Had that really happened? Was I seeing their real argument, or was my mind fabricating? I had no way to know. No one would be able to find out what went on in the cockpit before their plane went down. *Would they? Are there flight recordings?* I had no idea if small private planes even had black boxes, let alone recording systems.

I shovelled pad Thai noodles into my mouth, chewing and trying not to think. I had a full day of work tomorrow and no time to analyze why Robert's plane went down, why I was seeing him in my dreams, and why he had sent me this postcard a year later. I would never get answers, so I pushed the questions to the far, already crowded recesses of my mind.

I sent a text off to Nona, my mother, and Jarad telling them that I was home safe, wished Jarad safe travels, and went to bed. I dreamt of the bio bay. I dreamt I was cocooned in its warm wetness, floating, listening to the night sounds. Coquis chirped…no wait, that was my alarm, ringing me back to the present. I threw the clothes from the washer into the dryer and hopped into the shower. Off to work I went.

I had not jumped ship to the FBI as everyone thought I would. I was recommended, recruited, courted, and cajoled into spending a week at Quantico back in March, but decided it wasn't for me. Well, truth be told, I didn't think my secret ability would remain a secret if I worked for the FBI. I felt under constant surveillance.

There was no way I could continue what I was currently doing if I was partnered up and working for them.

I liked the freedom I had in my role as medical examiner. I felt like I had finally found balance. I would go weeks without the drums beating in my head, my body shivering, my hands tingling. I would just about forget the ripples and could almost convince myself that that part of my life was over and done…and then it would happen, and I would be with the person I had seen seconds before on my shiny cold steel table in the morgue.

I didn't always know when it would happen. A random body on my table, and suddenly I would be playing God. I would come out of my trancelike state knowing that somewhere, someone I didn't even know was alive after having died, and I was responsible. Uncle Ben's quote to Spiderman, "With great power comes great responsibility," always comes to mind.

I was well aware that a secret was only a secret if no one else knew about it. Although Kash and Sam shared in this secret of mine, they were trustworthy and I believed my secret was safe with them. Who would even believe this?

I did my work, kept the secret, and felt fulfilled. Mostly. I wished I had someone with whom I could share my life and ultimately my secret. Someone to vent to and to listen to. Someone to eat with, because eating alone is no fun at all. Thankfully I'd had Sam as a roommate for most of my twenties.

My parents were spending the bulk of their time in Alaska. We spoke or video chatted weekly, and although they always invited me up there, my vacation choice was the aqua blue waters of the Caribbean, not braving ice and polar bears and twenty-four-hour darkness in Alaska. I didn't care that there were, according to my mother, cute foxes appearing around their lodge looking for food.

Sam had worked for one year in LA and then relocated back to New York City. To hear her tell it, that year had been a decade long, and she had missed the city every single day. She opened a small private practice down by city hall and was building her patient list. She was deliriously happy, it seemed, every single moment. I was truly happy for her and Kash, even if her enthusiasm was a bit much at times.

Kash was now in medical school at City University, still working part-time as a paramedic. It was such a treat to run into him on the rare occasions when our paths crossed. He was still the same guy with boyish enthusiasm, crazy about his wife, and, to hear him say it, "killing it at school." I'd known he would.

The guy had it all: looks, brains, sense of humour, and most importantly, kindness. Sam was a lucky lady, and she knew it. I loved that my two best friends had found each other. Soulmates, they said.

Does everyone have a soulmate? I had thought Robert was mine; I'd felt so good when I was with him. That was a bust. No soulmate in Robert, just a life lesson.

I spent a lot of time thinking about the wedding in Vieques and the apparitions I had seen on the beach. I have never been one to see things that are not real. And yet, I could so easily picture the two teenagers melding into Sam and Kash. Who were they? Ghosts of love that had already happened? Nothing made sense to me. Why was my mind creating images that weren't real? My father and I had both seen the dog on the beach, and although he questioned what he saw, I doubt he thought about it constantly like me. I was popping acetaminophen again, a dozen a day. Not good.

And then there was my current almost-boyfriend. Another long-distance relationship that made me question why I could relate to someone far away and not connect with a person in the same city as me. Jarad was actively pursuing me, and although I enjoyed the attention, it was just that. Attention. No fireworks. He sent flowers, and called me in the evenings even though it was much earlier in LA. He was planning to come east for my Binghamton conference and again for Thanksgiving. The thought of Thanksgiving, when Robert had stood me up, made me feel steam come out of my ears. I was so pissed off about that memory taking up too much of my mind, my time, and my energy.

Robert had been my fantasy man. I had dreamt about him for over ten years. I met him as a teenager, and my fantasies grew as I grew. It's not often a fantasy gets realized. My fantasy realization had been like a million stars exploding inside me all at once. That was how our relationship hit me. Would I ever find that level of connection again? Did I even want that all-consuming feeling? I didn't know for sure. The cowardly part of me was opting for a safe relationship. One that wouldn't break me if it ended.

With Jarad, I felt an attraction, but there was also friendship. We had fun together. Easygoing fun. We couldn't rush things, since we were on opposite coasts at the moment. He was wooing me, and I liked it, but I didn't get butterflies like I had with Robert. *Will I ever feel fireworks again?*

I didn't want to spend the next few years comparing every date to Robert. He didn't deserve the time I wasted thinking about him.

Chapter 11

Back to Work in New York City

NARRATOR: SAM

Back in New York City! What a blast the last two weeks had been. I married my soulmate—yes, we felt we were soulmates, as corny as it sounded. Everyone had an amazing time in Vieques at my perfect beach wedding, and now I was excited to get back to my incredibly satisfying work.

Kash was already at class this morning and I was settling in with a grande moccachino from the gourmet coffee place in the lobby of my building. My office building. My address in New York City. I loved my little office space. I was thrilled every day to head downtown.

When I first admitted to myself that I had to move back to New York, I put out feelers with my professors and fellow grads. Through the social media grapevine I was sent a message about someone retiring. I was on the next plane to meet her and we hit it off like we had known each other forever. My grandparents and her parents were from the same village in India and had come to America for the opportunities America boasted.

I felt lucky and privileged to take over her lease and I even inherited a few of her patients. Win-win, Kash said. I still spoke with her once a week and she recounted the antics of her

49

grandchildren in their shared Hastings farmhouse. She referred patients to me and that alone made my practice viable.

I dropped my briefcase on my desk and turned on the lamp. My beautiful blue ruby ring sparkled in the light coming in the small window that overlooked Lafayette Street. The northern light was diffused, but I was grateful for the space and usually drew the privacy blinds when a patient was in session.

Pia found this ruby. I still couldn't believe that this gem existed and I was there, right beside her, when she first spotted it. To hear her tell the story, it took practically a sledgehammer to get it out of the lava rock. Juan had his own version of their morning escapade, even funnier than Pia's. But ultimately, she found this ruby. I had three beautiful chips of it on my finger and the rest was history.

The small museum in Vieques was still trying to trace its origins, as it was such a rare jewel. I was amazed she kept the secret from me, and although Kash, my brother, Juan, and Trez were in on it, I had no inkling that my wedding band would contain three perfect stones from a piece that chipped off the ruby. Pia said adamantly that it found her. If it weren't for the glint she saw while snorkelling at Navio, she would not have injured herself on the coral, and her fall in the bio bay later that night might not have given her the magic she was blessed with. Yes, blessed with. She was chosen. She had work to do with this gift. She was just getting started and I was honoured to know about it.

Enough cobweb-gathering, as my mother says. Now I needed to get back to my own work.

My first patient was new. He had an addiction problem, and had been court ordered to have therapy. I had a few minutes to review the documents before he came in at ten o'clock. His identity was very top secret. I sincerely hoped he was not a celebrity and not a waste of my time. This was not my favourite type of patient, but I volunteered to help out. This cause was one that Kash did volunteer work with, mentoring, tutoring, and taxiing teens to various medical appointments.

A caseworker would be bringing him soon. Pro bono. If he was a celebrity, he could certainly afford to pay for therapy, but alas, I signed up and now had to put in the time.

I quickly scanned the pages. Almost OD'd a year ago. Kid had been in rehab three times in the past year. Second attempt at therapy. Wouldn't speak to the other therapist. Not exactly a kid at twenty, but his troubles apparently started as a teen.

Therapy works in some cases, but mainly when the patient wants therapy and seeks it out. This patient was mandated. Summary: one troubled youth, possibly spoiled, with addiction problems and family money.

Jessie, my office manager/secretary, poked her head in. Today Jessie was dressing experimentally, apparently. But hey, no judgments. She was worth her weight in gold. Her flowing tunic and harem pants shimmered as she stood in the doorway.

"He's here," she said and waited for my nod.

A very tall, thin young man with dark bangs covering one eye trailed behind his caseworker, Fiona MacLellan, a force to be reckoned with. Feisty and fierce with a reputation for straight shooting. Her red hair and no-nonsense approach to people had seasoned lawyers and judges quaking in their boots. I really liked her. Her gruffness belied how very much she cared about her wards, as she called them.

"Dr. Sodhra, meet Joel." Her Irish brogue made *Joel* sound musical.

I stood up and leaned across my desk, put out my hand, and looked up at Joel. Then I realized who he was. "Pleased to meet you, Joel. Come on in and sit down." I gestured to one of two chairs facing my desk.

I thought about how Pia had described him to me and Kash, lying in his bed, OD'd, with his girlfriend lying next to him when she intervened for the very first time, able to somehow alter time and wake up the girlfriend, who called 911 in time. Pia saved him. She rippled time and now here he was in my office, with no inkling that he technically died a year ago.

I couldn't tell Pia about this patient. I couldn't tell anyone that he was here. But my mind was racing at seeing him in person, looking exactly like Pia described, right down to the spiky bangs flopping over his eye.

He slowly shook my hand. He had big strong hands that made mine look like a child's, but he had no grip, just apathy and sweat. He slunk over to a chair and slid in. One fluid motion, used to his long arms and legs and fluid body.

Graceful, I thought. *An athlete.* I remembered Pia telling me that he rode a unicycle. That skill takes concentration, balance, and strength.

I turned to Fiona, longtime friend of Kash and someone I instantly clicked with when I had crossed paths with her a few times before and most recently at Kash's birthday party.

"How's married life?" she said with a wink.

"Bliss," I answered. "You staying?"

"Nope. This one's all yours for the next hour. Good luck." She shut the door behind her, and I heard her talking and laughing with Jessie in the front room.

"So Joel…" I made my way around my desk and took the chair next to his. I stayed silent and I waited. Time ticked. I waited some more and after about fifteen minutes of this, an exasperated Joel said, "Well, aren't you going to try to fix me?"

I looked him straight in the eye. "What needs fixing?"

He looked surprised. Again, silence. Then, "Do you know why I am even here?" he asked, agitated and angry.

"Yes, do you?"

"Of course I do. My dad set this up. He controls everything. I can't do anything without his spies reporting back. I just want to get away from him!"

"So why don't you?" I asked, leaning back in my chair.

He was sweating and picking at his cuticles ferociously. "Why don't I what?" he stammered, shocked at my suggestion.

"Leave the city. Get away for a while. You are an adult. You can go freely."

"I can't just leave." He leaned forward and put his head in his hands.

"Why not?" I asked. "When you come of age, you're free. You don't have to answer to your father." His father, the mayor of New York City. Some people said he would run for president in the not-too-distant future.

Again he sputtered. "Leave? I can't. I mean, where would I go?"

"I'm not suggesting that you leave, but Joel, you are not a prisoner, other than in your mind. Your father doesn't control you."

He looked stunned as if I had morphed into an alien right in front of his eyes.

"But I can't."

"Why not?" I asked.

"Just go? Leave New York City?"

"You could if you wanted," I said flatly.

"My father would never allow it," he responded just as flatly.

"Joel, you are a grown man. He is your father, and wants the best for you. Maybe you could talk to him about it."

"Do you even know my father?"

"I don't, but I know of him."

"Yeah, well, it's his way or the highway." He crossed his legs and tucked his restless hands under them. He looked like a teen more than a twenty-year-old man. "The highway," he repeated quietly.

I wanted to launch into his addiction as his way of escaping his father's control, but my watch alerted me that our time was up. The session ended with a chime on my desk. He looked startled when he heard it.

He didn't move. He just sat there, head down, and for a second I thought he had nodded off. Then he jumped up and said, "It's pointless, Doc. He'll never let me out of his sight."

"Don't give up. Think about what you would like to do, if you got away for a bit. There are endless options. I'll see you next week." He didn't look at me. "Okay, Joel? Next week?"

He barely nodded and then was out the door.

I was left feeling like we had connected on a small level, but it didn't make any difference at all. I wondered if his father would ever come with him. Probably not; not good for his public persona.

Jessie knocked.

"Yes?"

"That was the mayor's son?" She knew things had to be kept confidential with regards to patients.

"Yes, and not a word about it." I smiled, but I was not kidding.

She knew. She ticked a lock with her fingers to her lips and asked if I needed anything.

"All good. I have the next one at twelve?"

"Yes, and your husband called." She winked and walked back to her desk.

My husband. Indeed. The thought still amazed me. I scribbled some notes in the chart and picked up my cell to return his call.

Chapter 12

Big Plans

My parents invited me to dinner. *My parents*. It still sounded strange. Twenty-six years of no father, and now my parents are blissfully reunited. So weird. They were in New York City for the week and then off to Alaska, to my father's business and home, his hunting/fishing lodge. My mother had been going back and forth for the past year. "Racking up the Air Miles," she said.

I had been crazy busy catching up at work all week and was really looking forward to a home-cooked meal. My mother's cooking is Michelin Star worthy. I learned at her side how to cook, how to create, how to improvise with food, but my cooking paled in comparison to hers. She made every meal look effortless. I had a trusty couple of dishes that I made well, but usually resorted to ordering out rather than cook for one.

According to my smitten mother, my father was a great cook, and he would be doing the honours tonight. Far be it from my mother to let anyone else take over her kitchen, but they had certainly grown together over the last year, and if she said he could cook—high praise indeed—then I was definitely interested in being a guinea pig.

I took extra care with my appearance and changed from my work clothes to a long gray shirtwaist dress and tall boots. I threw on a black leather jacket and wrapped a lacy scarf, that I am certain used to belong to Sam, around my neck.

I arrived with a bottle each of white, red, and Mik's Hot Honey, the perfect condiment to any meal. I was not sure what was on the menu but was craving killer spicy food, Puerto Rican, Indian, or Thai. Jarad's brother Mik had started his own bottling company making spicy condiments, and this one was fast becoming my favourite.

I buzzed up and was let into the second-floor apartment. As soon as I entered, I was shocked to see the apartment was almost empty. Nearly everything was either in boxes or gone altogether.

"What's going on?" I called out as I went to hang my coat on the coat rack, but it was notably absent from its spot just inside the door and there was nowhere and nothing to hang it on. I walked through to the kitchen and draped it on the back of a chair.

"Yes," my mother said as she came over, smiled approvingly at my appearance, and embraced me. "I am downsizing. Moving my things to your father's place."

"In Alaska?" I was in shock. My father turned from the stove and leaned in for a half hug.

"Yes, Pia, we are going to try the full-time thing. In Alaska," he said, turning back to the pot he was stirring. He looked so tanned and fit in faded Levis and a light blue checked button down.

"Full time?" I was horrified, and not sure why. "What about your job, Mom? You love that job."

"Yes, and I will continue to work remotely for now. Your father and I want to be permanent."

"Permanent in Alaska?" I was incredulous. Polar bears, darkness all day long, snow, winter, darkness ALL DAY LONG? "Alaska, permanently? Really, Mom?"

"Pia, I want to be permanently with your father. If he is in Alaska, then I will be in Alaska." Her tone said that particular discussion was over. "And," she continued, folding her arms across her white cashmere turtleneck.

I rolled my eyes.

"I saw that, Cassiopeia. Lose the attitude. Listen, I want you to have this apartment."

I couldn't even process what she was saying. She was looking expectantly at me. "Well, say something. Would you like to move back here? It's rent controlled, as you know, and it's much cheaper than what you pay uptown." She named the figure, one third of my current rent.

"Yes! Yes! I definitely would love to move back here. I love this neighbourhood. I can easily get a train to 34th and walk across town to work." Now, this was something to get excited about. My thoughts were going a mile a minute. Live in this fifteen-hundred-square-foot, rent-controlled, gorgeous two-bedroom pre-war apartment? Hell yes!

She hugged me, and I felt my father lean in behind her, and the three of us danced around until I bumped into the pot, nearly spilling its contents.

"Okay, fantastic. Both our names are on the lease, so there will be no problem," she said, sounding happy the matter was settled.

I walked over to the stove. "So," I said, looking in the pot, "what are we having?"

"Pizza soup," my father replied and turned off the burner. He saw my face and said quickly, "You will love it. It's all the ingredients that go on a pizza in a pot. Tomatoes, mushrooms, pepperoni, peppers, onions, cheese, salami, artichokes, basil, and olives. I put a couple jalapeños in just for you. Served with garlic bread." He brought his fingers together at his lips and kissed them. "Mwah," he said, lifting his hand into the air. "Delicioso."

"You'll love it, honey," my mother reassured me as we sat and my father served us.

I did love it. It was spicy and tangy and unlike anything I had ever eaten before. The hot honey was the perfect accompaniment to the soup and the bread. They loved it and said they would take the bottle with them to Alaska. I made a mental note to tell Mik.

After dinner we had coffee at the kitchen table; the living room furniture was already on its way north.

"Here are two sets of keys."

I took them and put them in my bag.

"Your bedroom is the same as you left it, and I am leaving the kitchen as is." My mother stood up and started clearing the table. "The kitchen at the lodge is well stocked." She stood with my father and he draped his arm over her shoulder. She leaned into him and I could feel her contentment.

"When do you leave?" I asked them, adding quickly, "not that I am rushing you." We all laughed. Part of me was already missing them, but the other part was excited about moving down to this West Side, pre-war apartment.

I called Sam the second I got home.

"Are you decent? Can we video chat?" I asked her, still breathless from jumping out of the rideshare van and running up the stairs. My nod to a workout for the day.

"Yes and yes," she said, then hung up and answered my video call. "So what's up? You're in an awfully good mood."

"I'm moving back home!"

"What? With your mother? Why?" She looked concerned. "What's happened?"

"No, nothing. Not moving in with my mother, moving into the apartment. Mom's going to Alaska. Full time." I could see her processing this.

"Wow. So they are really doing it. I mean, they looked so happy at the wedding, but this is a big move. Your mom is such an independent woman…and your dad is…and giving up New York City. I couldn't do it. She has been in the city her whole life." Sam sounded like she was talking to herself.

"Yeah, I know. The whole thing is crazy, but she is already packed. The place was practically empty. I have never seen it empty. It's so spacious. I love it. They'll still come back to New York once in a while to shop and visit me," I said hopefully.

"Sure they will. Pia, that apartment is to die for…Wait! What about your place? Our old place? Could Kash and I move in? We are so cramped here in his studio. I love living with him, but there's nowhere for him to study."

"Yes! That's perfect. You guys take this place when I move into Mom's." It really was a perfect solution for them. Kash's studio was serviceable for a bachelor, but two people in the one room was tight.

"I can't wait to tell Kash." She was distracted, and I could tell she was already mentally packing and moving less than a mile further uptown to my place.

"Where is he?" My phone chirped with a low battery.

"He's working tonight. He is doing two shifts a week. He should be home any minute."

"What else is going on? You two lovebirds are good?" I walked into the bedroom to grab my charger.

"Yes, we are. I am getting back into work. New patient today." She abruptly stopped talking, and it sounded like she wanted to say more, but didn't.

"And?" I coaxed.

"No, nothing, I was just thinking about him."

"Him, do tell. Anyone I know?" I laughed and plugged in my phone.

"No!" she said loudly and I almost dropped the phone.

"Whoa, okay, what's with you?" I asked her.

"Sorry, long day. I am going to hang up now and make some food for Kash. He's enjoying trying to be vegan."

"Yeah right," I said. "Cook him a Wagyu steak and he will show you what real love is." I laughed and said goodnight, promising to call her on the weekend to discuss our moves.

Chapter 13

Déjà Vu

Carol, our receptionist and all-round knew-everything-about-everyone greeter said, "I'm digging your tan, girl," as I walked into the medical examiner's office. She was the perfect first person for grieving families to encounter at the worst time of their lives. Carol preferred a spray tan to the real thing, telling me it was healthier. I shuddered to think of the chemicals in the tan in a bottle, though the real sun does damage too.

"Thank you, and again, Carol, thank you for setting me up with Desiree. She did everything for Sam and Kash and more. The wedding was so perfect. And I know that is almost impossible to achieve in Vieques."

"No problem at all. She's the best. Runs in the family." She winked and turned to answer her ringing phone.

Runs in the family, I thought to myself. *My father and I were both affected by the bio bay. Does that run in our family? Impossible. Absolutely impossible that what happened to us is real and is still happening to me.*

Unconsciously, I looked down at my fingers and did a double take. They were glowing bluish and tingling. I looked over to see if Carol noticed—she sees all—but she was still talking on the phone and typing away on her keyboard.

I went past her desk and down the elevator to my office. I threw my coat on the hook, dumped my purse, and made my way towards the cafeteria to grab a coffee. I was almost to the coffee maker when I heard my name.

I turned to see Dr. Bowman, the head of my department, signalling me by crooking his index finger to come with him.

I followed him to his office.

"Good morning, Dr. Bowman. What's going on?" He waited until I was in his office and then shut the door.

"We have a new case, arriving now, very hush-hush. Suit up, I will meet you in room 2."

"Okay, be right there." Coffee would have to wait. I made my way down to autopsy room 2. I pulled on full PPE including gloves and walked over to the log to see who this hush-hush casualty was.

As I walked across the room, I had an overwhelming sense of déjà vu. Why, when I was in that room almost every day? I could not imagine what was prompting this feeling, but it made me almost dizzy. I braced my palm flat against the wall holding the roster. The bluish glow had faded, but to my eyes was still there between my fingers and I scanned the names. *Room 2-John Doe.*

Okay, so it was a male. Maybe a celebrity, possibly an athlete, all shrouded in mystery.

I felt Dr. Bowman enter the room behind me and heard the doors whoosh closed behind him.

I went to the head of the steel table, and to my shock recognized the mayor's son, Joel. *Joel!* I screamed inside my head. *I saved your life over a year ago and now you are here again! Dead!* Anger welled up in me and I could barely stand.

"Cassiopeia, are you all right? Oh, I see you recognize him. The golden boy." Dr. Bowman pulled down the microphone suspended above the table and turned it on.

"Shall we begin?" he asked me, and I must have nodded, because he was beginning the autopsy and I was assisting, all the while remembering this teenager who had very nearly OD'd over a year ago.

That was the first time I was able to affect change. I reversed time and a paramedic was able to inject naloxone into him in time to save him. After a spike of two hundred thousand deaths a year during Covid, US opioid overdoses still led to eighty thousand deaths a year, many of which could be prevented with naloxone.

But naloxone wouldn't have helped Joel this time. As Dr. Bowman pulled the sheet off Joel's cold body, the cause of death became immediately clear. A bullet hole had torn through his chest, right above his heart. Another two had ripped through his abdomen.

My fingers still tingled, but there was no discernible glow.

I can't save you this time, Joel, I thought sadly and carried on.

As I left at the end of the day, Carol handed me a card for *Kash and Samsara*. Sam hates when anyone uses her full name.

"What's this?" I asked her.

"Just a little something for the newlyweds. Will you give it to them?"

"Absolutely, that is very sweet of you," I said as I tucked the yellow envelope in my purse.

She replied, "It's from all of us here, not just me. Kash is a good guy. We miss him. But he will be a great doctor. Give them my best."

"Thanks. He is and he will be. I'll get it to them right away. This is so nice of everyone," I said as I patted my purse. "Goodnight, Carol."

I fired off a text to Sam and Kash that I had something for them and to give me a call, then I made my way to the subway, still thinking about a young man's life, ripped away by a gun.

Chapter 14

The Mayor's Son, Again

I missed a call on the subway, so as soon as I came aboveground I fished my phone out of my purse to see who called. It was Sam.

I stopped at the deli and ordered a sandwich to go. I called her while I waited for it.

"Hey, what's up?" I asked, sounding a bit breathless.

"You home?" she asked.

"Downstairs at Ron's."

"Pia, not that three-meat sandwich on a kaiser roll," she laughed.

"Busted. You know I love his sandwiches. I may have to come uptown for a fix when I move." I paid at the register. The deli was the ground-floor shop of my apartment building, so it was a ten-foot walk. I checked my mailbox and then headed upstairs.

Inside the apartment, I flipped on the lights, threw my coat on a chair, and stretched out on the sofa to talk to Sam.

"So what did Kash say?"

"He's thrilled. We definitely could use more space, and he said his mother would be glad to have us closer. She can visit more often."

I could picture Sam's eye roll at this. Kash's mom came over with food almost every other day.

"I have a card from Carol for you two. Well, from the office people, not just Carol." I opened the sandwich and quickly took a bite.

"Which one is Carol? She's not an old flame, is she?" Sam's voice sounded strange. I had never heard her sound even remotely jealous of anyone.

"You know, Carol at reception. Sounds like Rosie Perez. Her cousin was the wedding planner."

"OMG! Of course, how could I forget that voice? I must write her a thank you for Desiree. She was amazing. I kept picturing all the things that could go wrong, and they didn't."

Neither of us spoke. I was chewing and she was probably reliving her blissful wedding.

Finally I said, "Something happened today."

Silence for a few beats and then she said, "Something…something?"

I said emphatically, "No!" and then I reconsidered. "Well kind of, related to, anyways."

"Hang up, I'm video calling you. And put down the sandwich, I can hear you chewing!"

I gobbled the rest of the sandwich, poured myself a glass of wine, and answered the call.

"So, what happened?"

"I was feeling weird on the way to work—"

She cut me off. "*Weird* weird?"

"Yes, *weird* weird. I could see the glow around my fingers and I knew something might happen."

She processed for a minute. "But nothing has happened lately, has it?"

I hadn't told Sam or Kash about my last few episodes of reverse ripples.

I fudged my answer, "No, not lately, but today I felt something was going to happen."

"Well, did it?" She sounded irritated or impatient, I couldn't tell which.

"No. Nothing happened except the body on the table—"

"Jesus, Pia, don't tell me about bodies on your table! Gross. I do not need a mental picture of the dead. I much prefer living patients, as you know."

"I wasn't going to describe the body, just to say that I felt something was going to happen. It didn't. The feeling, the tingling, faded away, and just wasn't present anymore, even though it had been all day. Sam, the body on my table was Joel. You know, the mayor's son."

I heard her gasp. And then silence.

"Sam, are you there? Are you okay?"

Sam and Kash were both aware that I had reversed time and saved Joel from an overdose the previous year. He'd had a second chance at life because of me. There was no third chance, though.

"Pia, he died?" She seemed to be sobbing.

It baffled me that she was so upset. "Are you crying?"

Through her sniffles, she said, "I'll call you back," then hung up.

I took the sandwich wrapper to the kitchen and tossed it in the trash can. I refilled my wine glass and sat back down on the sofa. The phone rang and it was Kash.

"Did you hear? The mayor's son died!"

"Oh, I know. Did Sam tell you?" It was going to be a long night.

"Sam, no. How would she know?" He went on to tell me the details. Who Joel had been with, where he was found. The mayor was up in arms, vowing to crack down on gang violence. The whole gambit.

My phone chirped a second call. "Gotta go, Kash, your wife is calling."

"Tell her I'm on my way home," he said cheerily and hung up.

I accepted her call. "Your husband was on the other line. Says he's headed home now."

She sounded serious. "Pia, I saw Joel."

"Where?" Interesting that she'd seen him and knew who he was.

"I'm not supposed to say. Patient confidentiality rules."

I got it. He was her patient. I knew the physician/patient privacy and confidentiality rules still applied to the deceased, and knowing Sam, she would kick herself for already saying too much.

"Wow. What are the chances?" I said, and waited to see what she would reply.

"Of all the therapists in the world, he had to walk into my office."

I laughed at the bad Casablanca imitation and said, "His father must be freaking. Kash said he is beyond crazy. Grandstanding. Threatening to hunt people down, sue who he can."

"I certainly hope he doesn't sue me," she said flatly.

"I was immediately sorry for what I said, and I tried to make light of it. "No Sam, suing the rehabs that repeatedly didn't work. And now he's coming after the gangs who were running the drugs he was buying, whoever he was tangled up with. But we don't even know yet if it was random."

I could feel Sam wanted to say more, but chose not to. "I'm going to say goodnight, Pia. Let's talk about the move in a couple days. Kash will tell his landlord he isn't re-signing his lease for this studio. The timing couldn't be better for us to get more space."

"Okay, goodnight, and Sam, don't worry about the mayor. He probably doesn't even know his son saw you."

I finished my wine and then jumped in the shower. The day felt about twenty hours long.

Joel. What happened to you?

Chapter 15

Morning Run Ripples

The next morning I had a work video conference scheduled for ten, but woke up with a headache. The pounding was intense. I popped a few tablets and when that didn't help, I decided to go for a run to see if the exercise would put my head right. No more multiple glasses of red for me in the evening if this was the payback.

I threw on old sweats, a hoodie, and a windbreaker, and laced my sneakers. There was still sand in them from Vieques. I dumped it into the trash can, did a few quick stretches to limber up, and went downstairs.

I made my way west to the Hudson River and then on to the ped path that ran a circuitous route around the entire city. Tax dollars put to good use. The illuminated and well-maintained pedway and bike path are a safe place for runners, cyclists, and dog walkers.

I could feel the endorphins working as my body found its groove. A much healthier solution than the pain pills I had been popping for the last year. My runner's high felt great.

The weather was a bit chilly and breezy, but my windbreaker, gloves, and wool hat kept me toasty warm. I had my phone zipped into my pocket and no earbuds today. I wanted to hear my breathing and the rhythmic cadence of my feet hitting the pavement. I was already picturing living on West End Avenue again and planned to make runs part of my routine instead of an occasional indulgence.

The jog to the Hudson River from West End Avenue was about five minutes compared to the twenty from my soon-to-be old apartment. I was going to be closer to the basketball courts and could start shooting hoops in the mornings, maybe with Kash. Sam could cheer for us from the sidelines. When I had lived at home with my mother, there was always a pickup game at the courts. Friendly, not too aggressive, but competitive. A great way to stay in shape. Not parkour shape, but good enough to get through my days when I had to stand for most of the time and practically drag my sorry ass home.

I dipped under the roadway and started south on the pedestrian route close to the water. I knew this route by heart. First mile was nothingness, the second mile was all what I called "the stumps," a few abandoned, collapsing piers and their pilings left rotting close to shore. The third mile was newly completed structures on the water side, and then I'd turn around and head back up.

There were few people out this chilly morning, a couple cyclists, one dog owner with a puppy who had a mind of his own. I hit my optimum stride, grateful for my healthy body, and relaxed into the run. My head was definitely feeling better and I was congratulating myself for thinking of running when I heard the slapping of loose laces from my sneaker. I leaned on one of the newly installed metal benches facing the water to tie it. When I took my gloves off, I saw a telltale bluish glow coming from my hands.

I just stared at the luminescence as things came together in my mind. Needing the run, my head pounding, the sense that I needed to be in this spot. I looked around for a reason for me to be there and saw none. And yet, my tingling fingers told me otherwise.

I retied my shoe, thinking I would replace these round laces with flat ones that didn't come untied all the time, then looked around with keenly alert eyes before I started up again. I hit my turnaround spot and leaned against the rail to take in the view of the sparkling water. The cliffs across from me and the reflective glass buildings of a new industrial park were visible between the tall tulip trees lining the path. Beautiful New York City seemed a bit ominous as the rising sun cast long shadows. A few runners had passed me on the path, showing me their intensity and speed as they blew by me. *It's not a race!*

A runner in head-to-toe spandex was stretching his hamstrings on the bench I had just leaned on. He was the only one around me. He didn't have a lanky runner's body; he looked more like a weightlifter, or a CrossFit guy, maybe. It was just him and me on this straight stretch of pedway.

No, wait, I could see a person up ahead on my left, on a short pier. She was bending low towards the water. What was she doing? Her pretty skirt hung just below her knees and was fluttering in the breeze. She was leaning over the low pier taking photos of the water. I looked at the water and saw ducks gathered.

I started picturing the warm, aqua blue water of Vieques, pelicans diving close to the shoreline, the sun beating down, and then my thoughts were interrupted by a short yelp. I looked toward the source and realized the woman on the pier was gone. I quickened my pace and ran the last twenty feet out onto the pier where she had been standing less than a minute ago. Yellow construction netting was strung haphazardly on the water side, and beyond a spot where it was mashed down, I could see her floating face down in the water, the waves banging her body into a short jagged metal piling just above the water's surface, her gray shimmery skirt still fluttering, now in the water. The ducks had fled.

Without hesitation, I lay flat on my belly and reached into the dark water. I could just grab her arm and pull her to me. Her body rolled over in the waves and I could see her head had hit the piling when she went into the water. Her mouth was open as if she was screaming. Her intense, dark brown, lifeless eyes looked at nothing.

I look at lifeless eyes all day long. She had been in the water maybe fifteen seconds at most, but I knew there was no reason for me to attempt CPR. She was sadly beyond that. She was very, very dead.

I removed my glove and grabbed her wrist again. As soon as my fingers touched her, I was standing next to her on the pier. Both of us were dry, and she was unaware of what was just about to happen. A freak accident. A split-second mistake and her life will be over.

I pretended I was taking a breather from running and I casually mentioned to her not to lean on the netting, it would give way. She seemed to consider this for a moment and then thanked me and walked to a more guardre area, with real metal fencing along the water's edge. *The city had better get the rest of this pier secured*, I thought. She gave me a quick wave and then bent low and aimed her camera through the gaps in the fence, her dry skirt billowing as the breeze ruffled it.

I calmed my breathing but could feel the adrenaline coursing through my body. I felt electrified. I used the feeling to move me forward as I left the pier and continued my run heading north, heading home.

"Hey, excuse me, miss," said a deep male voice behind me.

I stopped, turned, and saw that spandex man had rushed to catch up with me. "Yes, can I help you?" This was not running etiquette, bothering someone on a run.

"What just happened there?" he asked, breathless, hands on his knees.

"Where?" I asked.

"Back there. I saw that woman fall into the river. I'm sure I did." As he said it, he stood up and looked back at the pier, thirty or forty feet behind us. "She's dry now, like she never went in the water?" He said it as a question.

"I don't know what you're talking about." I turned to get away from his steely glare.

"The hell you don't." He sounded puzzled and said with intensity, "I saw what I saw."

"Look, I don't know what you think you saw, but she's fine and I've got to go." I started running again, praying he wasn't following me. How could he have seen her fall if I reversed time and she did not actually hit her head and die? How? I was still feeling the adrenaline, and a mild headache was forming again. Ugh. I kept running and didn't look back or pause until I was safely inside my apartment building. I had no time to consider the implications; I had to shower and then log on to a work video conference in thirty minutes.

The shower water washed over me. I willed my mind to empty all thoughts of the spandex-clad man and just feel the water. The wetness, the warmth, the cleansing. I let it run until I was out of hot water.

As I turned the taps off and stepped onto the bathmat, I felt strong. Resolute. Good. I'd saved her. I had felt compelled to run this morning for the first time this week. And not only to run around the park like I often did; I needed to be *there*, in that exact spot at that exact moment in time. Even my lace becoming untied seemed like a portent. Everything had fallen into place.

Well, everything except the CrossFit guy, who'd seen the impossible. How? How had he seen?

Was this something that could happen now? The thought that he'd seen before and after the ripples was almost as terrifying as the possibility of the advance warning that something may happen.

I pushed those thoughts away and concentrated on myself.

I felt powerful and…something else. Fulfilled. Like I had done a good thing, saving this woman who'd fallen accidentally. I always had a deep internal satisfaction that this absolutely crazy magical gift of mine was saving lives—or rather, giving people back their lives. But this time, with Joel's death, it somehow felt different. It balanced the scales for me. Had I somehow made the woman fall so I could save her, in response to Joel's dying? Was it a coincidence? Predestined?

I thought I might talk it out with Sam later. Her common sense and insight were reassuring, but ultimately I was doing the impossible, and even she couldn't provide anything other than a sounding board.

I wished I had some answers, but for now, the mystery remained, and I had work to do.

Chapter 16

Ripples Reverberate

I hadn't told Kash and Sam about my recent episodes, and this morning's encounter was no different. I longed to tell and I felt as if I would erupt if I didn't share this latest one. I struggled with wanting to blurt it out and just internalizing it. Sharing it somehow watered it down, the heady intoxicating rush I got from using the reverse ripples.

A complete stranger had no idea her story hadn't ended badly today. I'd altered her entire life. I still felt charged, electric, almost drunk with completeness hours later.

And spandex CrossFit man? What in the hell was that? It bothered me that he'd seen what he saw. *I can't be exposed*, I told myself. *The reverse ripples can't be seen.* But then, how did he see the ripple? Was it visible? A flash? A blink? How long did it last? For me it was a flash of milliseconds and time was reversed.

Kash was standing next to me the first time it happened at work. Mere microseconds, and he didn't see anything. So how could this stranger have seen her fall and then dry on the dock? It made no sense and was going to drive me crazy. Thank god I'd gotten away from him and wouldn't see him again in this city of 11 million. But a tiny part of me shouted, *This huge city is not so very huge and there are no longer six degrees of separation, it is more like 2.4 degrees.* I was going to seriously drive myself crazy.

Not confiding in Sam and Kash left me few options. I needed someone to talk to and I was leaning towards confiding in my father. He seemed my best and safest option. After all, he'd never told anyone about what had happened to him. Or at least I didn't think so. He hadn't told his therapist…or had he? Was that why Sam alluded to the fact that there was so much more to know about my father? I couldn't ask her about it because of confidentiality issues. The doctor-patient relationship is sacred and Sam is a stickler for the rules.

I was running late for work after my Zoom when I finally got to the subway. Worrying about the guy who confronted me, wondering who to confide in, I'd missed Jarad's call this morning. He sent a text: *You ok?* I responded, *Yes. Talk later.*

I gave the message a heart emoji and put the phone in my bag, tamping down the guilt that I only corresponded with Jarad when I felt like it. I didn't want to use him, but I knew that he was not foremost in my mind, and the safety of the long-distance relationship was probably the detriment of it too.

I caught the train immediately, slipping in as the doors closed. That rarely happened, even though I checked the MTA app before I headed out of my door. Trains in my neighbourhood tended to be late, for various reasons. I tried to be on time for everything and always heard my mother in my head saying to be late was a sign of disrespect. At my office there was no penalty for being late. I was the one who was stressed out about time. Most days I arrived early and left late, so a few minutes made no difference, except to me. I didn't like the fact that my head was elsewhere, my thoughts were scattered, and I couldn't seem to focus.

I sat down heavily on the one empty seat on the train and suddenly I felt the hairs at the back of my neck stand up. A shiver passed right through me. Apprehension clouded my vision and I felt dizzy. I made a point to breathe slowly. *I will not pass out on the subway. What in the bloody hell is wrong with me?*

And then I saw him. Or at least his feet. Spandex man. I knew it was him by his sneakers. He was about ten feet from me, standing and holding on to the top rail. There were a dozen people between him and me. I did not look upward and risk making eye contact. *Is this a coincidence? Or did he follow me here?* If he had, in fact, followed me, that meant he knew where I lived. What the hell was up with him? I kept watch on his feet and his black-jeans-clad legs, but they didn't get off at any of the stops. I pointedly pulled out my phone and look at the screen.

At my stop, I waited until the last second to exit, crashing into passengers entering the train through the open doors. There was some cursing behind me as I yelled back my apologies and I practically vaulted the turnstile and ran up the stairs to the street.

Without looking back, I walked east as fast as I could, and when I reached Second Avenue, I risked a quick look back. No sign of him. *Maybe it wasn't even him,* I told myself. *There are probably thousands of people with those same neon running shoes.* But my body knew it was him. That tiny reptilian part of the brain left over from thousands of years of fleeing danger, that part of me knew.

I made a point to regulate my breathing, and as soon as I was in my office, I called my father and arranged to meet him after work. He said he would be waiting outside for me at six.

Rather than second-guess my decision to confide in him, I got right into the day's work. Emails and phone calls to return. I had to send out a report on the video meeting I participated in and the day flew by. Thankfully.

At 5:55 I closed my computer, hung up my lab coat, and tossed the four empty coffee cups. Nasty habit. I wished I'd never started drinking coffee.

Chapter 17

Confession

My father is really a handsome man. I walked out of my office and towards him. It was amazing Carol hadn't honed in on him. Maybe she couldn't see him from her desk. He was talking on his cell and didn't see me at first, but when he did, he put the phone in his pocket and came the last few steps towards me.

"Pia, thanks for calling me." He leaned in and half-hugged me. Still a little bit uncomfortable with each other, but we were trying. "Your mother says hi. Helena is getting her hair done one last time before she has to deal with doing it herself at the lodge."

"No hair salons up there?" I asked. My mother was not a vain woman, but rather a woman who knew what she wanted and didn't mind spending money to get it. She had been going to the same hairdresser her entire time in New York. It would be a hard jolt of reality for her to be in a place with no Natasha at the Leoni Salon.

"Funny girl. She will text when she is done. What do you feel like?" My father looked intently at me. His green eyes sparkled like emeralds and his tanned face was smiling. No wonder my mother could never forget him. He had naturally assumed that I was inviting him out for a meal.

"How about we walk across town and eat at Teacher's?" I suggested. "Reliable and delicious."

"Perfect. I love that place." He started towards the crosswalk and I followed. His long, loping gait had me rushing to catch up.

Sam always complained that I walked fast, but this was too fast even for me.

"Slow down a bit." I grabbed his arm. Again I felt a little jolt of electricity. Or a spark. It seemed like every time I was in contact with him there was a frisson of energy that jumped between us. Could he feel it? He said nothing if he did. I did not know how to broach the subject I wanted to discuss.

"So what's up?" he asked casually, but I could tell he was more than curious as to why I would seek him out without my mother. "Is everything okay?" He stopped and placed his hands on my shoulders, forcing me to make eye contact.

"Everything is—well, good, I guess. Work is fine, Sam's great, it's all good." My answer sounded lame to me and I guess to him too.

"What are you not saying?" He led me over to a stone planter box and we perched on the edge of it, facing the street, not each other.

"I really don't know where to begin." To my horror, I started to sob. Huge, racking sobs that came out like I had been holding my breath for a month.

He sat next to me and said nothing. When my sobs had subsided, he put his arm around my shoulders. "I have to say, you're kind of freaking me out. Tell me what's going on."

I didn't know where to begin, what to say, how to word it.

"Is this about Robert?" he asked kindly, gently. His voice was soothing and supportive. He was ready to console me. I could feel it.

"No, not at all," I answered truthfully. Robert was on my mind, but not for the reasons he thought. I started, "Juris—"

"Will you ever call me Dad?" he interrupted. I could see the longing in his face.

"I don't know. Maybe someday. I barely know you."

He held his hand up. "Pia, you know me. I have told you everything about me. About the things that happened to me. You know the reason I left, and very few people know that whole story."

"I know. I appreciate that. But you have to understand that I went without a father for twenty-six years. I can't just suddenly refer to you as 'Dad' because I've known you for a year. But I'm not saying never, just not right now. Okay?"

He put his arm back on my shoulders. It felt good. I could feel the tingle where his arm was, but also his strength, his warmth.

I continued. "So the thing is…" I was stalling, but figured I might as well jump right in, so to speak. "I went to the bio bay last year with Sam." I stopped speaking, figuring out my next words, and he waited for me to continue. I was trying to figure out how to phrase what I wanted to divulge. What I needed to share. "It was magical." I took a deep breath. "That day, that morning, I had injured my leg and hands on the coral at Navio." I felt him straighten up and tense.

"Continue," he said.

"And I fell in. We hadn't planned on swimming. You're not supposed to. You and I shouldn't have been swimming there either. It's really frowned on now. Anyways, I toppled in and the next day, my cuts were healed like they hadn't happened at all."

He was excited. "The same as me! That's exactly the same thing that happened to me. I healed up. Barely a mark where I was cut. And I was cut deep." He rolled up his sleeve and pointed to where the injury had been.

"Yes, it was as if the water was magic," I said, feeling relief and also joy that I had revealed my secret. Well, part of it. The bigger part was about to be exposed. I shivered and he held me tighter.

"Do you want to grab a cab?" he asked me.

"No, but let's head to the restaurant, I am getting cold."

"Wait a minute." He stood on the sidewalk. "After I healed, I found out about the ripples. Time ripples. Does this mean that you experienced them too?" His voice was excited and an octave higher than normal.

I answered a barely audible yes.

"My god, Pia. You experienced it too. I am not hallucinating. It is real." He gathered me into his arms and hugged me tight. "I can't believe it! This is amazing."

He let me go and we stood facing each other. His reaction was different from what I had anticipated. I thought he would be full of questions, but rather he was just feeling validated.

"So it happened to you too. What about your friend?"

"Sam? No, she didn't swim. I was only in the water because I fell in. I wasn't even aware that I'd healed up until the next day." I looked at my hands, barely visible in the evening darkness.

He was shaking his head and laughing to himself muttering, "All these years, all these years, wondering and trying to convince myself. It is real."

"Oh yes, it's very real."

"Does anyone else know?"

"Know?" I asked him.

"About you? About the magic?"

The magic. I had never really dared call it magic. Magic isn't real. Magic is an illusion. Card tricks and pulling rabbits out of hats. What I could do was very, very real.

"Yes, Sam and Kash both know that I have experienced the ripples."

He was shaking his head in amazement. "They believe you?"

I could see his point. Friends taking my word for it would be difficult under normal circumstances. But, I explained, "They were aware of what was happening to me right from the beginning. The first thing was time kind of passed quickly or slowly or something. We were all skeptical at first. We all eventually kind of accepted that it was my new reality. It didn't make sense, but that didn't mean it wasn't happening to me."

He took his phone out of his jacket pocket and typed *Teacher's*, turned the screen so that I could see he was responding to my mother, and then put it back in the pocket. His eyes were back on me.

"They are truly great friends. Over the years, I have tried to tell a few people and they have all referred me to a doctor they know who could help. It's so easy to dismiss what we don't understand, but not so easy to live it."

"Exactly." He had nailed it. "Just when I convince myself that what is happening cannot be real, then it happens again."

"Wait, Pia. You have had multiple time ripples?"

"I have."

That sentence hung in the air between us. He absorbed the weight of it as I let the weight of the secret, lighter now that it was shared, dissipate.

We walked into the restaurant and were shown to a table in the middle of the back room. There were too many people around us for the conversation to go unheard. We concentrated on small talk, spoke of his impressions of New York City, and then my mother showed up, looking as perfect as always in a matching casual suede jacket and pencil skirt. Her hair looked beautiful and I told her so.

My father pulled out her chair and she said to both of us, "What's the secret? You two look like you're cooking something up." She laughed and accepted white wine from the waiter.

I was sure I blushed, but in the dim room no one could tell, and my father expertly deflected her question by complimenting her on what an amazing job she did raising me.

My mother fell for it, and I appreciated the surreptitious wink my father gave me.

Chapter 18

City Hall Meeting

NARRATOR: SAM

Jessie poked her head into my office. I was feeling lousy sitting at my desk reviewing our session notes wondering if there was more I could have done for Joel. Death is so final and I will never have the chance to make a difference with him.

"What's up?" I attempted cheerfulness.

"The mayor's office called. You're wanted over at city hall."

"Wanted for what? Is this about Joel?" I didn't need this. I saw him one time. I couldn't be held responsible for what he did. The mayor surely wouldn't press charges. Jesus, now I felt a major headache starting.

"Hey." She held up her hands. "Don't shoot the messenger. They said only to clear your morning and if you could get there by ten a.m., and I quote, 'It would be greatly appreciated.'"

I looked at my watch: 9:45 am. "Thanks, Jessie. I'll head over shortly." City Hall is a five-minute walk from my office. My office was central and one of the reasons I was thrilled with it was the location. Close to all the subway lines.

She closed the door quietly behind her.

I sat still for a few minutes and then gathered my phone, water bottle, and notes, shoved them into my laptop bag, and headed across the street to city hall.

This area of downtown was gorgeous. The park, the pedestrian walkways leading to the walkway across the Brooklyn bridge. Benches for office workers from Federal Plaza and the courts to have lunch. Newlyweds posing in front of trees and buildings, freshly hitched at City Hall. Traffic was gridlocked as I crossed the street diagonally to the entrance of City Hall.

I pulled my ID out of my pocket and handed it to the guard. He scanned it and handed it back.

I took off my jacket, removed my phone from my pocket, and passed my bag through the scanner. As I was putting my jacket back on, two plainclothes security guards came up to me, greeted me by name, and escorted me directly up a private elevator to the mayor's office.

He was standing behind his desk as I entered. "Dr. Sodhra, please come in." His voice was velvety and his smile was forced. His gray pinstriped bespoke suit was a perfect fit, tailored to emphasize his height and hide the paunch swelling above the waistband. His silver tie was loosened at the neck of a crisp white shirt. Shoes shined to mirror gloss completed the ensemble and I found myself standing taller as a reaction.

"Mr. Mayor, please let me offer my sincere condolences. I—"

He held up his hand for me to stop talking. *How rude*, I thought.

"Appreciated, Doctor. Now, let me get straight to the point." He gestured to one of the leather club chairs facing his desk. I sat.

I didn't like his brusque manner and could see why Joel had a hard time with this man, his father.

"You are under no circumstances to talk to the press. Do you understand?" He sat down and put his hands flat on his desk.

"Sir, I am bound by physician-patient confidentiality. I would never discuss a patient. With anyone." I sounded indignant, but how dare he?

"Good. See that you report any harassment or if anyone is trying to get to you." I must have looked puzzled. "Press, paparazzi, even the Republicans. It could be anyone trying to discredit me."

I looked at his manicured fingers adorned by a simple gold wedding band and thought about the fact that his only son had just died. He was here conducting business like it was a regular day. How must his wife have felt to have her husband go off to work? I felt anger rising up in me. The nerve of this guy. Taking a tragedy, the death of his son, and making it all about him.

"I will speak to no one about your son, sir. Rest assured. Now if you'll excuse me, Mr. Mayor, I have patients." I stood up. I wanted to get away from this slimeball.

"Thank you for coming, Doctor. Leave your notes with my secretary on your way out."

I turned to face him. "Excuse me?"

"My son's file. Your notes. Please leave them here, and if you have backups, please destroy them. I can't be too careful." He picked up the phone on his desk.

"I will not," I said firmly.

His mouth dropped open in surprise. There was steel in his voice now, almost menace. "You will not what, Doctor?"

"I do not carry around patient charts, and my notes are for my eyes only." I sounded stronger than I felt and turned to go, hoping he didn't sense my fear.

I could feel his laser eyes on my back. I managed to get downstairs without passing out. As I exited the building, I drew a deep breath. I hate a bully, and that's exactly what he was. He was the cause of Joel's unhappiness. I wouldn't kowtow to him.

I had an hour free, so I sat outside on a bench and people-watched. So different from L.A., where everyone drove everywhere. I gazed around this adopted city that I loved. City hall gardens are beautifully manicured, and other than the occasional rat jumping out of and running around the trash cans, it was spectacular. The sun reflected off the Frank Gehry building on Spruce Street. Kash and I toured one of those apartments when we came back from our honeymoon. Way out of our price league, but beautiful. Now we would be moving into the uptown apartment in which I spent my last years of med school. I loved that apartment.

We would have two bedrooms, and a separate living room/dining room combo. That was a huge upgrade from our studio apartment. The city noises were like music to my ears. I closed my eyes and listened. Passersby chatted, music came out of car windows, and somewhere a child was crying.

Groups of walking tours headed across the Brooklyn Bridge were gathering with one megaphoned leader asking them to stay together and follow his sign. I opened my eyes to see the sign, a hand-drawn, brightly coloured cartoon drawing of the NYC skyline with a red arrow held aloft above the heads of his group. No problem following that sign, but his arm must have ached from holding that up all day.

Street vendors were getting set up for the lunch crowd. I could smell charcoal in the air as the pretzel vendors started to warm their fare. This city made me glad to be alive. My stomach growled and I decided to pick up Halal for myself and Jessie. Maybe I'd pick up a third meal and take it home to Kash.

Chapter 19

Dinner with Friends

NARRATOR: PIA

I was so looking forward to the end of the week. I had been going through the motions at work just to get to Friday, when I was having dinner with Sam and Kash. The newlyweds. We had a lot to catch up on, and I had been going over and over whether to tell them about the woman on the pier.

I still had an uneasy feeling about the spandex man, who may have seen something he should not have. Then I would decide it was impossible he'd seen what had not actually happened. Then I would remember the reverse ripples themselves were impossible…so maybe anything was possible.

I thought back to Kash's confession after one of my reverse ripples episodes. At his behest, I had intervened with his work partner's mother. I was able to save her, but somehow afterwards, Kash remembered asking me to do so. It was shocking for him to have knowledge of before and after the event. We hadn't spoken about it since, and I wasn't sure if he'd ever told Sam. It wasn't a secret, but it was an anomaly that he knew what had unfolded. And now the runner had questioned me. Was something even stranger than the reversing of time happening? I remembered every detail, but I was living with these anomalies. How could Kash have been in the same mindset as me, and why Kash? What made him special? Why not Sam? I had known her for almost a decade. And now another person was aware of the before and after.

My head felt ready to explode and I knew I would tell my friends about the pier. I needed a new perspective. Any kind of perspective.

We arranged to meet at Pep's for the best lemon and garlic pasta on the face of the earth, or at least in Manhattan.

Sam was walking up to Little Italy from downtown, I was taking the subway, and Kash was using Bikeshare and zipping down from class on the designated bike streets.

We all arrived at the same time and were shown to our favourite table in the back. The owner was a college friend who became a restaurateur after completing his undergrad degree. He was super Italian, super fun and a superb chef. His effusive greeting and complementary coffee martinis set the tone for the evening. I handed over the card from Carol and watched as they opened it together. Inside was a very generous Visa gift card, which they both agreed would be used for things for the new, much bigger apartment.

"Like a new bed," Sam said, laughing. She'd told me more than once that she wanted a king-sized bed, and I always teased her that a single was more suited to her size.

"Or a huge TV," Kash replied, baiting her.

She swatted his arm and said, "The TV we have is perfectly fine and you know it. Besides, you don't have time to watch TV anymore." I laughed at both of them. My dearest friends. It was as if they had been together forever. Hard to believe that a year ago they were meeting for the very first time.

We ordered, and while we ate I dropped a bombshell. "So, I told my father about the bio bay and what happened to me."

Sam almost choked on her food. Sputtering, she asked, "What prompted that confession?"

"Honestly, I don't know. I just felt like telling someone, and I knew he would keep the secret. But something else happened." I twirled spaghetti on my fork and savoured the taste of the al dente pasta with garlic and a hint of lemon. *So good. I really have to ask him how it's made.*

Kash asked, "Something else, or someone else?"

"Wait," Sam said, "I thought you hadn't been experiencing any ripples lately." She looked intently at me.

"Look, guys, the other day something happened. Something really weird."

They both put their forks down on the table and waited for me to speak.

"I went for a run the other morning and saw a woman on Pier 87 fall into the water."

Kash thought for a moment and asked, "The one with the new construction?"

"Yes. I pointed it out to you once because it is the future home of pickleball courts and we were making fun of that."

Kash laughed. "Yeah, exactly. I mean, come on, who names a game 'pickleball'?"

Sam elbowed him and said "Shh."

"So I am out running, I see her fall in. I grabbed her in the water, she had hit her head. Definitely dead. Ripples. Boom! She's back up on the pier alive."

They both waited.

Finally Sam said, "So?"

Kash said, "That's what you do. You caused her to not die. You've done it before. I can't believe we're even having this conversation, like what you do is normal. But, I have to ask, what was so weird?"

"The weird thing was this guy who saw it." I could picture him and got goosebumps up my arms. I looked around quickly to make sure he wasn't in the restaurant. "He saw her fall in, and then he saw her when it had not actually happened and she was on the pier, safe and dry."

They both stared at me and said nothing.

I said nothing back.

Pep came over to ask us if we wanted dessert, and we demurred. He said he would bring us another round of martinis, we looked like we could use them. We thanked him, then continued to sit silently.

"He *saw*?" Sam finally asked.

Pep placed the three martinis on the table and quickly left.

"He saw her before and after." I downed half my martini.

"How do you know?" Kash asked.

"He chased me while I was running and asked me what the hell just happened. I was shocked. I blew him off, but…"

"But what?" Sam leaned forward and almost knocked over her glass. She righted it and took a sip.

"I think he followed me home, and I think I may have seen him on the train the other morning."

"Fuck." Kash let that hang in the air.

"Yeah, exactly, fuck." I drank the rest of the martini and sat back against the banquette.

Sam piped up. "That's not even possible. How could he see what actually didn't happen? You prevented her from falling in, so she didn't fall in, hit her head, or die."

Kash just looked confused, and was about to say something when he met my eyes and kept quiet. I said nothing. There was no answer. It made absolutely no sense at all.

Minutes ticked by, and finally I said, "So, good honeymoon?"

We all burst out laughing and the morose spell was broken. Sam talked about the resort they stayed in and the scuba lessons they took. Kash described the pig roast on the beach and Sam made gagging noises to accompany his description. A diehard vegan, Sam was not on board with the whole pig or any part of any animal being consumed. I laughed and asked how veganism was going for Kash. He made gagging noises as his wife gave him a dirty look.

Sam said, and Kash readily agreed, that they both felt as if they had known each other forever.

I thought about the ghostly image of them as teenagers on the beach at their wedding just as Kash said, "Sometimes when I look at Sam I can see her as a teenager." He laughed self-consciously and Sam replied, "The same thing happens with me, and I haven't even seen a photo of him as a little kid or a teen. It is crazy."

Maybe not, I thought and reached out to both of them.

Kash paid for dinner using a tiny portion of the very generous gift card and we grabbed our coats. We waved to Pep, busy at the pizza oven, and went outside.

Kash scanned the cars coming up the street for our rideshare license plate, and Sam took me by the arm and whispered, "Are you okay about Robert?"

Was I? I really didn't know how to answer that. "I was freaked out about it when I first heard. We haven't talked in almost a year and then out of the blue he sent a postcard." Sam still did not know about me being called to look at Robert's and Sofia's bodies.

"What? You never told me that. When did you get it?"

I tried to make my voice light. "Last week, when I came back from Vieques."

She was animated and intense. "What did he say?"

"He wanted me to forgive him," I replied flatly.

"Asshole!" Sam said, and I agreed, but I felt definite disquiet. He hadn't been an asshole when I was with him. He had been loving and kind. I didn't know what had changed him, but my feelings for him when we were together were very real.

Kash called over to us that the car pulling up was ours, and we went over and got in. I knew Sam would tell Kash when they got home, and I had a feeling she wasn't going to let this go.

The car dropped them off first and then me, farther uptown.

We were all going to spend the weekend packing our respective apartments.

Chapter 20

The Mayor's Agenda

"Fuck, fuck, fuck," I said to no one in particular. I was holding my phone, but felt like throwing it at a wall as Kash handed me coffee.

"What is it? Bad news?" He sat on the edge of the bed to drink his coffee.

"The mayor wants to see me again. No, correction, *demands* to see me. Jessie just sent me a message."

"The Joel situation?"

"Yes, the one you know nothing about. Right, husband?"

"Mum's the word. You want to shower first?" He got up and held his hand out to pull me into an embrace. God, I loved him.

"Yes, but I will be quick. I have to get downtown asap."

"You, quick? That'll be a first." He laughed and folded up the Murphy bed into its wall cabinet.

Jessie was behind her desk when I entered the office.

"You have two goons in there to escort you to city hall." She gestured over her shoulder at my office.

I froze. "You're kidding, right?"

"Yes, I'm kidding, but you are commanded to appear before your highness this morning."

I laughed. The best move I ever made was hiring Kash's brother's girlfriend. She was a gem. Manny, younger by three years, begged Kash to find his girlfriend a job. Gorgeous, dark-haired, dark-eyed Jessie. A talented guitarist and cook. Turned out she was exactly what I needed, and she had become invaluable in the year since my office opened.

"Okay, might as well get it over with. I'll just put my laptop in my office and then head over. What time is my first patient?"

"Ten o'clock. A couple. Marriage on the rocks, hoping for you to save them." She winked as she said this.

"Got it. Back in a flash. I hope." I pointedly left my briefcase on my desk and left the office.

"Where is your bag, doctor?" one of the security men asked as he escorted me to the top floor after I'd walked through the metal detector.

I ignored him but could feel my pulse rising at being questioned. I just gave him a withering look, which Kash assures me leaves no one uncertain of how I feel.

The door opened on cue and I entered the royal domain for the second time.

"Thank you for coming, Doctor. Would you like some coffee? I hear you love coffee in the morning." He slid behind his desk, snake that he is. His finger was poised above the intercom to order an underling to fetch for him.

"Mr. Mayor, can you please get to the point of this meeting?"

He seemed amused at my abruptness and smirked. "Yes, your notes, Doctor. You have been remiss."

"My notes, as I said before, are confidential, and I can assure you, will not be seen by anyone." I stood up and made to leave.

"I can subpoena them, you know." Steel in his voice.

"On what grounds? My one session with your son is not worth your trouble. I had hoped to help him. I thought we made some progress." And that was true. I thought maybe Joel could get out from under his father and do something for himself. I was starting to think that the mayor wanted the notes simply to see if his son had mentioned him.

Just then, there was a loud knock at his door and all charm left him. He barked, "Do not interrupt me."

The door opened and his frown turned to fury, but when he saw who was outside the door, behind me, he said with real concern in his voice, "What's happened?"

The security guard came into the office and stood next to me. "I'll escort you out, Dr. Sodhra," he said, waiting for me to exit immediately.

Again the mayor asked, "What's happening?" He seemed to forget my presence and was oblivious to everything except his top advisor, who was rushing over to him.

I heard two words of what they said, as I was steered out of the room. "School shooting."

Oh no! I processed what this could mean for Manhattan or one of the other boroughs. An active school shooter. Happening right now. As soon as I exited the building, I called Kash. He answered immediately, knowing I didn't normally call during the day.

"What's happened?" Kash's voice was full of concern.

"I just left the mayor's office," I said, carefully crossing the street and heading back to my office. "There's a school shooting. Right now. Have you heard anything?"

"I was in class. I haven't heard a word. I'll call you back." He hung up and I tried Pia.

The call went straight to voicemail, no surprise there. She didn't have her personal cell on her when she was working. I left a voicemail message to call me back, then went inside my office building and up to my office.

Chapter 21

School Shooting in NYC

NARRATOR: PIA

The place was a madhouse. Active shooter at an elite prep school uptown. Nine confirmed dead, the shooter among them. Madness. Teenagers.

Ten years ago, I was a teen thinking about homework assignments, doing parkour every day, and watching *Degrassi*. Now a student had brought a semi-automatic weapon into his school and let loose during assembly. It's a wonder more people weren't killed.

This type of crime, this tragedy, was happening over and over. I saw its devastation every single day lying on the slab in our morgue. Now ten sets of parents had lost their teenage sons and daughters.

I pictured my mother. How would she have coped if something tragic had happened to me? She would have become an activist against guns, of that I am certain. She would have been loud, focused, and would never have stopped her crusade. I raged at the unfairness of these young lives snuffed out in a flash. It was beyond heartbreaking, but I was a professional, and I would soon be face-to-face with these grieving parents.

I didn't take a lunch break, and when I got back to my office it was well past six p.m. I saw a missed call from Sam hours ago, but I didn't have the mental energy to talk to anyone right now. All I could do was change into my street clothes, grab my purse and jacket, and head outside.

I splurged on a rideshare uptown, way too exhausted to navigate the subway, completely missing that uptown would be a traffic nightmare due to the streets around the school being cordoned off. I would have been better off taking the subway, but it was too late now. I just rested my head and tried to relax as we crept along at two miles an hour. I knew exactly where the incident happened. It was directly across the street from my old high school. As we crept slowly up Broadway, I couldn't stop myself from peering out at the yellow police tape. I saw someone I thought I recognized and sat up straighter. I willed him to turn around, and as if he heard me, he turned slowly in my direction.

I recognized him even without the spandex. Today he was in a navy suit, and as my cab cruised slowly past, his eyes locked on mine. I couldn't look away. His gray eyes were hypnotic and the questioning look on his face was etched in my mind.

The other thing I noticed was the gold detective shield clipped to his breast pocket. *A cop? Good god, I didn't expect that.*

My heart was going a thousand beats a minute and I was starting to sweat. *A cop saw the ripple. That cop may have followed me. Why did a cop have to be out running that morning? Can he trace me? Does he know who I am?*

I closed my eyes and leaned my head back again. Traffic was moving now, and just as I dozed off, the cab pulled to a stop in front of my building. I now had the energy to call Sam. She would have an opinion on this latest development for sure.

Sam got right to the point. "A cop? And you are sure he recognized you?"

"Oh yeah. He had these steely gray eyes. He looked like…"

"A wolf?" She laughed.

"Yes, exactly like a wolf." Feral, wild. Something low down in my body reacted to the memory of that look he gave me. *Hmmm, I haven't felt that way in a while. Why with this guy? A cop, for god's sake?*

Sam continued, "This memory just popped into my head of this stray dog that came to our yard when I was a kid. He had gray eyes."

"Your brothers were talking about that dog in Vieques."

"Really. That's so weird. I haven't thought about that dog in twenty years. He was so friendly and attentive and then one day he just never came back." She sounded as if she might cry.

"Maybe you and Kash should get a dog," I suggested.

"No way. It's not fair to a dog to be cooped up all day in an apartment. When I get a yard someday, I'll get a big mangy mutt."

"I can't wait to see that," I laughed, "but in the meantime my spandex cop may be trouble."

Sam got a second wind. "Oh, speaking of trouble, that's the reason I called earlier. The shooting. I guess your office has all the details."

"Yes, too many." I definitely did not want to rehash the day. I got up off the sofa and went into the kitchen to grab a glass of wine.

I was pouring when she said, "I heard about the shooting when I was in Mayor Jerk's office this morning."

I put the glass down in the living room. "Again? What did he want this time?" I made my way down the hall to the bedroom, stripping as I went. I grabbed the bathrobe off the bed and picked up my discarded clothes as I made my way back to the sofa. I put the heap of clothes on the chair next to me to wash in the morning.

"Same shit. Wanted my notes, but we were interrupted by his aide. You know the guy who has hair plugs and thinks he's god's gift to women?"

"Treyon?" I could see him in my mind. All five-foot-five of him, strutting around importantly every time the mayor had a press conference. We had crossed paths a few times.

"Yeah. Treyon. Kash knows him. They went to school together or something. Anyways, I had an idea when I heard about the shooting. Are you drinking wine?"

"Yes, a Zinfandel. Waiting for Beaujolais to come out. What's your idea?" I savoured the aroma and then let the wine hit all my taste buds before swallowing it.

"My idea is that you stop school shootings."

"What?" I put my glass back on the table. "Are you crazy?"

"No, Pia. I am not. I'm not saying all school shootings. But locally. What if you could stop even one shooter from killing schoolkids?"

I let her sentence hang in the air between us. What if I *could* stop even one shooter from killing school kids? Could I do that?

Chapter 22

An Idea Forms

It was stuck in my head. What if I could prevent a school shooting? Any kind of shooting. I had saved Isiah from a bullet to the head by intervening, reverse ripple effect. He was a child who had caught a stray bullet. It was one of my happiest moments to know that child lived. I hadn't thought about him for almost a year. I hoped he was doing well. That whole night had been such a mess. No parents at home, shooter on the loose in the projects, the child hit by a stray bullet.

I turned my thoughts back to the question: Could I somehow prevent multiple deaths? The biggest hurdle was timing. I didn't know when my time ripple would manifest. There was no way for me to predict when someone was going to snap and take a gun to a public place or a school. How could I stop that kind of senseless killing? This question weighed heavily on my mind as I went back to work.

Gun violence. Gun violence. Gun violence. It was everywhere. Six hundred mass shootings in the United States every year for many, many years, the number on the rise and with no solution in sight. America stood for freedom and opportunity; kids should not be hiding from shooters or dodging bullets in classrooms. When I was in school we had fire drills. Now kids were being trained on what to do if a shooter came into the classroom.

How has this country gone so far off the rails?

I wanted to scream from the rooftops that this had to stop, but to whom?

I had ten dead teenagers in the morgue, a slew of injured in hospitals, and a city traumatized. Yesterday nine students got up, packed their backpacks, said goodbye to their families, and went to school having no idea that their lives would come crashing to a halt, at the hands of their unhappy, and perhaps mentally disturbed, classmate. Senseless. Could I change this kind of event? If I could find a way, I was determined to do it.

I answered emails and spoke with Kash between classes. We discussed logistics for the move and he offered Trez's help and van. I gladly accepted and agreed he and Sam should come up to the apartment to see what I was taking with me and what I was leaving. It was a normal, everyday discussion, a pleasant reprieve from the agony I felt for the shooting victims and their families. I would never get used to or immune to grief. Empathy was a part of life and a very necessary part of my job, but a hard part nonetheless.

Dr. Bowman popped into my office so we could update each other. After he left, I felt exhausted. I changed my clothes and grabbed my bag, thinking a walk across town to clear my head might be a good idea.

I would be moving on the weekend, I had the entire place to pack up, and hadn't even thought to ask for time off to do it. Work was crazy and it would have been a major inconvenience for me to take time off. So I walked and I focused on breathing and popped my earbuds in to listen to some music. I took my cell phone out of my bag and saw on the locked screen that I had missed a call. I didn't recognize the number, but I knew the area code was for Vieques, 787. My heart leapt to my throat and I immediately called my grandmother.

"Hola," her chipper voice said.

"Oh, Nona, I'm so glad you are okay. Did you call me?" I slowed my pace so my breathing did not sound so harsh.

"Cassiopeia, no, I didn't call. Are you okay? You sound breathless." She, on the other hand, sounded completely calm, and

I could picture her sitting outside, watching the water, drinking her herbal tea or a cocktail.

"I'm fine, Nona. Just walking across 32nd Street. It's busy and noisy. You know the city." I deftly avoided a collision with a super stroller, pushed one-handed by a nanny holding a dog leash in the other hand.

"Ugh, that place. I cannot stand the chaos. What's new, my darling Pia?"

"I got a call from a 787 area code. I don't recognize the number." I changed screens and recited the number to her.

"Does not ring a bell with me. Did they leave a voicemail?"

"No."

"Did you return the call?"

"No, I don't like to call numbers I don't recognize. There are too many scammers out there."

"Yes, very wise." She changed the subject. "How are the newlyweds?"

We talked as I walked across town to Penn Station and then I disconnected when I got on the uptown train.

I got off at West End Avenue and walked to my new, now-empty apartment and walked inside.

My mother had, of course, left everything spic and span. The floors shone and the windows gleamed with the orange streetlight glow pouring in.

The kitchen looked as it had, lived in and loved. I opened the fridge and found a bottle of sparkling wine with a purple bow tied around the neck. A sticky note on the ribbon said, *Only good things, Mom and Juris.*

The unknown call was forgotten as I sketched out my plans for the living room and dining room. I would make Mom's bedroom an office and repaint the bathroom. It was very exciting to have this gorgeous place to live in. I couldn't wait to be back here. But for now, I would head uptown to my apartment and start the tedious process of what to keep and what to throw away.

I locked up and exited the apartment, went outside, and stood on the concrete stoop. As a teenager, I'd spent many hours hanging out with my friends on this stoop, especially in summer. We would sit and make up life stories about all the people walking by. It was one of my best memories of this apartment building and community.

My elderly neighbour, Mrs. Seeger, who recently passed away, would sometimes join us and regale us with stories of her youth growing up on the Lower East Side. I was lost in the memory for a second, thinking about the time I'd spent with her. I was a latchkey kid from time to time, and she would often greet me as I came in from school and invite me in for cookies. I spent many afternoons listening to her talk about the old days, her children and grandchildren, and what she loved about New York City.

My mother found her passed away alone in her apartment and I have regretted ever since that I didn't spend more time with her.

The picture she painted of growing up in the 1930s in New York was the stuff of old movies that I could appreciate now but rolled my eyes at back when I was a teenager. She had a story about her father's shoe shop on Ludlow Street, and how she and her little sister would stand outside on weekends all year round selling shoes from a pushcart. When I went to the Lower East Side, I always looked around for the building her father owned, fantasizing that I would see her and her sister standing by a pushcart. She was a treasure and part of the fabric of my life, and now I was going to be living back in the building I grew up in. Mrs. Seeger put pumpkins on the steps in the fall, evergreens around the doors during the Christmas holiday season, and tulips in pots in spring. Our front stoop was always colourful and inviting and a good place to hang out.

Maybe I would be the stoop fairy now and carry on the tradition.

I had once told Sam about hanging on the stoop, but she didn't understand it. It's a New York thing. Everyone gravitates outside to hang out on their front steps because most apartment dwellers do not have backyards or air conditioners. It's a level playing field to sit outside. Sometimes lawn chairs appear and the group spreads to the sidewalk in front of the building. Then out comes a kiddie pool and everyone soaks their feet. Someone shows up with a little grill and another person provides hot dogs. Then music starts and a couple of flashlights or portable spotlights appear. That is summer in the city. That could be me next summer, hangin' out on the stoop, guessing about the lives of passersby and eating cookies. It saddened me to realize that as an adult with a job, I would not have time to stoop sit, but I might still decorate.

Chapter 23

Paranoia

I decided to walk uptown. I popped in my earbuds, selected my soundtrack, and set off two miles straight up Broadway. After a few blocks, I started to feel eyes on me. That hairs-standing-up feeling. Was someone following me? New Yorkers develop a sense for these things, and I was on high alert.

People were shopping and going home from work. But amid people hustling past me in both directions, I had a funny feeling that someone was watching me and keeping pace with me.

I stopped and plopped myself down on a bench. I looked around, but did not see anyone suspicious. I didn't even know what I was looking for. A trench-coated man surreptitiously looking into a store window, but in fact clocking me? A familiar face? A creepy face? Someone I knew, or a stranger? I sat for about ten minutes as people passed by the bench, oblivious to the fact that my heart was pounding. I was sweating and feared I might pass out.

No one was acting suspicious or standing out to me, so I started to walk again. The feeling was still there, humming inside me and making goosebumps appear on my skin.

I assessed the situation. There were people all around me. The street was populous and well lit. I had my cell phone and dug it out of my pocket and kept it in my hand. I took out the earbuds and put them away. I glanced behind me every block but did not see anyone. My nerves were clanging by the time I reached my building. I debated going around the block to throw off any would-be follower, but didn't have the energy. Was anyone really following me? I was making myself ill with the *what ifs*.

I quickly entered the lobby, raced for the elevator, and sighed with relief when it came right away. As I entered, turned around, and jabbed my floor number, my eyes were drawn to the glass front door entrance to my building. Standing outside and looking in was the spandex cop man. He wasn't wearing running gear, but that image was burned in my mind's eye. Silver flashing eyes met mine as the elevator doors closed and I went upstairs. I nearly fainted and leaned against the wall for support, and when the doors dinged open, I ran into my apartment, breathless and still sweaty. My sweat cooled and I felt chilled all over.

He followed me? What in the holy hell is he doing? Why? How? I knew something was going on. I should have listened to my instincts and gone around the block. That might have flushed him out. I should have called a rideshare. Now I'm screwed because he definitely knows where I live.

What does he want from me?

I dropped my coat and bag on the floor and made sure the two front door locks were bolted and secure. Then I went into each room and turned on a light, shut the blinds, and checked that all windows were locked. I had never felt so unsafe before. What the hell did he want from me?

But I knew the answer: He wanted me to tell him how the impossible was possible. He didn't even question if he was seeing things. He knew what he'd seen, but he couldn't understand it, so he was looking for an explanation from me.

I was too unsettled to make dinner. I was too unsettled to do anything but sit in the rocking chair and brood. *Thank god I am out of here this weekend. But what if he shows up when Sam and Kash are here? Or what if he follows me to the West End Avenue apartment? No, wait, he must have followed me from there tonight. Oh my god, this is a nightmare.*

I was so wired I could barely think. I toasted and burned a grilled cheese sandwich, ate it in three bites, and realized I needed to calm myself down. I was inside. Safe. But safe from what? From whom? What did he want?

I would read to calm down. I dug out Carlos's article on the Bermuda Triangle and promptly fell asleep in the chair. My morning alarm woke me and I dragged my stiff body into the shower. The fear I had felt the night before had receded somewhat, and I tried in vain to convince myself I had overreacted. Who did he think he was? Detective or no detective, he was freaking me out.

Chapter 24

DAYDREAMING

NARRATOR: SAM

When I was living in Los Angeles, everything flowed California style. No rush, no pressure. People became used to the traffic that could slow you down for hours, the immense lines at the local coffee place, and having to wait so long for parking attendants that it set you behind for the whole day. Patients missed appointments, cancelled at the last minute, or showed up when they didn't even have an appointment.

Californians thought therapy was as essential as breathing, but being on time was not necessarily part of the lifestyle.

They said, "Of course you're in therapy. Everyone is." There was no stigma to seeking help. People compared therapists at cocktail parties and therapists handed out cards like candy. There was a casualness to the city born of the beautiful weather every day that made you feel good, no matter what. Vitamin D doing its best work.

New York was the opposite. New York style was at a hectic, loud pace. People were unforgiving and could be rude at times. But they stayed. They stayed and they staunchly defended this city of craziness, anonymity, and chaos. New Yorkers believed in therapy because they had a problem and they wanted to be fixed. They did not discuss their problems at cocktail parties and many would not admit they were in therapy, but they went because they wanted solutions.

It was hard to live in a city of 11 million people. While some craved anonymity, others were swallowed up by the largeness, complaining how insignificant they felt and how hard it was to make connections. Depression, phobias, addictions, anger management, personality disorders, obsessions, rejections, grief, trauma, and guilt were the real issues New Yorkers in my growing practice dealt with.

But New York City got in the blood. I was so happy to be back in this city I loved. I embraced the brash loudness and vibrations that make the city pulse. The one year in LA felt like ten years. The time crawled and the days melded together into a blank canvas of nothingness. I made no meaningful friendships, had no amazing experiences, and mostly spent time comparing LA to NYC. No comparison.

I would have moved back to New York whether I was with Kash or not. I knew that the first month I was in practice out there. Pia knew it too. It's not that I wasn't happy, I just wasn't challenged or fulfilled. If I listened to one more patient spend an entire session complaining about a rude salesperson or that her daily cleaning lady didn't want to work weekends, I thought I would lose my mind. I didn't spend nine years in school to listen to entitled, bored housewives complain about their lives—or worse, listen to them complain about their children taking up too much of their time. That killed me. Why even have kids if you don't plan to interact with them?

I got in early to write up some patient notes. Jessie requested the day off; her dog was sick and needed a vet visit. I had only seen photos of the dog—well, videos, albums, TikToks, and a doggie calendar she kept on her desk—but I do believe that animal lovers are special people.

I begged my parents for a dog when I was a child. Every birthday, at Christmas, and when I brought home my straight-A report cards. My mother always laughed and told me she had her hands full with my three brothers and me. I wouldn't let up. I promised to do all the dog walking myself, I would feed it, it could sleep in my room, and everything fell on deaf ears. Then one day, out of the blue, a large dog just appeared in our fenced backyard. No collar, and we had no idea how he had gotten in. He approached me as if he knew me. He felt like my gift from the universe. I manifested this dog and now there he was.

I named him Wolfie because of his long bristly hair and wolf-like eyes and would sneak food out to the yard for him. He and I played and romped around the yard. He was my faithful friend and companion. My brothers joked that Wolfie was my protector. He didn't interact with the three of them, no matter what they did. He waited for me after school. He sat beside me when I did my homework and he came around a few times a week for over a year, and then he just vanished. I was heartbroken. I never stopped looking for that dog. Every time I went to my parents' house, I gazed out their kitchen window looking for him. Very unrealistic at that point. Where did he come from, and where did he go?

So Jessie took her very much loved little dog Cheeko to the vet and I talked to myself and still wondered where Wolfie went.

I turned on the lights, watered the plants on her desk, and then popped in a coffee pod. The cup filled and I poured in some vegan creamer. I had fifteen minutes before the first patient arrived and I loved this time of preparation and expectation. I was meeting the mother of a recently deceased child. Brutal. The sadness was overwhelming and the finality of death was something that you had to learn to live with and eventually accept. She wanted therapy to help her deal with this new life without her only child.

The shrill ringing of my cell jarred me out of my tranquil state. I heard Treyon's voice: "Mr. Mayor needs to see you immediately."

"Nope, can't do it. I have a patient arriving momentarily."

"Cancel it. This is more important." He sounded so pretentious, as if he were the mayor himself, not the mayor's lackey.

"No, Treyon, I will not. My patient is much more important. I will check to see when I have a break and call you to reschedule." I hung up before he had a chance to start blustering. I knew how he operated.

The door to the waiting room opened, and I ushered in the mayor's wife. She was impeccably dressed and reminded me of Helena, Pia's mom. They had the same taste in clothing and the same elegant bearing. I directed her to the chair in front of my desk and sat down next to her. I waited a minute and then in a very calm voice introduced myself. She looked so forlorn, and when she made eye contact with me, I could see her son in her face. I was pretty certain she didn't know that I had treated Joel, and she would never find out from me.

I waited and finally she let her feelings pour out in a jumbled rush. She told me she was embarrassed to be seeing a psychiatrist and hadn't told her husband. He thought she was at her salon. Our session would be the first of many and I was immediately taken with her intelligence, inherent kindness, and fragility.

Our hour flew by and we scheduled her next appointment for two days hence. As she exited, she turned to me and said, almost pleadingly, "I would do anything, give anything, to have him back. No mother should lose a child."

I thought of how Pia had saved Joel last year. Now this mother was grieving her son for real.

I would see her twice a week going forward. It appeared I was tangled up in the mayor's family, and there seemed to be no escape from it.

No mother should lose a child, I thought to myself. I'd heard my own mother say it many times, when tragedy had struck one of her friends. I thought again about the school shootings happening too often and about bringing it up again with Pia. Could she do anything? Was I dreaming? I felt deep inside me that Pia might be able to intervene. Maybe this was the reason for her impossible power. Her reason for being magic.

I loved Pia with all my heart. She was the sister I never had; however, when these episodes first began, I did doubt her. But not anymore. She had a gift, the reverse-ripple effect, and I believed she could make a huge difference in our world. For real. It was crazy, but it was real. This world was messed up on a global scale, but right here at home in the United States we were perhaps the most out of control we had ever been. Pia couldn't help the world, or even make a difference nationally, but here in our backyard of New York City I believed she could work her magic.

Enough daydreaming. I had to get back to work.

I reluctantly pulled up the day's calendar on my screen to see when I could fit His Majesty into my schedule. I called Treyon back and scheduled another meeting for three p.m. This was ridiculous. What could he possibly want now? A whipping boy? I would need another couple of cups of coffee to fortify me for being face-to-face with our slimy mayor.

Chapter 25

A Smooth Move

NARRATOR: PIA

No sign of spandex man all week. I was exhausting myself keeping an eye out for him at all times, and then I would admonish myself for being ridiculous. I had nothing to fear from this guy—or did I? *He cannot prove a negative*, I kept repeating over and over. *If he confronts me again, I will simply accuse him of being delusional.* I just really did not like the idea that he might confront me. There was something about him that intrigued me or irritated me. I couldn't decide which. I reacted to him viscerally, although he would never know that. I barely acknowledged it myself.

I had to get my apartment packed up and had only a few days left to do so. I made a mental note to coordinate with Kash and Trez after work and was already planning on cooking them a huge paella thank-you meal at my new place. I had to make two versions, one regular and one vegan. Way more ingredients to shop for. I would be doing a huge online order to fill my new kitchen and fridge and I had to stop at the market to pick up fresh ingredients for the dish. A lot to do in the next few days, and as daunting as this move would be, I could feel the excitement building. Sam and Kash had already moved into my place in their heads. They had everything planned out for both bedrooms and I was certain their packing was completed and boxes were labelled. I hadn't even taped up the boxes I got from the downstairs deli. They were flattened and in a pile in the living room.

The week was hectic and I was surviving on too much coffee and an evening deli sandwich. The "three-meater" as Sam called it. Whenever I went into the deli I would be handed a few boxes to go with my sandwich. I would lug them upstairs and throw them into the pile.

I did go through my clothes, sorting them into piles: keep, donate, and throw away. My donations had been picked up by the Salvation Army, and each morning I lugged a suitcase full of my things and a plant over to the new place to make the move quicker on the weekend.

Friday night I wished Carol a good weekend and went outside to find Trez and Juan waiting in Trez's van. I did a double take. Juan, from Vieques, in New York City! My dear friend had flown from Puerto Rico to help me move—or rather, to be with Trez, and as an added bonus, help me move as well. I was so excited to see him I felt like crying.

We went straight to the apartment, and while they were assessing how many loads the panel van would hold, I went downstairs to order deli sandwiches. Sunday night we would feast on my homemade paella, but for the next few meals, we would be eating ad hoc deli.

I walked outside of my building and the ten steps to the deli. I went straight to the back and called my order to Oskar, whom I had known for years.

He called back, "Pia, someone was asking about you."

I froze, then slowly turned around and asked, "Who was it?" But I knew.

"To me, he looked like a cop."

He saw the look on my face and added, "Don't worry, I said nothing." Oskar was Hispanic and could do a perfect broken English accent, though he grew up one street over from me and had lived in the US his entire life.

"What did he say?" I didn't need to ask him to describe the person. There was only one person who would be asking about me.

"He asked if I knew you. He described your beautiful self. To a tee. But I told him, 'No, I not know her.' And then he left." Oskar went back to slicing meats for my triple sandwich order.

"When was this?"

"About ten minutes ago. I smelled cop right away. What'd you do?" He laughed as he composed the sandwiches.

"I didn't do anything!" I said in outrage, and when I looked at his face I saw that he was laughing and so I added, "Yet."

"I am going to miss you, chica," he added, and I reminded him that Sam was moving back in.

"Yeah, she doesn't eat meat," he said in a mock sad voice.

I started to walk towards the door, then turned and said, "But her husband does, and he is a big eater."

I could already picture Kash and Oskar getting along very well.

I took the sandwiches upstairs and popped open three beers, then we ate, using the deli wrap as plates.

I had moved into the West End Avenue apartment by Sunday evening, and Sam and Kash had settled into my old apartment. What a whirlwind.

I had a mountain of organizing and unpacking to do, but I was pretty sure Sam had the entire apartment fully settled the night they moved in. Her organizational skills would give Marie Kondo a run for her money.

I looked around at the piles of boxes and bags. My first priority was the plants. Once they were off the floor and onto window ledges and shelves, I could start hanging clothes and sorting through what would go in my home office. I had a desk and a brand new bedroom set. My old one was dated, and the full-size bed was too short for me. I can't get comfortable on any bed smaller than a queen. I threw my sheets into the washer and poured myself a glass of wine. A quiet ringing interrupted my planning. I walked around trying to locate my cell phone to answer the call. It had stopped by the time I found it discarded under sofa cushions.

A 787 number I didn't recognize and again, no voicemail. Dammit! Who was calling me and not leaving a message?

I switched the laundry, put my few dishes away in the already full kitchen cupboards, and finished the wine. As I made the bed with the new sheets, I found myself wishing things had gone differently with Robert. Maybe that 787 call had twigged my thoughts of him. How I would have loved to try out this new bed with him. How I missed the intimacy we had. It was so easy with him. Never uncomfortable. Never forced. Our bodies fit together so perfectly. It was as if we were one person. Would I ever feel that spark again with someone new? I used to love strange new bodies, and now, I just wanted comfortable, familiar, and compatible.

Next weekend was the conference in Binghamton, and Jarad would be joining me. I was not nearly as excited as I should have been at the thought of seeing him again. That was so unfair to him and to us. I should have been thrilled he was willing to fly across the country just to be with me in the evenings after my all-day meetings. I texted him that the move had gone well and I was in the apartment, up to my ears in boxes, but content. He had responded to my text with a very flashy fireworks screen display of thumbs up.

I made the bed, undressed, and fell into it. And then I suddenly remembered. I jumped up and double checked all the locks on the door and windows. That cop was out there somewhere, and he knew where I lived.

Chapter 26

Making Plans

New place for Kash but old stompin' grounds for me. I spent five years in this apartment and didn't realize how much I loved it and missed it. It was perfect. The commute was just a few extra stops on the train. Well worth it to get a separate bedroom and living room, not to mention the second bedroom for a study. There was so much space compared to the studio.

Kash's TV looked so large in our studio and now I saw that he would definitely want to upgrade. I warned him that there would be no TV in our bedroom. He could put one in the study. He was agreeable to just about anything, this easygoing husband of mine. He was in there now, planning out a man cave. His brother Manny was here and they were laughing like loons. I loved this man.

"Do you want anything?" I asked the two of them as I walked into the study.

"Do we have beer?" Kash asked.

"Yes, the fridge is stocked. Thanks to Pia." I took a wedding-gift wine goblet down from the shelf above the sink and poured myself a glass of wine.

Kash and Manny joined me in the living room, each drinking a bottle of Bud Light. Kash lit a patchouli candle and we sat enjoying the feeling of space. I rested my head on my husband's chest, put my feet up on the coffee table, and sighed.

"How you holding up?" he asked me.

"I am beyond exhausted. So tired that I feel like I'm glued to this sofa." I laughed, but the lethargy was very real. I had been tired all week, overdoing the planning, packing, and organizing. In the evening I had been writing out thank you notes for all the wedding gifts that kept coming in. I was trying to stay on top of everything, but the past week had kicked my ass.

"Oh man, I'm sorry. I'll get out of your hair." Manny stood up.

"No, Manny. Stay. We are grateful to you for all your help. How's the dog doing? Jessie said he wasn't feeling well after the vet visit."

"Cheeko's tough, but he is old. The vet said it's just old age and arthritis. He'll be okay, I think." Manny was still standing. "I'm gonna head out."

"Do you want to take the paella?" I asked him. Pia had sent the leftovers home with us.

"Yeah, sure. If that's okay with you guys. It was fantastic." He went out to the kitchen and came back carrying the large food container Pia had foisted on us.

I could see Kash looking longingly at the paella. "She sent the vegan one home for us as well."

"Oh yeah, vegan. Great," he said with no enthusiasm, and I laughed so hard the wine came out my nose.

Manny left happily with his food and the place was strangely quiet.

"What are you thinking, Sam?" Kash asked. He placed his empty beer bottle on the coffee table.

"I was actually thinking about this dog I used to feed when I was a kid." I hadn't thought of him in years and he had really been on my mind since the wedding.

"Whose dog?" he asked.

"I have no idea. I was around nine or ten and this huge wolf-like dog appeared in our backyard. I fed him and he would play just with me." I was lost in my memories of Wolfie.

"Was this your parents' fenced backyard?" He had been to my parents' house the previous Christmas and we had hung out in that yard.

"Yes, why?" I turned to look at him.

"How did he get in?"

I hadn't thought about that, but I did now. On the other side of the fence were woods for miles. The fence was about five or six feet tall, and the only gate was next to the house.

"Maybe he dug under the fence. I don't know," I answered, racking my brain. I would ask my brothers. They were older than me, and maybe there had been an opening I do not remember. "He would just be in the yard, sitting waiting for me."

We were silent for a while and then Kash asked me, "Do you want to get a dog?"

"Eventually, but not now. Not in this apartment. Besides, we are both too busy to give an animal proper attention."

"My wise wife," Kash said contentedly.

"What about you?" I asked him.

"Oh yeah. I want the whole nine yards, kids and a dog. White picket fence. Trampoline."

"Trampoline?" I laughed.

"Yes, I only ever saw one on television. Looked like fun." He laughed self-consciously. "City kid here. No trampolines in Harlem."

"Then you shall have a trampoline someday." We got up, turned off the lights, and went into our bedroom. Kash closed the door simply because we now had a door to close.

I couldn't stop thinking about how Wolfie got into our yard.

Chapter 27

School Safety Seminar

NARRATOR: PIA

"Hey, just checking in with you. I'm about to board. See you in Binghamton." Jarad sounded excited about his trip, involving three different flights. It would be a miracle of aviation if all the flights were on time and he actually made his connections.

"Okay, great, safe travels. I will meet you at the airport." I disconnected, feeling a bubble of discomfort take root.

I wanted to go away with him. I wanted to take our relationship to the next level, didn't I?

Even if I had second thoughts, it was too late now. He was on his way. Flashes of Robert popped into my head, and the pure physical excitement I had felt when I was with him. How completely and utterly physically satisfied I'd been. Would I have that with Jarad? Did I even want that again? What was he expecting from this weekend? My thoughts were all over the place as I threw my clothes into my overnight bag.

The conference was taking place in a Q hotel, known for its spacious ballrooms and conference facilities. Attendees would be housed in the same hotel and for three days all meals would be provided. I was really looking forward to the lectures and had signed up for a full agenda, including teen suicide and cyber bullying.

I landed an hour before Jarad, so I sat and watched the airport arrivals board for his flight. He came through the passageway smiling and enveloped me in a bear hug. My nerves settled at his easygoing manner and we grabbed a cab to the hotel. My first meetings were the next morning. We were both starving, and the plan was to drop our bags in the room and head out of the hotel for a late lunch.

As we entered the hotel lobby, my nerves started to clang. We were sharing a room; for the first time we would be spending our nights together. I realized that I was really nervous. We checked in, each receiving a key in a wallet size folder, instructions for WiFi, and passes for the buffet breakfast.

We went to the elevator and up to the sixth floor. As we went down the carpeted hallway, Jarad broke the heavy silence. "Are you as nervous as I am?"

I was so relieved, I laughed. "Petrified," I admitted.

"It's cool, Pia. No pressure." He put his arm around my shoulder as we continued to our room.

I was so grateful for his thoughtfulness that I was able to relax and knew the weekend would be just fine.

We ate a delicious meal at a local diner: hotdogs, fries, and coleslaw. Strawberry milkshakes to accompany. It was perfect. *Sam would go ballistic if she saw me eating like this*, I thought, then said it aloud to her brother.

"Oh, you should have seen her when we were younger, she would school our mother if she was using too much butter, which she always did, or if the food on the plate wasn't colourful enough. All these years later, I still remember her saying we eat with our eyes first."

"Yes, she said that to me. I'm surprised she can't cook."

"Oh, she can cook. She just doesn't want to," he said laughing. "Our mother had us all in the kitchen from the time we were little kids. We all know how to make tikka masala and vindaloo blindfolded."

"That sounds yummy. Maybe you'll cook for me sometime," I said hopefully.

"I have tasted your cooking and it beats mine hands down."

"Flatterer."

He was sweet, but was sweet enough?

We walked back to the hotel and fell asleep watching a movie. In the morning we had quiet, gentle sex that was exactly what I needed. No fireworks, but a feeling of contentment washed over me and I knew this was a good man. A man who cared about me. I felt twinges of guilt that this was one-sided, but maybe my feelings would grow. Maybe I was just nervous and afraid to commit.

The first presentation was a complete bore and I fought to stay awake. My mind was elsewhere, and during the intermission I called Sam.

"So, how's things with my brother?"

I knew what she was asking, and answered, "He is a gentleman."

Sam laughed loudly and countered, "No, seriously, Pia. You guys okay?"

"Yes, we are great together, in and out of bed." It was true, but anyone can have sex. Not everyone makes it earth-shattering like Robert did.

Silence. I'd shocked her. She recovered quickly, cleared her throat and asked, "Any interesting lectures?"

"This one is a total snore, but this afternoon there is a series on cyberbullying in schools. We're actually going to a school to speak with students." I realized this was my main focus for the three days. This was what I had come for. Ever since Claudia Baskin's suicide, I had been seeking answers. Maybe now I would get some.

"Sounds great. A very hot topic. Did I tell you I had my meeting with His Highness?"

"No! How was it? What did the slimeball have to say?" I had forgotten how furious Sam had been at being told the mayor wanted to see her again.

"Get this…" She paused for dramatic effect. "He wants me on the task force."

"What task force?" I asked, perplexed. Sam was apolitical and not affiliated with any organizations other than one Kash was involved in. I couldn't even think of its name, but it was something about mentorship and volunteering.

"Remember the school shooting last month?"

"I'm still involved in the collateral damage from that tragedy." Parents were still emailing me every day, even though all the autopsies and funerals were over.

"That task force. The one he put together after that shooting. It was all over the news."

"Oh wow. Yeah, I can see that. You'd be a great addition."

"I had no choice, but I must say, I feel like I will be an asset. I just hope the others accept my input. There's a cop, a school guidance counsellor, and some Columbia professor. We meet next week."

"You will be amazing. I want to hear all about it. Gotta go. Love you and love to Kash."

"Okay. Say hi to my brother for me and tell him to call me when he gets a chance. There is something I want to ask him."

"Is it about me?" I laughed.

"No, it's just a question about when we were kids."

I replied, "Okay, sure, will do," and hung up.

Chapter 28

Reversing the Outcome

I caught the last of the boring seminar, then met Jarad for lunch. I relayed to him my conversation with Sam and he said he would call her. We thoroughly enjoyed shrimp scampi in the hotel restaurant, had interesting conversations on various topics, and I had the disturbing thought that I enjoyed eating with him more than anything else we did together. I silently fought with myself to lighten up and stop pressuring myself about him.

By the time lunch was over I was feeling good, and decided not to let one boring lecture ruin the rest of the seminar weekend.

I went to meet the group for the afternoon field trip, but as I hugged Jarad goodbye near the hotel elevator, I could feel a headache coming on. I carried pain medication in my purse, so I kissed him on the cheek, saying I needed to visit the restroom before my afternoon session, and went straight to the lobby bathroom.

Once inside, I pulled out the bottle with shaky hands and swallowed three capsules. I hadn't had a headache since the day of my run along the river. I held my hands up and could see a very faint bluish glow between my fingers. *Not now! Not again.* The banging of the drums pulsing in my head were faint, but I could feel them building. I could feel the damp chill of sweat starting under my clothes. I shivered and rubbed my hands together.

I splashed warm water on my face and made my way out to meet my group. Twelve of us filed into a shuttle bus to drive the half mile down the road to the local high school. This area of Binghamton was all strip malls, car dealerships, and low brick schools. Twice we passed buildings I assumed were our destination but turned out not to be. Every building looked alike out here.

The bus driver acted as a tour guide on the ten-minute drive, giving us the history of the city. He recited, in a monotone I partially shut out, that the village was founded in 1834 by a Philadelphia merchant named Bingham, it bordered Pennsylvania, was an agricultural area, incorporated as a city in 1867 yadda, yadda, yadda, and we finally arrived at the squat, brick Binghamton High School, home of the proud state champion Panthers.

The school looked exactly like every other rural school I had ever seen. Lots of land to spread out, no need to build up and put the play area on the roof like in New York City. It looked as if there was a corn field abutting the sports track. How different it must be to go to a large, expansive school like this. My city schools had utilized every square inch of space and classrooms doubled as storage rooms, assembly halls as art studios. Wire cages covered all of the windows; at first look, schools in Manhattan look like jails.

The shuttle pulled up in front of the school and honked loudly and repeatedly at a muscle car parked right in front of the double glass doors. The bright green car stayed where it was, engine running and the front window down with a hand holding a cigarette giving the bus driver the finger. The driver finally laid on the horn, inched closer, and the vehicle sped off, kicking up gravel and dust in its wake.

"Teenagers," the driver mumbled, and I laughed, thinking we were about to enter the teenagers' domain. School shootings were most commonly the work of teenagers. This was their home base. Their mother ship.

The twelve of us exited in an orderly fashion, adults and professionals. Four men and eight women, all holding briefcases or laptop bags. This being the first day of the conference, I didn't know any of them yet. We fell into single file as the driver directed us to go inside to the lobby and told us that Detective Rogan would meet us there.

A woman wearing a beige cardigan over a navy blue suit dress approached and introduced herself as Principal Paisley. She gave us stick on name badges and asked us to write our names and where we lived on the labels. We did, then stuck them on our jackets. I was wearing a black, belted trench coat, and the white label really stood out. *Dr. C. Barnes, NYC.*

Her heels clicked on the stone floor as she led us to a classroom to the right of the lobby. It contained stadium seating, dim lighting, and a podium. As if by arrangement, we all sat in the last three rows of the six rows of bleachers and waited for the guest speaker. Four students filed in and stood nervously behind the podium. I opened my bag and pulled out a pen and notebook. My hands were glowing. I looked around quickly to see if anyone had seen, but no one was paying attention.

There were two boys, two girls. Probably fifteen or sixteen years old. The tallest was an African American girl, close to my height, six feet. She looked nervous and was almost wringing her hands. Next to her was a short, chubby girl with acne, who looked directly at me as I scanned the front of the room. Her piercing green eyes startled me with their intensity and intelligence. I smiled at her. She kept staring at me. Could she see my hands? I put them in my lap. Next to her was an all-around preppy-looking kid. He could have been at any private school on the Upper East Side. Beige khakis and a robin's-egg-blue polo shirt. His light brown hair was expertly cut, streaked with blond highlights and styled to look naturally tousled. Next to him was either a wrestler or football guy. His shoulder and arm muscles rippled under his gray sweatshirt. He had a buzz cut and no neck, and he seemed to vibrate with an intense energy.

Detective Rogan followed them, took his place at the podium and my heart did a little jump. I recognized that walk. I recognized everything about the spandex man, and as soon as he looked up at his audience, his eyes met mine and he winked.

Winked! What in the hell was it with people winking? This could not be happening. Spandex man was leading this session. Wait till Sam hears about this. The last time I saw this man he'd been staring at me through my apartment doors.

I would finally get to ask him why he had been following me. No, I couldn't, because then he would bring up the pier. Of all the cops in New York, it had to be him. As Sam would say, there is no such thing as coincidence. This was fate. *Fate, my ass. This is bad luck.* And on a day when my fingers were blue and now beginning to tingle and my head felt like it was going to explode, I had to spend the afternoon with him. I made a rash decision to exit the room for a brief minute, miming a phone call with my hand up to my ear. He nodded distractedly and turned to speak to the students standing behind him. I exited the classroom and the principal was right there.

"Is everything all right, Doctor? You look quite pale." She had a kindly, almost motherly concern in her voice.

"Fine, yes thanks. I just need the restroom, if you could direct me."

She pointed across the hall and I headed to the girls' restroom. Once inside the empty room, I stood in front of the long mirror. If I stood straight I couldn't see the top of my head, but if I bent a bit, I could see my whole self. I did look pale. My hands gripping the washbasin looked translucent in the harsh fluorescent light. I ran the warm water and let it wash over my blue hands. They stayed blue. I shivered, not with cold, but with dread. I didn't know how long I was in there. I felt the seconds ticking in my head. What was I waiting for? The lecture was about to begin.

Time seemed to stop as I gathered my courage to go back into the classroom and face Detective Rogan—and then suddenly I heard it. Loud and sharp. *Rat-a-tat-tat.* I knew it was gunfire, but part of my mind thought it sounded like loud popcorn. Ridiculous. It was gunshots for sure. Was there a movie playing in one of the classrooms?

I skipped the hand dryer, shaking off the excess water as I left the washroom. There was Principal Paisley, on the ground, blood pooling around her open sweater and belted dress. The smell hit me first. Blood and something else. Metal. It coated the back of my throat and I took short breaths through my mouth as I looked down at her. She had a surprised look on her face, and her empty eyes stared at the ceiling. Her glasses were on the ground next to her. There were two dark round holes in her chest and a dark stain around her body. I was frozen as if in a dream. *She has been shot,* my rational brain said. *How? Where?*

I stood there, fingers tingling, head exploding, until I heard it again. *Rat-a-tat.* The shooter was here, in the school, right now. *What should I do?* I didn't have my phone or laptop; I'd left them in the presentation room despite telling Detective Rogan I was taking a call. I made my way back, tiptoeing and slinking along as quietly as I could into that room, and saw carnage. Detective Rogan was on the ground, lying flat on his front with his head turned at a weird angle. I instinctively crouched beside him, making myself as small as possible. His suit jacket was open, revealing his leather holster snapped closed with the gun intact. The four students were also shot and were lying in a heap, all arms and legs and blood.

This cannot be happening, my mind screamed. The room was dark and smoky, and then in my peripheral vision I saw the gunman leaving through the door the students came in on the opposite side from me. The eleven people I'd come with were cowering on the ground being quiet, but I could hear the breathing and a gasp as someone tried to keep the horror from escaping their mouths. *Of course; that's what you do when someone opens fire.* We'd all seen this in movies. Instinct causes you to drop to the floor, cover your head with your hands as if that would fend off a bullet, and make yourself as small as possible and make no noise.

I heard the door close with a bang as I assessed the situation. I had almost stepped out of myself. Detective Rogan was not moving. Blood was on the floor all around him, and the crazy part of my mind said killing a cop was serious business. More so than killing a civilian, or even five civilians. The four students who had been going to give a presentation on cyberbullying and how it had affected them, and the school principal. I had all of these thoughts in seconds and with no hesitation at all I lay my wet hands on Detective Rogan's wrist.

My hands were shaking, but I made contact with his cold skin and I felt it immediately. The electric charge zapped me as I was transported back to the moment I left the classroom to go to the washroom. I heard my heart beating and a loud whoosh, and I saw my cell phone in my hand, and when Principal Paisley asked me if I was okay, I said no. I told her in a strong, firm voice to lock the school doors immediately as I dialled 911. She was a no-nonsense educator who saw the truth on my face and did exactly what I said.

We watched together as Billy got out of his muscle car parked in front, pulled out his gun, and walked with menace up to the school doors. When he found them locked, he started screaming and shooting. I saw it in slow motion, although it was happening in real time. He shot the glass and it fractured but didn't shatter. I heard the principal saying it was designed to withstand storms and would not break. He continued to shoot and get more and more angry. He was cursing and spittle flew out of his mouth.

Three police cars arrived in minutes and begin to negotiate with him to put down his gun. The scene played out like a movie, the cops crouched behind their car doors and someone on a megaphone. I stifled the urge to laugh at how movie-like the scene was, except that it was real. Mrs. Paisley and I stood there watching the horror unfolding as Billy was now lying face down on the pavement, being cuffed.

I went back into the auditorium to retrieve the rest of my things and saw that the room was exactly as I had left it the first time I went to the restroom.

Detective Rogan was at the podium addressing the room and the students were waiting to give their presentations. The principal followed me in and announced that there had been an incident and the school was being evacuated. Detective Rogan looked at me sideways, as if waiting for me to say something. I picked up my bag and headed out the door closest to me. The one Billy had used after he shot six people.

Principal Paisley took Detective Rogan aside and told him about the shooter. I could barely catch my breath. Adrenaline was racing through me. A school shooting, Sam's task force, Detective Rogan here, and his silver-gray eyes boring a hole through me.

My hands were shaking, but losing the bluish glow. Everyone filed out of the room behind me, talking excitedly and nervously as they moved towards the school exit.

And then he was next to me, guiding me, telling me to stop for a minute before I went outside. All the others were being ushered towards the rear of the school. The hall lights were bright and unforgiving. I was exhausted. Exhilarated. Fearful. I just wanted to go to sleep. I wanted it to be tomorrow already. This day had been way too long already. My shivers had turned to shakes. He took off his suit jacket and draped it over my shoulders. He probably assumed I was in shock. I was not, but my teeth were chattering too much for me to speak. I gazed down at his waist and again saw the leather holster.

"You knew." It was not a question. He was speaking quietly in case anyone came in. "You knew."

"I knew what?" I looked up, directly into those mesmerizing silver eyes of his, looking like Halloween contact lenses one of my friends wore once.

"I don't know how, but you knew. You left the room. Just in time, it appears." As he said it, I could see confusion on his face. What he was saying was ridiculous and he seemed to realize that even as he said it. How could I know about a shooter unless I was complicit, which was insane? I had never even been to Binghamton before.

"I saw him get out of his car." I started to stand up, hating that I was leaning on him and still shaky. Inside I felt great about what I had just done. I had stopped it. I had reversed time and six people shot dead were now walking around, never to know that they had been massacred by a teenage boy with anger issues and access to guns. "His car was in the way of the bus when we pulled up. He had to move. He was furious."

He looked at me, trying to make sense of what I was saying.

Was that why he did it? Because the bus driver honked at him? Or had he already been there with intent to shoot when the bus pulled up? He'd brought the gun to school. More questions than answers, and more than likely, I would never know the reasons for this teenager to decide to bring his gun to school.

Detective Rogan shrugged, acknowledging that I had nothing more to say. I was still shaking as we started walking where we were directed, towards the rear exit. I could feel his body touching mine as we walked side by side down the narrow hallway. It felt good. It felt electric. He felt solid and very, very masculine. I shouldn't even have been thinking about how good his body felt next to me, but I was. He was taller than me and yet his size was comforting, not intimidating. I reprimanded myself for these thoughts as we made our way outside. I felt physically ill, as if this whole incident had drained all of my resources. My headache was returning, and the nervous chatter of my group echoed and bounced around inside my skull. I wanted to put on noise-cancelling headphones and sit in a darkened room. Instead we were clustered outside in the bright sunshine behind the school while a police officer went from person to person writing down names and numbers.

The shuttle was waiting, the driver looking at his phone. He had been parked behind the school the entire time waiting for us and had not seen or heard anything. I watched as a police officer spoke to him and by his open-mouthed expression, I could see he was in shock. He would tell them about the car being in the way of the shuttle when he made his statement and the pieces would all come together.

This was real. A school shooting averted, an actual shooter apprehended on the premises. An eleventh grader known for his volatility and truancy. We were all aware of how differently today could have gone. The chatter stopped as reality sank in.

Detective Rogan was right behind me, and said as I stepped up into the shuttle bus, "I still want to talk to you." He smiled, but his voice was serious. "I haven't forgotten that woman on the pier, Doctor." I took his jacket off my shoulders and handed it back to him. He took it while never breaking eye contact with me. His face was set in stone. His silver eyes flashed.

There it was. This was exactly what I had been waiting for him to say. This was exactly what I had been dreading. I needed to get back to the hotel. I needed to calm myself, or I wasn't sure I would be able to be rational with Jarad. I felt as if I had lived one hundred years and exhaustion had finally caught up with me. Jarad would be considerate and sweet, when I really needed someone to let me scream in frustration. I felt like taking up boxing so I could legitimately punch something.

On the bus, I sat and put my head in my hands, holding it tight to prevent it from exploding from the inside. I stayed like that, not talking, not engaging with anyone.

The bus was silent like a tomb, everyone struck dumb by the close call. After all, no one had expected the eruption of violence on the weekend devoted to sessions on teenage violence and bullying.

We had to wait for our police escort to arrive. The word was out and news vans and cameras had arrived en masse. The school was cordoned off, students were standing huddled in groups waiting for their parents to pick them up or being escorted over to their vehicles, and progress through the mayhem was slow.

We were all dazed and in our own heads, and then one of the attendees broke the silence with, "So no bullying presentation?"

We were all still mute, and then someone laughed and it broke the tension for a minute.

"You're back early." Jarad looked up when I entered the room. He could see I was far from all right and got up out of the chair and headed towards me. He took my hands in his and pulled me into a tight hug. I sagged against him as he held me.

I stepped back and said, "It's a long story."

I sat on the bed and took off my boots and then went straight to the minibar. I took out a bottle of vodka and downed it while Jarad looked at me, waiting. I sat down again on the edge of the bed and told him a watered-down version of what happened. He sat down next to me and I leaned against him, mentally comparing the two men I had relied on for their strength in the past hour. I berated myself for feeling so weak and ready to cry at a moment's notice.

I understood that adrenaline was leaving my body now that the crisis was over, but I still hated that my reaction was tears. There was no point in fighting, so I let them come as I leaned on Jarad. My thoughts kept returning to walking next to the detective, feeling his body so close to mine, and I was furious at myself for thinking that if he had come back here with me I would be horizontal and naked right now with him. Hot, sweaty sex was what my traitorous body wanted and needed.

Finally I was empty of tears and I nodded when Jarad said he would go out and get us some dinner. My phone chirped and I ignored it. I had no energy to talk to anyone. I dreaded the news vans and the reporters and the media circus that had already begun. tSomewhere that boy's family was also getting the news. It was going to be a rough ride for everyone involved. Another shooter. At least this had ended without death. T was very often the outcome in any mass shooting event. Again, gun violence had taken over a peaceful school that hadn't seen it coming. Or had they? Had this boy been flagged in any way in the system?

I needed Sam's common sense right now, to talk me through this. No watered-down version for her. I needed to recount every single detail from the second I'd gone into the bathroom. She would listen and I would feel whole and not insane.

Sam and Kash were my anchors in the craziness that is my new reality, the only ones who knew everything. This reverse ripples episode had saved many lives today, but my mental and physical health were suffering.

I still had two days of conference left, and sweet Jarad to deal with, and I felt as if I could sleep for a month.

Chapter 29

The Impossible is Possible

"So you actually pulled it off? You did it!" Sam said smugly after saying nothing at all while I described what had happened. She just sat, still and serene, and let me spill every last detail, observation, thought, and feeling from the time I got on the bus until I was back in the hotel room. It felt so good to unburden myself.

"This is what you are meant to do. I can feel it," she said emphatically as she sipped the delicious Beaujolais, first batch of this year. Kash surprised us with two bottles each.

Four different wineries compete every year against each other with young grapes to see who will come out with the top-ranked favourite. We were holding an official tasting at Sam and Kash's new place, my old apartment.

"I have the winner," I announced and held up my goblet.

"Kash, I do believe Cassiopeia is drunk." Sam laughed and raised her glass. I had gotten home from the conference a day earlier; the rest of it had been postponed due to the thwarted shooting. It was rescheduled for January, in a new location, with a new focus on shootings, with no new gun restrictions and with the same people who still hadn't come up with any solutions. I was non-committal about attending. I would go alone if I went at all. I wondered if Detective Rogan would be participating.

I wouldn't go with Jarad. He was much too sweet and considerate for me. If I had any hope of staying sane, I needed a strong, take-charge guy who would listen, distract, entertain, and ravage me. I needed a guy like the cop with the wolf eyes to make me feel alive and allow me to work off this crazy, pent-up energy boiling up inside me. Jarad was not my type. My hope was that we would still have a friendship, especially because his sister was my best friend.

He had left Binghamton at the same time as I did, and although he was disappointed in how the weekend had turned out for us, he was very understanding. Too understanding. Too easygoing. I needed him to be upset or angry, not accepting.

I offered for him to come down to the city with me, but he had something come up with his older brother and figured he may as well go back out to LA.

He said he still planned to come to NYC for Thanksgiving, and I was more sure than ever that I didn't want that to happen. But that was not up to me. He could have Thanksgiving with his sister and brother-in-law if he wanted. I may or may not be there.

I had to be open with him. I would not lead him on and end up hurting him. I knew firsthand how that felt thanks to Robert. Robert, who had felt like fireworks compared to Jarad's candle. Now I knew how my mother felt all those many years, pining away for my absentee father. At least my father had been alive. I was still thinking about a dead man.

"Yes, I am quite drunk and may stay here on your sofa." I lay down and mimed sleeping.

"You are welcome to stay, Pia. Anytime." Kash jumped up and covered my legs with a throw.

Sam started laughing. "You need two throws to cover those long legs of hers." We were all laughing, relieving tension and avoiding any talk whatsoever about the shooting. The shooting had been thwarted because of me and reverse ripples. Magic. Not possible, but indeed, possible.

"Pia, are you awake?" Sam asked in a serious tone.

"I'm drunk, not asleep. What's up?"

"You know this is exactly what I was talking about last week. You prevented a school shooting. It's really kind of a monumental coincidence that this event happened when you were there. Don't you think so?"

Kash looked questioningly at his wife.

"What are you saying?" I opened my eyes.

"Just that we were talking about it and then it happened. At the exact time that you were at the school. I find that strange."

I could see her point, but did she think it happened *because* I was there? That I somehow attracted the event? I started to sit up, woozy with wine and too many thoughts swirling through my brain. "I find it strange too. A freaky strange coincidence and almost impossible to believe. But I live with the impossible every single day." I closed my eyes again and leaned back against the sofa. My head felt so heavy I could barely hold it up. "Are you saying I caused this?"

"No, not that you caused it. But you live with the impossible. That's what I'm saying. Your impossible is possible. Maybe you were drawn to it—you know, destined to be there. Not the other way around."

Kash added, "Like you were meant to be there at that exact moment to stop it."

"I don't know about that, but I can tell you that one shooter less in this world is a win."

I lay back down on the sofa and closed my eyes. I could picture this teenager's rage when he'd found the school locked and he started shooting. How had he gotten that angry? I spoke without meaning to. "He's a kid, for chrissakes. He should be out skateboarding or working at a fast food restaurant. Not shooting up his high school."

"Agreed. So frickin' tragic." Sam put her hands on her face. "One more little drink and I am off to bed. The useless task force meets tomorrow." Sam emptied the bottle into her glass and stood up. Kash got up as well and asked me, "You sure you are comfortable?"

"Completely. See you in the morning." I turned onto my side facing the back of the sofa and was instantly asleep.

Chapter 30

The Task Force

NARRATOR: SAM

My day went smoothly, from the second I stepped into the downtown train, which arrived the second I passed through the turnstile. All of my patients showed up more or less on time and at five p.m. I made my way down to Broadway and the spectacular Woolworth Building, where the task force was holding its initial meeting. This was an introductory session chaired by His Highness. I was told there would be no press, just introductions and some brainstorming. I knew that the mayor, as well as the others participating, would each have an agenda. Did I have one? All I could think about was Pia and the near miss in Binghamton and the impotence I felt at not being able to contribute anything useful.

I checked my email for the room number, stepped into the ornate golden elevator, pushed the button, and then made my way down the carpeted hall. The door to the suite was open and I entered the massive space containing only a long board table and eight office chairs on castors. Five seats were occupied. The mayor was at the head, Treyon sat to his right, their heads bent together in a whispered conversation, Fiona MacLellan sat next to Treyon and two men I did not recognize sat across from them. Fiona made eye contact with me and gave a head nod to indicate where I should sit. Everyone appeared to be watching, poised, waiting for the mayor to break off his private conversation and begin the meeting. I wasn't sure if he even saw me enter. He gave no acknowledgement so I sat and waited with the rest of the group. I felt as if I was in front of the principal at school, which had never happened to me personally, but nonetheless the tension in the room was bringing butterflies to my stomach.

This was shaping up to be an interesting evening to say the least.

The mayor finally looked up and looked around the table studying each of our faces. He seemed pleased with his choices and after a nod, suggested we introduce ourselves to each other. Of course it was implied that he would need no introduction.

Treyon started, and then Fiona, Detective Rogan went next, and when he made eye contact with me, I had an overwhelming feeling of déjà vu wash over me. Intense, visceral. I stared back into his silver-gray eyes, reminiscent of the eyes of a wild animal, a predator like a wolf, and felt my heart jump to my throat. Why was I reacting like this? I scolded myself. I felt the hairs on my arms stand up and a buzzing in my head. I knew this man, but in fact, I did not know him. I had never seen or met him before. But part of me knew him, or recognized something about him. I felt as if I was on high alert. This feeling lasted mere seconds and then as the introduction by Professor Schella ended, I cleared my throat and stated my name.

The mayor looked directly at me as I spoke, making me wonder if at some point I should bring up the fact that his son died by gun violence. Surely that sad fact had prompted this task force. I decided to wait on mentioning anything outloud. I would wait and see where this went.

We had all listed our credentials and specialties and what we hoped for the task force. I said I hoped it wouldn't be a waste of my time, at which point Fiona laughed out loud and agreed with me. She seconded my statement and the mayor assured everyone that it is a very necessary step in the right direction to understand what was happening under our noses in the schools and on the streets. Not just under our noses, but across the entire country in cities, towns, and rural areas. No school, not elementary, middle, or high school, was safe. The need to protect students and staff from shootings was not simple, and we had our work cut out for us if we hoped to make a difference.

I felt personally that gun laws needed updating, but this was clearly not the time for my gun agenda. NYC had successfully bought back guns in previous campaigns, but there were rumored to be more guns in private citizens' hands than the amount owned by the NYPD.

I stole another look at the cop sitting across from me. Why did wolf man look so familiar?

"Mr. Mayor, there are many issues at play here," Fiona continued.

Treyon cut her off. "Of course there are. That's why we are here."

Fiona was used to people listening to her sage counsel, not cutting her off. No one cut her off. She stood up and asked Treyon what his credentials were and what he was contributing to the meeting. He started to sputter and the mayor held up his hand to quiet them.

Professor Schella cleared his throat and suggested we take a break.

"We don't need a break, we just started," replied Detective Rogan.

I was laughing inside with my face remaining impassive. *This is a joke*, I said to myself. *We will get nothing accomplished as it is, so far, a battle of egos.*

Detective Rogan continued. "I think we need an educator here. Someone in the trenches, familiar with students, the kids who have issues."

Professeur Schella spoke up with a sour look on his ruddy face. "Excuse me, I am an educator. Tenured." He put the emphasis on *tenured*. But just because he was tenured at an Ivy League school didn't necessarily mean that he had expertise.

The cop looked right through him and went on as if he had not even spoken. "I was in Binghamton last week when a shooting was averted. There was a principal on site that afternoon, and she was very knowledgeable about the students and their issues. I think we need someone like her on this panel. To give us insight into the kids. The kids these days are different from when I was a kid. Would you agree, Dr. Sodhra?" He turned his silver eyes on me. Everyone at the table looked in my direction.

I stood up and put my palms on the table in front of me. I was mimicking the mayor's posture from his meeting with me a few days previous. This posture meant business.

"Yes, completely," I answered him. "The issues have changed over the years. The family dynamic has shifted and kids are now tethered to their phones, looking at screens morning, noon, and night, and there is the ever-present social media pressure that affects their every move, their clothing, who they hang out with, and what they eat. I could go on all day." And I could. In fact, I had written a paper recently on that very topic. Maybe that was why I was here and not because I'd had the mayor's son as a patient.

"Absolutely," Detective Rogan agreed. "That is why we need an educator on the high school level."

Fiona seconded this. Professor Schella fumed. This panel was going nowhere fast.

The mayor agreed with the cop. He looked at each of us individually and then turned to Treyon. "Find a local principal who has a stellar reputation and is willing to join forces with us." We all knew the mayor meant someone supportive of his politics. I hoped that wouldn't make the pool of candidates too small.

Treyon was taking notes, and said he was on it.

I looked over at Fiona and she rolled her eyes. She put her thumb into her chest to signify that she would find the principal and pass that info along to Treyon so he could be the one to recommend the person to the mayor.

Suddenly the mayor stood and said, "Come along then, Treyon, let's let these folks get to work."

And then they exited. The four of us looked at each other warily across the boardroom table. Where to begin?

After a boring but informative hour of statistics recited without notes by Schella, a review of city and country gun regulations given by the detective with the wolf eyes, and a discussion regarding school security plans, we all agreed to break for the evening.

I had wanted to ask the detective about the shooter in Binghamton, but couldn't find a moment to do so. He was on his phone the second the meeting broke up.

Fiona and I left together. "So what's your take, Doc?" We were walking to the same train. I knew she was asking about the meeting, but I had the cop on my mind.

"That detective kind of seems familiar to me," I said.

"He's a hunk, that's for sure. Those eyes of his. I can see how he unnerves suspects. They bore into you somethin' fierce. But what I actually meant is what's your take on this so-called task force?"

"I don't know if there is a point, other than politically. It looks as if the mayor is doing something, but I feel as if we are spinning our wheels. How can we make a difference?"

"My opinion is that something is better than nothing. And who knows, it could turn out to be useful, as long as Treyon keeps his mouth shut." She laughed and I joined her.

We decided to stop in a pub for a quick bite before we went home.

Over tapas and, at her insistence, appletinis, we reread the report on the recent shootings and the demographics of the shooters, and we talked about where we thought we could make a difference. She had a lead on a principal and was planning to reach out that evening to see if he would be willing to join the group. Only then would she pass his name on to Treyon.

"If only we could see into the future," she said wistfully.

I agreed, silently thinking about Pia, a secret weapon in the fight against untimely death.

"What's got you smilin'?" she asked me. "You thinking about that handsome husband of yours?"

I said yes I was and she responded, "You can go home and *Kash* in on that. Get it? *Kash in.*" All the patrons turned around to see what was so funny as she roared with laughter at her own joke. I told her about the rainshower videos I had filmed in Vieques and was pleased to see the unflappable Fiona, quite flabbergasted by my revelation.

"Why, Dr. Sodhra, you never cease to amaze me. Looks like Kash is the one who cashed in." She was still laughing at her joke when we parted.

CHAPTER 31

The Cop Pays a Visit

NARRATOR: PIA

I spent the early morning searching for flights and locked in my Christmas Alaska visit. Three flights, a long layover, a short flight on a puddle jumper, and I would arrive in the land of ice and snow. I hated the thought of an entire day's travel with no beach at the end, but it was necessary if I wanted to spend Christmas with my mother and father in Alaska. New York to Chicago, Chicago to Seattle, Seattle to Fairbanks, and then a bush plane to my father's wilderness camp. Yikes. Just the thought of that little pontoon plane flying over hundreds of miles of wilderness was enough to make me revisit the Caribbean option.

Last Christmas I had floated in the Caribbean Sea. Last year I had found the amazing blue ruby wedged in volcanic rock at Navio. Last year I had reunited with my birth father. Last year I'd had an affair with a man I still couldn't let go of. Last year I'd had my heart broken and my life-changing bioluminescent experience. Last year. What a difference a year makes.

This year's holiday would be the exact opposite, and although I really dislike the cold, I was looking forward to seeing my father's lodge and spending time with him and my mother. I invited Kash and Sam to come along with me, and after they finished laughing at the idea, they told me they were headed to California for the holidays. Lucky them. They tried to entice me to

"

come out there instead, with the bonus of spending time with her brother, but I demurred, saying that I had promised my mother that I would finally visit Alaska. Not exactly a lie.

I knew I did not want to spend the holidays with Jarad, and I was kicking myself that he was not enough spark for me. I liked him. He liked me. Why wasn't that enough? I wanted to feel explosions of excitement, feel my pulse race and have that "take me right this minute" feeling again. I'd been lucky to have it with Robert; maybe that was my once in a lifetime. Jarad was tame, and I felt as if I had a wildness inside me. I felt wild with Robert, uninhibited, like I could say or do anything. With Jarad, I felt like I could easily shock him, whether that was true or not.

I grabbed a coffee from the cafeteria and went up the stairs to my office. Detective Rogan was leaning against the doorjamb of my closed office door. I wasn't even surprised to see him; I was surprised it had taken him this many days to seek me out. We now knew each other's names and line of work. His steely eyes tracked me as I came down the hall.

"So, Detective, what can I do for you this morning?" I said with forced civility, completely aware this man affected me in a strange way. I tried to slow down my racing heart, not wanting him to know he had any effect on me. I felt fear, but I also felt my attraction to him buzzing and humming in my entire body.

His answer surprised me. "How are you, Doctor? You okay after what happened?"

I carefully weighed my words before I spoke, knowing that the shooting he was talking about had been averted (by me, but he had no idea about that) and fortunately no one was injured. After the event was over and he'd said to me, "You knew," I knew trouble was brewing. But how could he possibly have known I had something to do with it? This man unnerved me—in an interesting way.

"Yes, thank god it ended as it did. No one was hurt and the young man will hopefully get the help he needs." My mind drifted to Sam and her practice. How she had met with Joel just the one time and had hoped that he would be all right. But clearly it had been too late, and it had ended badly.

"Yeah, yeah. That young man is disturbed, and he's in the right place now. A jail cell. You know that's not what I am talking about, Doc." He followed me into my office and sat down. His suit coat opened to reveal the holster I had seen before. I could still picture the bullet entry wounds on his chest, red on the pristine white shirt. I dragged my eyes off his chest.

"So, Detective, what is it that you want to know?" I hated the way that came out. Leading him right where he wanted to go and where I wanted to avoid.

"I don't get you, Doc." He leaned back in the small seat he dwarfed and rested his palms on his thighs.

"What don't you get?" I asked and wished I had instead just asked him to leave. There was something hypnotic in those gray eyes of his. They were like flint or steel. Piercing. I felt like his eyes could see right inside of me and it made me uncomfortable. Uncomfortable in my own office at my place of work. *Ridiculous*, I chided myself. *Get a grip.* But he was magnetic, and I found myself staring.

"There's something going on with you, and I can't quite figure it out." He crossed his arms on his chest and continued to stare at me. He had a way of being absolutely still, like a statue. I was about to speak when he said, "But I will."

"I can assure you there's nothing going on with me. Nothing. Nada." I shoved my hands into my lab coat pockets.

"I want to believe you. That would be simple. The end of it. But, you see, I saw that woman go into the Hudson River. And then she was dry and hadn't fallen in. And there you were. And I saw that boy come into the classroom with his gun and then he wasn't there, but you were there and he was locked out of the school. Nice and tidy. Crisis averted." He smacked his palms together and then rested them flat on his knees again. "Twice."

I was shocked. He could remember what I knew had happened in a millisecond, before time rippled back as if it never happened. My head was starting to pound.

He continued, "I sound like a crazy person, and I tried to convince myself that I couldn't be remembering things correctly, and yet…" He paused midsentence and locked eyes with me. "I saw what I saw." He sounded too sure of himself.

"Look, Detective—"

"Please, call me Kevin."

"*Detective*, I am not in the mood for your fishing expedition. I have a lot of work to do and I am scheduled for an autopsy right now." I did have an autopsy, but I set my own schedule and as long as the work was done, I could map my own time.

He was not taking the hint. *Like a dog with a bone*, I thought to myself, then realized that…I liked him. I didn't want to like him, but I could feel the pull he had on me, almost feral and very exciting. I hoped nothing showed on my face. I worked to make my expression stern and refused to let the laugh I felt inside come bubbling out of me. That would be completely inappropriate and he would probably think I was batshit crazy.

"Listen, Doc, may I call you Cassiopeia?"

My withering stare disabused him of that notion, but I saw no reason to antagonize him further. "Pia. My friends call me Pia," I said, thinking, *He is no friend of mine yet*, but it was too late to take it back.

And then he smiled. A real smile. My breath caught in my throat. Again my laughter itched to burst forth and I could feel my heart racing. What was it about this guy?

He seemed surprised at the change in my demeanour. "Thanks, Pia. I won't keep you, but I would like to discuss this situation in Binghamton further. Could we meet for a drink later?"

I was so surprised by his question, I just stared.

"Or coffee. Could we meet for coffee?" He laughed self-consciously.

"I don't see the point, but if it will put an end to your questions, I can meet with you at six." *What in the holy hell am I doing, agreeing to go out with him?* "Coffee or a drink. Either is fine." I could feel my excitement building.

"Great," he said, standing up. "I'll be back at six. See you outside."

He turned and left and the small office felt strangely empty and cold. But I was smiling like a loon.

I found myself clock watching and waiting for six o'clock to come. And it did, seven long hours later.

Chapter 32

Yoga with Sam

Saturday morning dawned bright and clear. I rang the buzzer of the very familiar apartment building even though I still had my old spare keys.

"Hello," came the disconnected voice from the intercom. Sam asked, "Are you coming up or am I just coming down?"

"Come on down. I just want to duck into the deli and say hi to Oskar."

"Okay, be down in a sec," she replied.

I walked into the deli and took a bottle of water out of the first refrigerator cooler. I went to the back and looked to see if Oskar was there. He popped his head up from behind the counter and caught sight of me.

"What's up, Doc?" He grabbed me in a full-body embrace. I leaned into his stocky, heavy body and sighed.

"All good, Oskar. Sam and I are headed to yoga on Randall's."

"Oh yeah? My brother Max is training out there to be a firefighter. Say hi if you see him."

"Highly unlikely unless he joins our class." I laughed as we separated. It was good to see him and be back in my old neighbourhood.

"Have fun, Doc. Tell Sam I got in that tempeh she asked for."

I waved over my shoulder as I paid for the water and walked out. "Will do, and yuck."

Sam was on the sidewalk and hugged me as soon as she saw me.

I gave her Oskar's message and we chatted on the way to the bus stop. The crosstown bus was almost empty when we got on, and we were able to sit side by side. Sam looked so happy and fit in her Lululemon gear, all matching black and red with a warmup jacket zipped up. I had on an old Columbia U sweatshirt and gray sweatpants.

"Is that what you're wearing for yoga?" She looked down at the baggy sweatpants.

"Yeah, they're super comfy," I said defensively, laughing and about to tease her that she sounded like my mother.

"Pia, yoga is about getting your body in the correct positions to maximize the flow and effectiveness. You can't even see your legs in those baggy pants."

She was right. I had a lot of yoga pants my mother had foisted on me for years. "I promise to unpack my yoga pants and wear them next time. I'm on call this weekend, so I might have to duck out."

"Yeah sure, just a lame excuse to not do yoga." Sam laughed. "There *will* be a next time. I love yoga, and this new instructor has such a soothing voice. You'll love her. I know it's not parkour, but Pia, really, it's fantastic." We got off the bus and began our walk across the pedestrian bridge over the East River to Randall's Island.

"A soothing voice?" I looked at her. "I don't want to fall asleep."

"No, not that kind of soothing. More like a phone sex voice, and a throaty laugh."

Again, I looked at her. "When have you ever heard phone sex?" I asked her, and winked.

She smirked. "You know what I mean."

Aly was everything Sam promised. She had on one of those headsets that made her voice loud and clear. Her voice was perfect, with maybe a tiny hint of a Canadian accent. I recognized it because my assistant Olivia is Canadian. The group of about twenty people was set up on a field at the base of the ped bridge.

Randall's Island has over five hundred acres of parks, a few buildings, and about sixteen hundred lucky residents of a low brick apartment complex. The last time I had been on Randall's Island was a couple of summers ago for the Electric Zoo music festival. Being there again reminded me how much I needed to get out more instead of working all the time. I made a silent promise to myself to do something fun every weekend. This yoga class was a great start.

The history of this island was like an urban folklore tale, complete with quintessential haunted psychiatric hospital and adjoining facilities. Years ago the place had been run down and terrifying looking. A real eyesore. But Odyssey House was rebuilt and now offered state-of-the-art treatment for drug and alcohol abuse. Sam pointed out the building across the field from us and just past a stand of willows.

She did a summer residency there in college. I had forgotten about that. For a brief period, she had considered working with addicts when she graduated. She described the institution and how much she enjoyed being there.

"Oh, yeah. I forgot about that. Why didn't you stay with that?" We spread out our mats on the cool ground. Fall in New York is a gamble, but today was bright and looked as if the sun would make an appearance.

"It was too depressing. I struggled with the failures. I mean, look at Joel. He had everything going for him and still he couldn't conquer his demons. If he hadn't still been using…"

I agreed, all too familiar with the collateral damage of drugs and alcohol and the violence tangled up with them. "Yeah. Sometimes you just can't help." Sad but true. "But…I don't have that problem with my work." She looked sharply at me with a serious look on her face and then we both burst out laughing. Aly, the instructor, cleared her throat, clearly waiting for us to stop so the class could begin. We worked hard to stay focused during the class and I managed to bend my tight body into some new yoga positions.

After class Sam introduced me to the teacher, who was almost my height and very complimentary. After a brief chat and promise to take another class, Sam and I headed straight across the field to the smoothie bar.

"That was fantastic!" I was pumped. I had been running along the river on weekends all year, but this felt as if my entire body had engaged the same way it did when I was doing parkour as a teenager. More than a few years ago. I was sadly out of shape, but muscle memory is a powerful thing, and this morning my muscles were simultaneously complaining and thanking me.

"I told you," Sam crowed, clearly proud to have been the organizer. "Even Kash likes the class."

"What? Kash does yoga?"

"Don't tell him I told you. He would kill me." She was smiling, clearly thinking about her fabulous husband who did yoga with her. Probably picturing him in stretchy pants.

I would keep that little tidbit a secret, for now. "Well, if he likes it so much, why isn't he here?" I realized I had been so preoccupied since the almost-shooting in Binghamton, I hadn't been in touch with Kash. I missed seeing him all the time, but his hectic school schedule and only part-time paramedic job meant our paths seldom crossed anymore.

"He went on a boys' weekend with Juan and Trez."

We took our juice smoothies outside and sat on a bench overlooking the East River. There were only ferries on the river going back and forth, no tugs or police boats.

"A boys' weekend? What on earth are they doing?" I could not think of any weekend activity the three of them would have in common.

"You'll never guess." She took a long draw of the smoothie, barely suppressing a laugh.

"Fishing?"

"No, try again."

"Antiquing?" I asked sarcastically.

"Not even close. I'll give you a hint. They took their passports.'

"They flew to Vieques for the weekend." I figured that guess was right.

"Nope. Any other ideas?"

"I give up. Tell me."

"They went to Montreal, Canada, to pick up a Dachshund puppy for Trez and Juan."

"Really?" That struck me as so funny, tears escaped my eyes and were rolling down my cheeks. "Come on, you're kidding, right?"

"No, really I'm not. Juan and Trez saw this little puppy online and they want to adopt her. They have a nice apartment with a little back garden and Juan works remotely…so, they are doing it. It's all good." She slurped her smoothie.

"A puppy. A silly wiener dog. That is kinda cool. What will they name him?" I asked.

"Her. Ruby. Get it?"

I did. They named her after the gem we'd hacked out of the lava rocks. "I need to be more in touch with them. I feel bad that since Juan moved here from Vieques, I have only seen them once."

"Everyone in New York is busy. That's how it goes. I've only been over a couple times. I plan to do Thanksgiving this year. You're coming, right? Jarad is flying in."

That last statement about her brother sat heavy in the air between us. I knew Jarad was coming and of course I would be there. But a full vegan Thanksgiving—I wasn't sure about that.

It seemed easier to just go along at this moment. "Absolutely. I have to bring the turkey, right?" She elbowed me in the ribs, almost spilling my shake.

She apologized and we sat quietly for a few minutes.

"I happen to love Tofurky," I said in a very serious voice, and she mimed elbowing me again. "So, change of subject, how was the taskforce?" I asked her.

"I don't know," she responded, all gaiety gone from her voice.

"What do you mean? You were there, weren't you?" I put my empty cup on the bench next to me and turned to her.

"We've had two sessions, but I don't think we can accomplish anything. What can we do? We can't get the guns. We know that people with mental illness and other issues are not all being helped. Mental health problems are increasing every year. And we can't turn the schools into prisons to protect the kids. You would not believe the stats."

"I *would* believe the stats. I am well versed in this area." I spoke with conviction.

"Oh Pia, yes, of course you know. And you saved everyone at that school. You are our secret weapon."

I leaned back as much as the hard bench would allow, stretched out my legs, and said, "Yeah, well, that was unbelievable. That poor, messed-up kid. That's the real problem."

"Yes. Hence the task force. But Pia, you saved all of those people."

"Yes, I suppose I did, but there is the additional problem of the detective."

"Ah yes, spandex man. Does he have a name yet?"

I said nothing.

"Pia, what's going on?" Sam knew me well, probably better than anyone in the world. "OMG. Tell me you didn't?"

I looked at her. I raised one eyebrow. She knew.

"How? When? How? Wait, what? How?" She was positively sputtering.

I actually savoured the moment of Sam's inarticulateness, which is very rare indeed.

"Tell me everything," she ordered, and to make her point she sat cross-legged on the bench facing me.

And so I told her. I told her about Detective Kevin Rogan meeting me after work for a drink, which became two drinks and then a leisurely dinner. And then, long story short, he walked me home and we couldn't keep our hands off each other, so he came upstairs with me to my apartment and it was amazing.

She was looking at me strangely.

"Honestly Sam, his eyes had me. I can't explain it. We connected, and even though he is suspicious about what happened in Binghamton, he didn't press me."

Still she said nothing. As a psychiatrist, her silence was a tool. And I fell right into her trap.

"It was visceral. We couldn't keep our hands off one another. I felt—well, I don't know. Like we were meant to be. Not just fucking, but something else. Connecting."

"Like with the captain? The same."

"Yes, the same but different. You know how hurt I was by him. I loved our long-distance thing, but part of me wanted to keep it long distance. I liked him being away from me for days on end. It made our being together more special. I know that sounds juvenile, but at that time, the distance was okay. It was the lies I couldn't stand. Robert was the first guy I ever trusted and let into my heart, you know. I felt as if I had been waiting for him ever since my first crush on him as a teenager. There was love; in fact, he said it to me first. But then there was hurt, and that was all too real." I met her eyes. "I still miss that friendship. That back-and-forth thing we had going on. Sending each other funny memes and texts. Checking in. That was the best part of us."

Only children have a different take on being alone. I told Robert all the mundane things brothers and sisters share with one another. I had Sam and my mother, of course, but with Robert I had a person who shared my sense of humour and my quirky take on my crazy job. He listened and he always responded with something equally weird or crazy.

The air between was still. Neither spoke for a beat, and then Sam broke the silence.

"Can I add my two cents?" She stared directly at me.

"Of course. Your two cents are gold."

"You were hurt by his behaviour, but I think it was your ego that was wounded, not your heart."

I started to interrupt her, but she continued.

"I know the sex was great, I've been privy to that tidbit, and you did have a crush on him for years, plus it was exciting when he would fly into the city, but was there any other connection with him?"

I thought about that. Had I been connected to him?

"It's hard to explain." I stared straight ahead at the East River and soul searched. Would she even understand? She had brothers and cousins galore. I had none of that.

Sam, well practiced at the art of drawing people out, said nothing.

As she expected, I started to talk to fill the silence.

"Sam, the feelings were real. And we connected and were affected by how amazing we were together." I was defensive now. "I missed his presence in my life even though he was thousands of miles away."

"Great sex is just pheromones and hormones. But did either one of you talk about the future?" She adjusted her small body on the wooden bench.

"No, we didn't. We were in the early days. We were just enjoying the here and now. You know how I felt. I'd had a crush on him since I was a teen. Now we were together as adults. It never felt truly real. It was too good to be true. When I was with him, just being next to him, I felt at peace. I felt like I had waited for him all my life and now he was here.

"Remember what I was dealing with then. I was figuring out what was going on with me, you know, and that on top of my full-time job left just enough space for me to have that kind of relationship. I thought we were okay and could go on like that for a while longer. The only future event we discussed was him flying in for Thanksgiving, and we know how that turned out."

"Yeah, asshole didn't show or have the decency to explain why."

I replied quickly, "Oh he explained why, making up lies as he went. He didn't mention he was married, for example. Yes, he behaved like a real prick and that surprised me. I didn't see it coming."

"Maybe things happened like that for a reason," Sam said matter-of-factly.

"What do you mean? That he would hurt me?" I was puzzled.

"No, not at all. I would never think there is a reason anyone should be hurt, but I guess what I am saying is that it was better to find out early on what he was like rather than later, after you have invested more time."

"Wait. Are you and Kash okay?" The way she spoke made me worry for a second that things were not perfect in paradise.

"Yes, yes, Pia. Kash and I are fine. I just see so much heartbreak in my practice and most of the time there were early signs that were ignored. That's all I am saying." She reached for my hand and squeezed it. "Trust your instincts, that's all."

"And don't fall for a prick again?" I asked.

"Let's not speak ill of the dead, but yes," she said somberly. "But tell me this."

I waited.

"Did you at least make it to the bedroom this time?" She couldn't keep a straight face.

I laughed and replied with more information and details than she'd bargained for.

There was something soothing about talking with Sam. She was a fantastic therapist. She knew when to talk and when to listen. I always felt lighter and unburdened when I spilled my guts to her. I used to think psychiatry wasn't a real science. Just mumbo-jumbo and chatting. I knew differently now. Whether all of the anguish happening now, the overdoses and suicides and shootings and the extra stress Covid added, could be solved by therapy alone, I wasn't sure. But Sam knew her shit, and every person she treated was going to be better off than before they saw her.

"I have a couple more questions." She reached for my hand.

"Shoot," I said and realized that was a saying we should all probably drop from our repertoire. I didn't think I had left out any pertinent details, but hey, if she had more questions, I would give her some answers.

"Okay, where to begin?" She paused for effect. "His name?"

"Detective Kevin Rogan."

"Kevin Rogan?" She practically screamed his name.

"You know him?" I asked.

"He's the one on my task force." She paused, then put her index finger up to her closed lips and tapped it a couple times. "Oh yeah, his wolf eyes. I get it."

Wow. Of all the cops in New York City. "Six degrees of separation, huh, Sam?"

"This is not a coincidence, Pia. Oh my goodness, this is incredible." She crossed her arms in front of her body, an indication that she was deep in thought.

"You had other questions?"

"Yes, okay. I assume you're seeing him again?"

"Tonight," I said flatly for affect and when she looked up into my face, she saw me blushing.

"When were you going to tell me about this?" She sounded a bit hurt.

"Today, I was bursting to tell you. I wanted to tell you in person. I haven't felt like this since Robert. But I am scared. I don't even know what happened with Robert. Do I even want to start something again?" I covered my face with my hands. Suddenly I was drained.

"Yeah, I get that. But you connected and that is something. Just be careful."

"Careful?" Was she giving me a safe-sex talk?

"Pia, I know how hurt you were after Robert. If you feel this much of a connection with this guy, then just guard your heart. You know I love you. I don't want you to get hurt again." She reached over to hug me. "Can I ask one more question?"

"Sure, go ahead. Like me saying no would stop you."

"Ha. Ha. What about my brother?"

Yes. Her sweet big brother, Jarad, who was coming for Thanksgiving. How could I answer? What should I say? I said nothing.

"Forget I said anything. You're both adults. None of my business. You connected with the guy with the wolf eyes. That's it."

She laughed and we stood up. The spell of intimacy was broken. We dropped our empty cups in the trash can, linked arms, and made our way to the ferry.

Chapter 33

A Weekend Away

Monday morning, back at work after an amazing weekend spent in bed. Well, bed for all the time that I wasn't at the office. Carol, her acute antennae always on high alert, smirked at me as I passed her reception desk.

"Well, Doctor, looks like you had a *restful*"—she raised one eyebrow—"weekend." She laughed at her own comment and didn't wait for my answer.

I responded, "Good morning to you, Carol," and proceeded into the elevator.

I had indeed had a restful weekend. Somehow I was able to relax completely with Kevin. At first I kept waiting for the inquisition, but as we started to get to know one another, I figured he had pushed his questions about those incidents aside. And I was grateful for that. I just wanted to be free, myself. No drama.

I felt as though I had known him all my life. We compared schools and clubs and activities, but could not find a single common denominator. He was only a couple years older, although he had left the city after high school to attend university in Virginia. We didn't appear to have any early friends in common, but he knew Kash and Trez by sight.

I fell asleep watching a movie with him at my place on Friday night. He teased me about snoring with my mouth wide open and it felt natural, not combative. I really enjoyed his company, if not his taste in action movies. I had to work Saturday; my new contract said I had to cover one weekend a month. Two overdoses, one jumper, and three gunshot fatalities were my weekend lineup.

When Kevin picked me up Sunday evening and we ate takeout pad Thai at his place, how could I possibly be expected to stay awake? The food coma kicked in. He woke me to drive me home, knowing I needed to change my clothes before making an appearance in my office Monday morning.

So over the weekend I'd worked, had a yoga class and two dates, and had thoroughly enjoyed every minute of it. I was rested and ready for whatever the week brought.

I made my way down the hall to my office.

I had recently been upgraded to a larger space that had a real window, from which I could see a couple of trees if I stood on my tiptoes. I didn't care about the office space one way or another, but after my first trial year was up and I signed a new contract, I was given, with much fanfare and a huge sheet cake, a decent-sized office with an en-suite bathroom. Don't get the wrong idea about my new digs. They boasted gunmetal gray walls, a beat up L-shaped metal desk, room for my intern to camp at one end, an empty wooden bookcase, and two worn though serviceable club chairs. The best part was the state-of-the-art computer/x-ray/monitor tech system that rivaled Quantico's. For that alone I would put up with a janitor's closet. Every day I look forward to turning it on and getting to work.

I hung my jacket, dropped my purse in the bottom drawer of the desk, fished my phone out of my coat pocket, put on my lab coat, and slipped the phone into the outside oversized pocket. I turned on the computer system and made my way to the cafeteria to grab a coffee before the weekly catchup/update Monday morning mandatory staff meeting. What would this week bring?

Monday morning's meeting was over, but all cell phones rang simultaneously the second we left the conference room. We all looked at each other because we knew what that meant. My intern, Olivia, looked panicked. She was not issued a work cell and could only look to the rest of us for an explanation. Her eyes met mine, wide with terror. The rest of us, two other forensic scientists like myself, Dr. Bowman, his secretary and our three assistants all stared at our respective screens all the while heading to our individual offices. Olivia was right on my heels.

"What is it?" she asked, unable to keep her voice level.

"School shooting in Connecticut," I responded flatly. There had been too many damn shootings. This was the fourth in this area since the school year began only two months ago.

"What do we do?" she asked, dropping into one of the two guest chairs in my office.

"What *can* we do?" I could hear the defeat in my voice. This was not the answer she was hoping for.

"It's Monday morning. Who goes to school with a gun and starts shooting? Why? How can this keep happening?" She was looking through her bag to find her personal cell phone.

"Someone probably plotted and planned all weekend, disgruntled about some perceived wrong, or they just mentally snapped. We should know more soon. Connecticut authorities may need some extra hands on this."

My week was crazy, and by Friday, I could not wait to hole up in my apartment binge-watching some Netflix series and ordering in Thai and tacos. Maybe even at the same time. Heaven in a paper bag. My detective—I loved thinking of him like that—was working all weekend and we both bemoaned the fact that we wouldn't be together. I still held out hope that he might call after work, admonishing myself because that would be a booty call, and my booty-call days were way behind me now.

If there ever was anyone to booty call, it was him. He was exactly what I needed. Big, strong, forthright, insightful, and open to anything. I felt alive in his arms and couldn't get enough of him. The taste, the smell, the muscle, his mouth. Perfect, all of it. I hoped he felt the same way. One tiny part of my mind cautioned that maybe he was a liar, or a user, like Robert had been. But the larger part said to go for it, and I was listening to that.

Sam argued with me after I tried to beg off leaving the apartment for anything that weekend.

"No, Sam." I used my serious voice. "Between the shooting and dealing with Olivia constantly, I am toast."

"What? Why? I thought you liked your intern?'

"Oh, I do. She's great, but she's super keen and super engaged. All the time. And the questions…they never stop." I took another bite.

"Remind you of anyone?"

I knew Sam was referring to me. I have never met a mystery I didn't want to solve. My mother always encouraged me to ask questions, and so I'd told Olivia on her first day, "Ask away!" That had come back to bite me in the ass.

"What are you up to?" I asked, thinking about the leftover tacos waiting for me in the kitchen.

"I am packed for the weekend and am about to meet Kash downstairs to kidnap my best friend for a weekend away."

I groaned but realized I might as well get ready, because Sam does not take no for an answer.

Kash pulled up outside the building and Sam texted that they were downstairs waiting. I had no idea what they were up to, so I wasn't sure if I should pack a bag for a yoga weekend or just bring extra warm clothes in case they were planning a hike.

I threw a mix of everything into a bag, wolfed down the rest of the tacos, and went downstairs.

Kash drove us out to the tip of Long Island, where they had rented an apartment overlooking the ocean. They told me we were going to walk on the chilly beach, eat seafood (not Sam), do hot yoga at a spa, and take in a couple art galleries. Very civilized.

Kash parked and grabbed our bags, leaving Sam's hands free to put in the unlock code on the door.

"I love this place," I said as I walked into the great room. Comfortable white leather furniture flanked a red wood stove, already stoked and burning. Whitewashed walls, gray plank wood floors, and soaring windows completed the picture-perfect rental house. The room was toasty and made me think of my father's lodge. It was probably a lot like this.

"Kash saw it online. It's our thank-you gift for all you've done for us. This weekend you relax here, or go out, or do absolutely nothing if that's what you want. We will cater to your every wish."

Sam had already thanked me profusely and had presented me with a gorgeous locket for being her maid of honour. I had already put my mother's picture inside it and was wearing it now.

I fingered the locket and said, "This is so unnecessary, but it is wonderful. I am glad to just do nothing." I sat on the sofa and stretched my legs out.

They sat on either side of me.

"Okay, what should we do now?" I said in a serious voice.

We all burst out laughing.

"I win," said Kash and he held out his hand, palm side up to Sam.

She reached across me and put a twenty dollar bill in his hand and then explained. "We had a bet as to how long before you were restless and wanted to do something. I bet an hour, Kash said five minutes."

I laughed and realized that number one, I was predictable, and number two, I didn't really know how to slow down and actually relax.

I vowed to make a huge effort to just be in the moment with my two friends in this gorgeous house in Montauk. I would stop overthinking, planning, and checking my phones. Today I would relax. Tomorrow we could do things.

When I got back to my apartment on Sunday evening, refreshed and ready for a new work week, my detective was there on my stoop. He had his phone in his hand and looked up as I walked up to him. For a fleeting second I remembered Robert doing the exact same thing a year before. Robert had ambushed me, but Kevin was simply checking that I'd had a good weekend and presented me with a bag of my favourite pad Thai, probably as a bribe to get invited upstairs. As if he needed one. I laughed as we traded bags, me carrying the takeout and him carrying my backpack.

His weekend had been uneventful and mine had been delightful. He listened to me talk about the beach, the art we saw and the hot yoga I had nearly passed out in. We ate, caught up, and then went to bed, the thing we had both been waiting for since the previous weekend.

Chapter 34

No Volunteers Here

NARRATOR: SAM

"This damn task force is stressing my last nerve!" Fiona was drinking from a takeout coffee cup and watching me as I gathered my papers and put away files. We had a meeting tonight and she popped into my office unannounced to walk over with me.

But I knew she had an ulterior motive for this little impromptu meet up.

"It's a drag," I agreed, still resenting that I'd been railroaded by the mayor. "Why did you volunteer?" I asked her.

"Volunteer? Oh no, honey, I was drafted."

I wasn't sure whether to ask for her to elaborate or not. I waited.

She tossed her empty cup in the trash can near the door and said, "Three points."

I wasn't sure the distance in my office qualified as a three-pointer. I smiled and waited.

"I wanted to be promoted and let it be known that I wasn't happy with the mayor's choice of appointees at my office. His highness called me to come meet him at city hall, like that would impress me, and said that he had a better option for me. Better option? Humph." She snorted and continued. "You know I have a law degree, right?"

I shook my head.

"I do. I took a job as a caseworker with children's services because there was a hiring freeze at the DA's office when I graduated from Yale."

I figured she was top of her class there.

She continued, "I did all right in law school, but I worked two jobs to pay my way and still came out with a mountain of debt. Nowhere near the top of the class, but not at the bottom either. I needed a full-time paying job and took one at ACS."

I nodded.

"So that first year was brutal. Working all hours, every weekend, but what really got me was the disorganization and no one sharing notes. Kids were lost in the confusion. I mean lost, as in ended up dead."

I remembered reading about some abused children who'd been let down by the system that was supposed to protect them.

"So I went to my boss and suggested an overhaul of the system. I had a comprehensive plan for interoffice communications, etc., you get the gist, and I was shut down and basically labeled a troublemaker."

"So you don't practice law?"

"Oh yes, I do. I didn't bust my ass to pass the bar to be told to be quiet. I have a nice little home office and private practice, but my loyalty has always been to the city."

"Why? Why are you loyal if you won't be heard?" I was really curious now.

"Because, the system worked for me. I was one of the lucky ones who was saved by it, and I want to pay it forward."

That was heavy. She'd been saved. "So the mayor...?" I asked, wondering how he'd bribed her.

"His highness knows all. He knows about my history and my current frustrations. So..." She paused for dramatic effect. "He has promised me the reins if I make this task force work."

"Ah, that's impressive, but this task force is getting nowhere," I said, almost as a question.

"True, but we are all smart people. We have got to figure out what can be done. Any ideas in the Columbia-educated head of yours?"

I didn't let my surprise at her knowing my school show. "We need to recognize the kids with issues. Kids who may, for a multitude of reasons, be at the highest risk of becoming volatile. If we could coordinate with a system for tracking kids, even anonymously, and preferably get them help before it's too late—" I paused to take a breath.

"Yes!" She slammed her hand down on the desk so loudly that Jessie opened the office door.

"'Everything okay in here?" she asked hesitantly.

We were both laughing, so Jessie retreated.

"I spoke to Vince. That's my principal friend. He is the head of an at-risk high school in the Bronx."

"At-risk high school?" I had heard "at risk" used to described children who weren't safe in their homes, but not applied to a whole school.

"The entire population of the school's students are at risk of dropping out or failing, and they have no support system. I was an at risk kid."

I sensed that she wouldn't want any personal questions, so instead I asked, "So, he's in? He'll join up with our merry band?"

"Yes, you'll love Vince. Just wait till you meet him."

"I can't wait," I said.

We made our way over with the beginnings of a plan to the Woolworth Building to see the others.

Chapter 35

Surprise Thanksgiving Plans

My cell rang as I entered my office, and I fumbled it out of my oversized purse. Olivia rushed over to take the bag and my coat. I nodded to thank her, answered the call, and headed to the cafeteria for coffee.

"What are your holiday plans?" His deep voice boomed. I loved his voice. I was sinking too deep, too soon. I needed to rein myself in, because this guy could be trouble.

Kevin meant Thanksgiving; he was well aware of my Christmas trip to Alaska. He made fun of it constantly, saying he was getting me a fur bikini to wear.

"My friends are hosting, actually in my old apartment. You know, a Thanksgiving/Friendsgiving, as Sam's family is in California."

He said nothing for a beat and then asked, "Dr. Sam Sodhra from the task force?"

"Yes, right, that Sam. Her parents-in-law, and her brother-in-law and his girlfriend, will be there. About seven or eight people." I was blabbering because my mind was racing. Jarad was planning to be there so I couldn't invite Kevin. Jesus, this was a mess. I did not know what to do.

I was about to come up with an excuse when he said, "Would they miss you if I spirited you away for the weekend?"

"Well, Detective, what did you have in mind?" I exhaled the breath I had been holding, already formulating my excuse for Sam and Kash. I knew they would understand, because Sam was thrilled just to be hosting this Thanksgiving in their new place. She was positively obsessed with having enough room for her new table that seated twelve with the leaves added.

I would have to reach out to Jarad and end what never really got a chance to turn into something meaningful. That made me sad for a second, and I berated myself for even letting it go as far as it had. I hadn't intended to lead him on, we just fell into a long-distance friendship/relationship that was comfortable and easy. But having no sparks whatsoever on my part made committing impossible for me. I vowed to call him as soon as I got off the phone with the detective.

I wasn't even listening to his plans, I was so caught up in my own head when he asked, "How does that sound, Pia? You up for it?"

I laughed as I realized I had no idea what the *it* was and what he was planning. I replied, "I am up for anything."

He said great, we agreed to talk later, and we hung up.

I was up for anything except calling Sam to cancel and then telling Jarad I had made plans that did not include him.

Sam took the news like a trooper. She was so overwhelmed with cooking her first turkey—all Kash's family ate meat—that my news barely registered until I mentioned Jarad and she quickly said, "Oh Pia, I forgot to tell you. He is not coming east after all. Mik needs him to do some business-related stuff. He sends his apologies. I told him I would tell you."

I was so relieved and silently sent a prayer up to the universe, thankful I would not have to call him after all, chickenshit that I am. It seemed strange he hadn't reached out directly. Was the universe sending him a signal that I was not interested, or that my interests lay elsewhere?

"Thanks, Sam. No worries. Kevin and I are doing something, and I have no idea what."

"Is it a secret?" she asked. "He's making some clandestine arrangements?" I could hear the laughter in her voice.

"No, nothing like that. Honestly, I wasn't listening to him when he told me the plans. And I didn't want to tell him that I wasn't paying attention to what he said, so it will be a surprise."

We caught up on family news and promised to grab a drink one evening before the holiday.

"I miss you," Sam said in a serious voice. "Remember last Thanksgiving? Your mother met your father for the first time in twenty-seven years."

Oh, I remembered, all right. That was also when I found out my lover was a liar. It was not a good memory. "Yes, and look at them now. Together forever. They are so lucky," I said wistfully.

"They are and you will be too. Maybe the detective is the one."

"Maybe he is, who knows, but at least I'm going in with my eyes wide open." But was I? I wanted to be with him, couldn't stop thinking about him, but I didn't want to fall too fast too soon, and I sure as hell didn't want to be hurt again.

"Pia, look at Kash and me. Take a chance and give it your best shot. That's all you can do."

"Yes, I know. I really like him. I keep telling myself to just go with the flow, but you know how it is. I overanalyze things."

"That's an understatement. More like you pick things apart until they are sorted, categorized, and filed."

"Guilty. I just really like this one." I really, really liked him. "Okay. Give Kash my best and see you soon."

Sam and I lived together for years, and we could read each other's energy. I had a niggling feeling there was something up that she wanted to tell me but she preferred face-to-face. Whatever it was could wait until we were together. Now I had to figure out what Kevin and I would be doing for our four-day weekend.

Chapter 36

Pre-Thanksgiving

The night before Thanksgiving I met up with Sam at Teacher's. She was seated in a booth drinking a martini. I had gotten soaked walking from the subway, but rather than running, I took my time and let the rain wet my face and head, and when I got into the restaurant I realized I look like a bedraggled mess.

I nodded to the bartender as I walked by and he said, "Martini coming right up, Pia." Gotta love the local haunt; even though I hadn't been there in a while, he remembered my usual and he handed me the drink and a clean bar towel to dry my hair.

Sam started to get up, but settled for leaning into me as I squeezed in next to her on the banquette.

"You look good," I said to her, always in awe of her stunning looks. Red lips, heart-shaped face, dark eyes, glossy long hair, and the smile that lit a room. She had not been caught in the rain.

"You too," she said, cocking her head to the side. "That wet look really enhances you. No, seriously, you do look good. Satisfied. The detective must be good for you." She smirked as I knew she would. "So did you crack the secret?"

"What secret?" I asked, genuinely perplexed.

"Where he is taking you for the weekend."

"Oh yeah, no big secret. He has a cabin up in New Paltz and we'll sort of camp out, cook on the fire, and rough it for a few days. He is so excited, and I'm getting on board with the idea."

The waiter put my martini in front of me and I signalled that we would order in a few minutes.

"Does the place at least have electricity?" Sam lifted her glass and clinked mine. We sipped our dry martinis.

"I certainly hope so. But who knows? It's been in his family for generations." I told her as much as I knew from Kevin's description of the log cabin his grandfather had built. We looked over the very familiar menus and then ordered the same dishes as always.

"So where is Kash this evening?" I had seen him earlier in the day, just by chance. We waved to each other across three ambulances parked in the bay.

"School. I'm amazed that he has any energy, but he does. He loves school, loves studying, and still has enthusiasm for all of the department bullshit and his part-time job. The man is my hero." She batted her eyelashes comically.

"Yeah, yeah, I know." I teased her, knowing full well how fabulous her husband is. I lifted my almost empty glass. "Here's to Kash!" We clinked glasses and downed our martinis.

I had a delicious chicken Caesar salad and Sam a veggie stir fry while I talked her through the entire turkey preparation and she took notes. She was excited and nervous, and her happiness shone through.

"So I have Kash's parents, of course, and Manny and Jessie. And probably Cheeko, you know, her dog. Now Trez and Juan are coming with their pooch Ruby, and Trez's mom is also coming, and I asked Fiona, you know her, right?'

"Yes, I love Fiona. She's a riot. I met her through Carol at work. You'll have a great time with her there."

"Yes, but you know, Kash's mom is kind of conservative." Sam sounded worried.

"Kind of?" I quipped and we both laughed. The waiter deposited new martinis in front of us. He knew us well.

"She is always hinting that it's time to give her grandchildren. It isn't time, is it?"

"You know, Sam, we never really talked about kids. Do you want them?" I had never told her I didn't plan on having any. I'd kept that to myself ever since I saw the horrified look on my mother's face when I told her. She assumed it was something she had done wrong in raising me. But it was really the fear of losing a child that would keep me from bringing one into this world.

"I do. And Kash does too. But not now. I'm not even thirty yet." She gulped her drink.

"Thirty is the new twenty."

"I'll drink to that," she said and we clinked glasses again.

I said, "It will probably be the most amazing Thanksgiving ever. Just get Juan telling Vieques stories. That will distract Kash's mom from grilling you, and he will keep everyone entertained." I felt a pang of loss that I wouldn't be there with those people I loved and enjoyed spending time with. We sipped our martinis and picked at the remaining croutons on my plate.

"So are you and the detective serious-serious?"

"Well, I am. I've jumped in with both feet. I can't imagine seeing anyone else." I hadn't thought of Robert in weeks and I enjoyed every minute with Kevin. Even the texts and phone calls make me break into a ridiculous smile.

Olivia had even mentioned my goofy smile earlier when he had sent a funny meme about Little Red Riding Hood and told me to remember to bring my cape because he had the basket. I almost told him he reminded me of a wolf. His eyes. Sam called them bedroom eyes, but they were much more than that. They looked right inside me. A tiny part of me was scared that if he looked too intently, he would see my bioluminescence secret, and another part of me wanted him to know. Some of the time I wanted to confide in him, and other times I was afraid of how he might react.

Sam drained her glass and asked, "What about him?"

"Who knows?" I replied. "Look how it was with you-know-who. I thought that relationship was great. And it was, until it wasn't. I don't think I am the best judge. I am just enjoying the present and not expecting too much. I don't want to be hurt, but damn if I will let what Robert did cloud this relationship. Kevin is thoughtful, kind, and most of all, he is here in this city. And he doesn't crowd me. You know what I mean." I drained my glass as well and nodded when the bartender looked over asking if we wanted a refill. Sam put her hand on hers to indicate she had enough.

"Yeah, I hear that. Men can take over. I hear it every day in my practice. I am so grateful for Kash. We're equals, although he did try to mansplain the new coffee maker to me. Then when his instructions didn't actually work, he got all flustered. I called him on it and we both read the instructions after that."

"You like it?" I asked, knowing it was a wedding gift from the school faculty.

"Yes, it is my favourite part of the kitchen. And I'm working on cooking some meat for him once in a while."

I laughed. "How's that working for you?"

"You know Kash. He would eat shoe leather if I put it in front of him."

I agreed. Kash was a true gentleman and would not want to hurt his wife's feelings if her food was less than par.

"Kash is a great cook. He can do the cooking," I added, remembering him cooking me ribs before Sam came into his life.

"Yes, true, and he is willing. But he is messy and I like the kitchen, well, you know, spotless. So I volunteer to cook."

We made small talk about her penchant for neatness and my lack thereof, and finished our drinks.

I kept waiting for Sam to tell me what was really on her mind, but nothing came up. It was not like Sam to keep any secrets from me, so I just chalked it up to me being oversensitive with the new romance and Sam being preoccupied as a newlywed, with a new practice, a husband in school, and the task force responsibilities. Jesus, how much load could she shoulder?

My life, though crazy at times, seemed simple compared to hers.

We were both a bit tipsy as we left the restaurant and headed in opposite directions, counting on our respective walks to sober us up. The air was chilly as I started down Broadway. We turned at the same moment and waved to each other. I heard my phone buzz and fished it out of my bag.

You home? Kevin's text read. I replied: *Will be in 15 min.*

I practically skipped home and ran up the stairs to the apartment. I dumped my coat and plopped down on the sofa to await his call. I looked around, realizing that I hadn't yet packed, so I went into the bedroom and started pulling sweaters out of the closet and dug around for tights and warm socks.

The phone rang and I picked up immediately, butterflies already fluttering inside me.

"Hi."

"Hi yourself," he said in his deep voice. "All packed?"

"Yes," I lied, "are you?" I continued pulling articles of clothing out of drawers. The pile on the bed was threatening to topple.

I sat on the edge and reached underneath for a duffle bag that I had shoved under the bed from my weekend in Montauk. I pulled it out and held it in my lap.

"Just checking," he laughed. "I can hear you pulling clothes out of the dresser. I'll be out front at eight tomorrow morning. Is that too early?"

"No, that's perfect. I'll be outside. I'll pick up two coffees. You sure you don't want me to bring anything? Something to grill? Anything?"

"No, I got it, really. I am looking forward to grilling, it's been awhile. See you in the morning, my love."

My love? Hmmm.

Chapter 37

A Peaceful Weekend

Thanksgiving weekend went by in a blur. We drove up I-84 through the Hudson Valley area. We listened to oldies from the eighties and argued about who was the best guitarist in history. We stopped for coffee and pastries and talked about hiking, possibly horseback riding, and exploring the small town of New Paltz, population 7700. Kevin described the eight-thousand-acre Mohonk preserve in detail; he spent every summer of his childhood exploring the park.

He laughed so hard he almost went off the road when I said, "So that's where you'll hide my body?"

"I will be doing things to your body, Pia, but hiding it is not one of them."

Good answer, I thought to myself.

Detective Kevin Rogan's "little cabin" was a huge log home situated on over a hundred acres of forests and streams. It was immense and breathtaking. "Cooking on the fire" meant an enclosed backyard pergola with grill, firepit, heated patio, and view of a gently sloping valley. There was an outdoor sauna, a hot tub, and a three-sided heated casita complete with a heated infinity pool.

Every time I turned a corner, there was another amenity. I was already picturing describing this place to Sam. I quickly snapped a couple photos with my phone and planned to take many more.

I had never seen anything like it. Growing up in the city, my friends and I had apartments, brownstones, or lofts. We didn't have yards, hot tubs, or in my case even a driveway.

The stone fireplace in the great room was over twenty feet wide and tall. His grandfather had been the stone mason. He had been a judge in Ireland, and when he emigrated to New York could only find work as a labourer. He gambled on his newly learned masonry skills, formed a company, and grew it into one of the largest and best known stone distributors and contractors in upstate New York. I loved hearing the pride in Kevin's voice when he spoke of his family.

He insisted they had once cooked a full-sized moose on a spit there when he was a kid. I wasn't sure if he was kidding, but a moose could easily fit in the massive fireplace.

The flagstone floors were heated, and the exposed wood beams lent a warmth and hominess to the place despite its cavernous size. I told him about my father's lodge and wondered how it compared size wise. The kitchen was larger than any I had ever seen and could accommodate a staff of twelve cooks.

The second floor was more of the same opulence, tastefully done. Each of the five bedrooms boasted en suites. Our master was bigger than my entire apartment and housed a velvet settee, should one feel a fainting spell coming on, a reading corner complete with two leather armchairs with reading lamps over each, two large walk-in closets, and his-and-hers en suite baths.

Wow was the only word that came to mind.

Kevin saw the look on my face and told me, "My parents had it redone a few years back. It was a rustic hunting lodge in my grandparents' time, but my parents are anti-gun and pro-opulence." He laughed self-consciously.

"I'll say. It's amazing. I mean wow, I have never seen anything like it." I spun around and then flopped onto the California king bed.

"Do your parents use it much?" I asked, staring at the shadows cast by the ornate light fixture in the centre of the ceiling.

He didn't answer. I waited and then sat up and looked over at him. He was standing by the window. He turned. "No, they both died last year. In a home invasion. They were both shot."

I got up and went over to him. I put my arms around him and laid my head on his chest. "I am so, so sorry. I had no idea. That must have been awful."

"It was. It was brutal. I started running just to wear myself out." He stood still like a statue.

He was a tough guy, and in true tough-guy form, he brushed it off as if showing emotion was just a nuisance. He gradually relaxed into me, but I knew he did not want to discuss it anymore. I had a million questions. Had it happened here? When was the shooting? Had the shooter been caught? Had I seen his parents pass through my morgue? Is that why he wanted to be on the mayor's task force? I kept quiet, though.

He took my hand and we went back downstairs.

"I'll bring up the bags, and then I have a Thanksgiving dinner to cook over a fire." He disappeared down the hall to the foyer where we had both deposited our bags.

"Help yourself to anything in the fridge," he said over his shoulder as he went outside.

I wandered into the kitchen and opened the oversized refrigerator. It was as big as my entire kitchen and was fully stocked. I called up to him asking if he wanted a beer, but he was five miles away upstairs in the bedroom at the far end of the hall and he didn't hear me. I took out a bottle of rosé. I stood there holding it, wondering which of the thousand drawers held a corkscrew.

Thanksgiving dinner turned out to be a complete turkey dinner with all the fixings and then some. Premade, ready to heat from Delmonico's in the city.

As we were eating on the floor next to the huge fireplace, I teased him about cooking over the fire.

"Did I say cooking over a fire? I just wanted to impress you. What I meant was eating by the fire and cooking on the grill outside." He laughed his deep rumbling laugh and his silver eyes sparkled in the firelight.

"It's perfect, and I am impressed." He impressed me with his down-to-earth manner amid this complete decadence, his thoughtfulness, and his sense of humour. He could laugh at himself and that really mattered to me. We can't take ourselves too seriously, as my mother used to always say. Laughter is the key to happiness.

I was so looking forward to an entire weekend out of the city, in this amazing house, with this amazing man. What a difference from last year, when I'd lost Robert and gained a father. A story for another time.

"Tell me one thing you're grateful for this Thanksgiving." Kevin, stretched out, leaned back on his elbows. He was staring at me looking wickedly sexy. I wanted him right then and there.

I took a sip of wine, my third glass since we got here, and replied cautiously. "Honestly, there are too many things in my life to be grateful for. It's hard to pick one."

"Come on, that's a copout. No pun intended. Pick one." He sat up and took my hand. My stomach flip-flopped.

"Okay." I gulped. *Here goes nothing.* "I'm grateful to be here with you." I looked into his eyes, wanting to see the same feelings I felt. And I saw them.

"Your turn," I coaxed, feeling confident that we were on the same page.

"Same thing. So much to be grateful for." I saw a shadow pass over his face. Probably the shadow of his lost parents. "I am so grateful for you."

He leaned towards me and we kissed. The food was pushed aside as we slowly undressed and explored and loved. Tender, cautious, unlike our previous rushed, frantic pairings. This was new—gentle and deep—and it felt like it meant something new for us; a cementing or solidifying of this relationship that had started with a morning run and suspicious circumstances, to say the least.

Afterwards we lay back on the floor and both became aware of its hardness and the embers burning down in the fireplace. He stood and reached a hand to pull me up to him. We stood naked, holding each other for what seemed like hours. I breathed in the scent of him, sweaty, sweet, and manly, and was truly grateful for the fact that he'd sought me out and now we were becoming something special. I banished all negativity from my overthinking brain and enjoyed the moment. Skin on skin. His tall, strong body next to my shorter, strong frame. His arms were around my middle and mine up around his chest. Our bodies were sweaty and breathing heavily and it was the most wonderful sensation to be next to this man, uninhibited and together.

The weekend of eating, hiking to burn some of the calories we consumed, naked swimming in the heated pool, eating some more, and a lot of horizontal time proved to be the best four-day weekend I had ever experienced. It beat the beach, and that was saying something. I told him about Vieques and promised to take him there in the future. He said he loved the beach, a must for any partner I could have. Maybe I was projecting, but I felt the connection and believed he did too. I was slowly letting my guard down and pushing away the fear that something bad or unexpected would happen, or that he would disappear like Robert.

On the drive back to the city, in stop-and-go, end-of-the-holiday traffic on the thruway, I asked him if he had siblings.

"No, I am an only child. What about you?"

"Same. I'm used to it, but being a single child is very much different than someone who has grown up surrounded by brothers or sisters and aunts and uncles. My mother was also an only child," I explained.

"Ah, yes, that *is* an only. I grew up with lots of cousins. My mother was one of three and my father had four brothers. I have over a dozen first cousins alone, most of them in New York. You'll meet them."

"I will?" I turned in my seat and faced him. I smiled at the thought of meeting his family.

"We are close. Especially in this last year. I couldn't have made it without them. My closest cousin, Rich, has a daughter down at I.S. 239. I see her every week. She's a real sporty girl. I'll take you to one of her games sometime." His face showed the depth of his feelings, but as he looked over at me he smiled.

"Yes, you are lucky to have them. I feel the same about my best friends, Sam, whom you have met, and Kash, her husband. Couldn't have made it this last year without them." I turned to face the road.

"Why?" He sat up straighter, interested. "What happened last year that you needed them for?"

Oh my god, I am such an idiot. Why did I open my big mouth and say that? Now what am I supposed to say? My mind was racing. *There is no way I'm going to tell him what happened to me in Vieques and how I can reverse time and save people who are dead, or that for the first few months after it happened to me, I thought I was going crazy and Sam and Kash were my anchor. Especially with him already questioning me on what he saw the day we first met, running on the West Side. This is the answer to every question he has had for me since that day.*

"I had a bad breakup." Simple. Concise.

"Oh, honey. I am sorry to hear about it. His loss, my gain." He reached over and squeezed my hand.

I was glad he didn't pursue the topic and at the same time, mildly irritated that he didn't. Maybe that's a male thing, but if our roles had been reversed, I would have been insanely curious about his bad breakup, if he had one. Especially if it meant he had to reach out to others for support.

My year had been a rollercoaster of reverse ripples, losing Robert, meeting my father, navigating my new job, seeing my best friends get married, moving back to my childhood home, and my mother moving to Alaska. I needed some peace in my life. Peace and predictability.

Chapter 38

Holidays Approaching

Time flew, the city garbed itself for the Christmas holidays, and traffic was as always at a standstill. The weather was at least cooperative, and I was able to walk home a couple of nights a week, which allowed me to think, process, rehash my cases, and come to conclusions.

There is always an uptick in holiday-related suicides and gun violence starting in December, going through to March. The dark and cold and the feelings of isolation are factors. Domestic violence always rises during this stressful time of year. By the time my Alaskan vacation was looming, I was counting the days.

Olivia, my intern, had become invaluable, and my relationship with Kevin was on secure footing. He'd received the Carol seal of approval; she couldn't stop talking about him and always had a pun ready when I came in through the main lobby. "I bet he does great work under the covers," or "Do I detect a satisfied Pia?"

I always laughed. I felt good about the relationship and vowed to just enjoy myself.

Then I had an incident of reverse ripples. Although Olivia was by my side at the time, she was oblivious to the fact that when a ten-year-old girl struck by a bus and instantly killed came to us, I was able to send her back to the time before her mother let go of her hand and she absently stepped off the curb in front of a Fifth Avenue Christmas window display precisely when the Staten Island Express bus was trying to make up some lost time.

I knew it was coming from the headache and tingling in my fingers that morning as I hurried to work. I looked at my bluish hands repeatedly on the subway, felt the tingling intensify as soon as I donned my lab coat. I had already consumed four pain pills for my burgeoning headache as I made my way down the hall to room 1.

Olivia trailed behind me into the autopsy room, but I was barely aware of her existence. I knew I needed to see the girl. I could already see her. It was intense. I went to the sink and washed my hands. I heard Olivia offer me gloves, which I ignored as I lifted the sheet on the small body.

I saw the mangled mess the brutal accident had wrought. I lifted her wrist, dainty and fragile, wearing a multicoloured string friendship bracelet, and instantly I was standing beside her on the sidewalk.

The air was crisp and cool. I could even smell the burnt yeasty tang of street pretzels roasting on a cart nearby. People were packed ten deep waiting to see the light display on the store windows. Music blared in time to the changing coloured lights. The red glow from the display made all of the upturned faces look ghoulish.

I looked down at our hands. Mine with my gold wristwatch shining, hers smaller and paler. I held tightly to her wrist, even though she was oblivious to my touch, and as she started to step down into traffic, I tugged her hand as hard as I could. She was startled and stopped moving forward. She looked back towards where I was standing to be able to grab her, surprised that her mother was not there. She stepped back up on the curb as the bus blew by in a whoosh and I was back in the morgue, standing next to Olivia, who was talking about her plans for the Christmas holiday.

Why this particular girl at this particular time? Once again, I had no idea, but it didn't really matter. All that mattered was that she was spending a magical Christmas with her family, not in my morgue on a cold steel table.

Olivia walked over to the list on the clipboard, then crossed the room to the bank of drawers to start on our next case.

Chapter 39

Heading to Alaska

The night before my flight, my mother called. I was coming out of the shower, dripping across the living room to grab my cell phone off the coffee table.

"Hello?" I panted.

"Oh honey, did I catch you at a bad moment?"

"Hi, Mom, no nothing out of the ordinary. Just me racing to do things last minute."

"Good, Cassiopeia." I don't think she was even listening to me. She had her agenda and she continued. "So how are you?"

"Good. How are you and Juris? How's the cold?"

"We are excited, and you get used to the cold. I am driving Juris absolutely crazy waiting for you." I could hear the excitement in her voice.

"I'm excited too, Mom. I'll see you tomorrow evening."

"Then everything is set, and you fly in the morning? I can't wait to see you here at Lost Lake." I could positively feel her happiness through the phone. It made me smile even though I was dreading the next day's travel marathon.

"That really is a terrible name for a lake, Mom. If you ever get lost, I guess that's the first place searchers would look."

"Very funny, Pia. Getting lost is nothing to joke about. Over two thousand people get lost and perish every year in Alaska." Trust Mom to know the statistics.

"Relax, Mom. I don't plan to be outside. I'll be cozied up by a warm fire. You do have a fireplace, don't you?" I knew the lodge had wood-burning stoves and radiant-heat flooring. It was in the brochure she sent me.

"Of course we do. We're not barbarians up here," she said indignantly.

"I'm just kidding, Mom. You have my schedule. I won't miss my flight. The weather is fine and my rideshare is booked. I'm not looking forward to the day of travel, but I miss you and will see you soon."

"We miss you too, honey. See you very soon. We'll be tracking your flights." She was smiling through the phone.

"Tracking my flights?" That sounded a bit creepy.

"Yes, you know, through an app. Carlos showed Juris the best ones."

Ah yes, I could see that. My grandmother's boyfriend, the retired pilot, was involved. Made perfect sense. These parents and grandparents of mine were more tech savvy than I was.

We disconnected after air kisses into the phone and her last-minute request, with profuse apologies, for fresh mozzarella. I was way ahead of her. The cheese was already packed in a cooler bag beside my suitcase. That and a loaf of her favourite Italian crust bread thanks to Pep and his Italian restaurant. Pep had also given me a couple pounds of pizza dough, so I wouldn't be jonesing for his burrata pizza while I was away.

When the packing was done I had nothing to do but wait for Kevin to arrive for a last evening together. I sat on the sofa and drank a bottle of water. My mother had reminded me to hydrate before the long flights. I figured I would get a head start.

I wasn't sure if Kevin and I would be exchanging presents with one another. One of those weird new-relationship worries. What if he got me something and I had nothing for him? What if I gave him something and he was embarrassed that he had nothing for me? I hated that our sweet relationship was fraught with this waste of thought energy. Our relationship at this point was three months old. At the three month mark with Robert, I was ghosted. I pushed those negative thoughts away and replaced them with loving thoughts of Kevin. He was not Robert. He was everything I could want in a partner, however, I still I had no idea if he was coming over with a gift or a card or nothing at all. With the loss of his parents, his holiday might be a gloomy affair, or he could go over the top to make up for his loss.

After his initial grilling of me about what he saw on the pier and then questioning me again at my office, he had mercifully dropped the topic and we were in a really good place.

Some people say you can't really know a person until you hit the five-month mark in a relationship. I hated thinking of it. If it were true, it would mean that he could turn out to be a completely different person in a couple of months. I pushed that notion away. Right now was what mattered and even though part of me was bracing for the worst, which would be a repeat of what Robert did by ghosting me, the other part was content and trying to relax and enjoy this new man.

I had decided to err on the side of caution and had ordered a gift card for him to go wild at Runner's World. It was personal, but not too personal. We'd met while running, so we had that in common, and we had gone for a couple of slow runs over Thanksgiving weekend.

He was in far better shape than I was, but a slow two-mile run left us both winded. He had claimed it was the elevation and I gladly agreed. Otherwise I would have to join a gym to get my strength and stamina back.

I figured if it turned out that we were not exchanging gifts, or if he was anti-holidays, then I could use the gift card myself.

He arrived with takeout Thai and a tiny box wrapped in silver paper. It was flat and rectangular in shape, not a ring box, but my heart leapt worriedly at the thought that he might have bought me expensive jewelry and I was giving him just a gift card. He set the food down on the coffee table and handed me the box. He looked nervous.

"I wasn't sure we were even exchanging gifts, as we didn't talk about it, but then I said to myself, screw it, I'm crazy about her and I'm getting her a Christmas gift." He sat on the sofa, making the three-seater look small.

I smiled and he relaxed. I reached into my nearby handbag and handed him the envelope containing the gift card.

"Thank you Pia," he said as he read the card and tore the gift card envelope open. "Now open yours."

I carefully unwrapped the silver paper and opened the box. Inside was a silver necklace. The serpentine chain was long and very dainty. There was a silver sneaker-shaped medallion with a tiny diamond chip in it. Diamond is my birthstone, and I was surprised that he'd remembered. I looked up at his smiling face, thrilled with this memento of how we met.

"Wow," I said.

"Wow good, or wow bad?" He asked.

"Definitely wow good. Thank you, yes, I love it. It is perfect." I got up from the armchair and sat beside him.

"I thought it was a cool reminder of how we met running that first day on the water. That's your birthstone, right?" He looked so eager, so intense. His silver eyes sparkled with what looked like tears.

"Yes, it is perfect, I really love it. Thank you." I threw my arms around his neck and then put the necklace on as he re-read his humorous card and looked at the gift card.

His card was an illustration of Santa Claus panting and trying to catch up with his sleigh, and the caption read, *I should have asked for a treadmill!*

He chuckled and said, "I guess we both had running on our minds." He paused and then took a deep breath. "I love you, Pia."

I felt an overwhelming rush in my ears. My heart was beating out of my chest. *He loves me and I was worried whether we were even exchanging gifts.*

"I feel bad about the gift card. It's not—"

"It's perfect. I need new gear. You saw what I ran in. Spandex, for god's sake. A gag gift from the guys at work."

We laughed and he held me. I whispered, afraid to say it too loudly, "I love you too." I hoped he heard me.

Kevin left early and the ride share was late. Even the app can misread the gridlock holiday traffic of New York City. Suffice it to say that started my nightmare travel day. The flight to Chicago was oversold. I ended up giving my third-row window seat to the female half of a separated honeymoon couple and got stuck in the back of the plane in the groom's crappy aisle seat. The bathroom door swinging open and closed constantly was my travel entertainment.

There was no coffee left for a refill and I was sporting a huge headache by the time we hit the tarmac at O'Hare. I had seventy-five minutes to kill in the airport, so I grabbed a breakfast sandwich and coffee from the nearest kiosk—fourteen dollars, thank you very much—and sat at the gate to wait for the boarding call. My seat assignment was in row sixteen, the exit row. Extra legroom and very comfy, if there was no need of me inflating the emergency slide. If the plane did in fact go down, it would be over forest and mountains, and no slide was going to help in that crash.

My plane came in, the passengers disembarked, and lastly the crew left the boarding area. I daydreamed about my flight back to New York after my summer in Vieques, surprised that Robert, my then one-night fling, was the pilot. It hurt my heart to remember those fun times with him. Damn him, damn him to hell for still affecting me all this time later.

Now he was dead, and I was involved with a New York City detective. *And I am over Robert. I am.* I filled my mind thinking about Kevin, absently twirling the pendant in my fingers. But Robert flashed in my mind and was impossible to erase. We'd had such a connection. And now I had given my heart to a new man. My head was starting to hurt. I willed myself to focus on the here and now. I knew my mother would grill me about my latest romance. *Oh, stop!* As Sam would say, stop overthinking. Enjoy the present. I forced my concentration back to the waiting lounge and gulped the last of my overpriced designer coffee.

The screen behind the desk remained unchanged. No changes or delays had been posted. I checked my emails on my phone, tracked my baggage with the electronic tags inside them—a Christmas gift from Carlos and Nona—and saw they were on the move to the plane. So far so good. I had no idea what to expect when I arrived at camp, as Juris called it.

Sam and I had looked on Google Earth and knew what the lodge and camp looked like from aerial views. It was a huge star shape in the barren wilderness of the Chena River. The lodge specialized in hunting and fishing, no animal too large or too small. The website showed a beaming hunter holding up a beaver! As if they pose a threat or are a worthy adversary. There were also caribou, bear, moose, and fox strung up as trophies. My stomach roiled at the thought of eating beaver, or bear, caribou, or any other wild animal. Somehow a burger or piece of chicken just didn't feel the same in my mind. I thought of Sam and how she would react if such a meat were placed in front of her. I may convert to the dark side, as I call vegetarianism.

The leg to Fairbanks is the longest. It is the second largest city in Alaska. I'd seen movies of people dog sledding in the city streets.

I was planning to sleep this leg of the trip. Sam used to joke that I should put sleeping on my resume. I could sleep leaning against a wall, waiting in line for show tickets, on the subway, and sitting outside a fitting room while she tried on clothes.

My head was still feeling a bit off, and I felt a chill shudder through my body. I hoped I wasn't getting sick. Rubbing my hands together, I saw a slight bluish glow from my fingertips. *Holy shit! Not now, not on my vacation.*

I rubbed my eyes and looked again, opening my palms and examining the front and back of my hands. Maybe I was seeing things?

I still felt the chill in my body and thought about my recent, very expensive, shopping trip to Patagonia in Soho. I seriously hoped my outer and underwear gear delivered as promised. I do not do well in the cold and here I was headed to the cold top of the earth. I expected to spend my time huddled by the fireplace, wrapped in wool or down and drinking a hot beverage.

I watched the blue glow fade from my hands as boarding was called.

Thankfully, we boarded on time. Kevin texted me a kissy face and I sent the same back to him, smiling like a moron. This man said he loved me. I said it back. I hadn't even told Sam. I was savouring this newest tidbit for a little while longer.

I hoisted myself up out of my seat, unplugged my charging phone, and made my way into the queue. My legs were leaden, and I sank gratefully into the exit row seat of the plane.

I had never been on a plane that had gone completely dark before. As soon as the doors of the plane closed, the entire plane went dark. The power was off. No lights, no emergency lights. Nothing. After about ten seconds the pilot's voice came through the sound system explaining there would be a slight delay because the plane needed to reboot! Seriously? The reboot took about thirty minutes, and everyone on board breathed a sigh of relief when the seatbelt and no-smoking lights began to flash. We almost stood up and cheered. The plane was emptier than the previous flight and I was able to stretch out with both of my arms resting on arm rests as the middle seat next to me remained empty for the flight.

I slept. Deeply. I dreamt of Vieques and floating in the tranquil sea. I saw Robert's face smiling at me, walking towards me. He was holding his palms up as he came slowly towards me, in an apologetic manner. I reached my hand out to his but before our fingers touched—

Thud! The wheels hit the ground and I jolted awake. A long flight and a really long nap. The food and beverage cart rolling by had not even woken me. My mouth was dry and my lips were cracked. I attempt to lick them to ease the dryness and wake myself up out of my fugue.

I shook off lingering memories of Robert and questioned again, why was I still seeing him in my dreams? I dreaded the thought that every time I flew, I would think of him. Not dead Robert, but alive and usually in a pilot's uniform. My brain would not surrender the image. I couldn't seem to shake him no matter what I did, even getting involved with someone else. Someone I'd fallen in love with, could see a future with. *Go away, Robert! Get out of my head.* Sam told me that I had fantasized about him for so long, it may take just as long to let go of him.

Kevin and I had agreed to be exclusive. We spoke about our monogamy during our Thanksgiving weekend. He tentatively broached the subject, and although we both knew that there is no standard time frame for deciding to be exclusive, we both jumped right into that boat, with no second thoughts, at least on my part.

My only "committed" relationship in my life had been with Captain Robert, and that hadn't exactly worked out. So what did I know? The one thing I knew for sure was that my one-night-stand days were over. I was committed to Kevin, and I felt the same vibe from him. We just fell into the commitment part naturally. We weren't kids and New York City was a tough place to meet someone not looking for a dating-app hookup. I had deleted the apps from my phone. Sam told me how proud she was of me for doing that, in a mock mothering tone, with an eye roll thrown in for good measure.

On my part, committing was frankly laziness. I had no energy for or interest in pursuing any other relationship or situationship. On his part, he'd been burned in his one-and-only marriage to a nurse who'd cheated on him with a patient. He told me that no one else had "turned his crank" in a long while. I quipped that I was the lucky "crank turner," pun intended. He laughed and we fell into an easy agreement about being exclusive.

But right now, I was mentally gearing up for the last leg of my trip—the dreaded puddle jumper to the lodge. My mother described the plane as an adventure in itself. I would be flying in a sardine can with water floats, very similar to the puddle jumper over to Vieques from San Juan, except that we would be actually landing on a lake. If that lake was frozen, we'd still be landing on it.

We all trudged single file down the plane's stairs and across the cold, windy tarmac. The electric doors opened and I broke off to sit and wait for my next flight. The rest of the passengers went on past me to the baggage carousel.

I tried and failed to picture landing on a lake. How would it feel to splash down, essentially? When I had flown from Vieques over to San Juan the flight was over water. LaGuardia airport in New York is also next to water, and as you take off and land over Long Island Sound, you feel precariously close to a dunking.

I had researched the Beaver bush plane and knew it could hold gear and people. It was the plane that opened up the North, and in the mid-1900s the pilots were revered as gods by the Inuit communities they served. I gave passing thought as to what kind of person my pilot would be. Living in the extreme cold and ferrying people and supplies back and forth for a living. Not much of a life—or maybe that was harsh and judgmental on my part. Perhaps the pilot loved his work. Flying to remote areas no one else could get to.

I pictured a crusty old-timer who had been flying since the beginning of time and would spend the flight chewing tobacco and pointing out wildlife. I could visualize his worn flight jacket, a week's stubble on his weathered face, and could hear his raspy voice. It would surely be entertaining, if not too terrifying.

I pulled my brand new parka out of my suitcase and grabbed the flap hat. I put the hat in my backpack for easy access, pulled the warm parka on, and zipped it halfway. It felt like I was wearing a sleeping bag. Not unpleasant at all. I texted Sam with an update on my travel so far, snapped a selfie of myself in my new jacket, knowing she would be amused.

Chapter 40

Pia's Detective

NARRATOR: SAM

Pia had gone to Alaska and we were headed to California. A warm Christmas going to the beach, hanging with my brothers and their families, and seeing some childhood friends. *With my husband!* The trip would be perfect if I could talk Kash out of Disneyland, and if not, maybe I could convince or bribe one of my brothers to go with him instead of me. I did not do rides, hated the long lines, and couldn't stand the smell of fast-food grease.

My only trip there had ended with me vomiting on a ride all over myself and the two people behind me. The auto photo snap captured the moment the vomit left my mouth in a wide arc. My oldest brother, Mik, bought the photo and brought it out at every family gathering. I guessed Kash would be the new viewer this year. Whenever I thought about it, I could taste bile in the back of my throat.

If he paraded that photo, I would share our wedding photos. Every single one, over five hundred.

I was feeling some concern about Jarad. He hadn't been texting me regularly like usual. He was kind, sensitive, and way too quiet lately. He had been disappointed when Pia went away with Kevin for Thanksgiving. I didn't tell him about how serious they were. That was not my place, but Pia, honest to a fault, told him she was in a new relationship. He didn't get mad, he got quiet, and it's always the quiet ones with whom we psychiatrists are most concerned. Kash knew my concerns and had promised to spend some extra time with him, if only to assure me that he was doing all right.

At last night's task force meeting, the Connecticut Elementary School shooting was the only topic on the table. The mayor and his sidekick attended and were as shell shocked as we all were.

There was a pervasive feeling of impotence among us, an overwhelming sense that nothing we did could change anything. We quoted statistics and probabilities, but there were at least two mass shootings, meaning at least four people besides the shooter were injured or killed, every day for the last four years and authorities were useless in preventing them.

As always, the conversation turned to gun legislation, and Kevin got defensive.

He educated us about the type of weapon used in the Connecticut shooting. I had never heard of it. He called it the auto switch, also known as the auto sear. There had been over one thousand shootings in the US in the past year where this device was attached to a semi-automatic weapon, turning it into a machine gun. The fact that they were illegal was moot. They were used on the streets every day. They could be fabricated in a 3-D printer. As fast as they were confiscated, new ones appeared.

At the end of Kevin's talk, the feeling in the room was dejection. *How can we combat this surge in gun violence?* was the only question, and there was no answer.

The mayor said we were doing our best, and then we all squabbled and put in our two cents. I stated that we were not doing our best, because talking about the issue was the same as doing nothing. Our best was not good enough if schools didn't get more staff and funding for counsellors and programs, and gun legislation had to change. It was exhausting to go around and around and not get anywhere.

I couldn't wait to get out of there and head home, but was waylaid by Pia's detective.

"Excuse me, Dr. Sodhra, could I speak to you for a minute?" He pushed the elevator button and we both got in.

The doors shut behind us and he cleared his throat. Stalling.

"Detective?" I prompted.

"You know Pia and I are seeing each other?" It wasn't really a question. He knew that I knew.

In fact, I knew a lot more than he could imagine. Pia was very forthcoming on every aspect of every date with him and I closed my mind to the more intimate details about his body that she'd shared. One tattoo in particular was hard to get out of my mind. I prayed I wasn't blushing.

I nodded and he continued. "She is really something. Did she tell you how we met?" I knew the story of her early morning run and encounter with him. Was this what he meant? I wasn't sure where this guy was going. I was not about to talk about the reverse ripples on the pier that saved a woman's life.

Again, I nodded and told him I was aware as the doors opened at the lobby level and we both started through the foyer towards the street doors.

Outside on the sidewalk, he stopped and turned to me. "Can I buy you a coffee?" he asked, hopeful and cautious at the same time.

"I have an early flight tomorrow and don't want to drink coffee now, so please detective, just say whatever it is you want to say." I started walking towards the uptown train and he had no choice but to follow. His long legs easily caught up with me.

"Okay, sure. It's just that…she is very unusual. Would you agree?"

"Unusual?" I stopped and looked up at him. "Pia is my best friend. There is no better person than Pia." I knew I sounded super defensive, but I didn't see where he was going with that statement. "Unusual, no, but I will say she is one of a kind."

"Yes, that's what I meant. Unique, like a rare gem."

He smiled as if thinking a happy thought. I could certainly see the attraction. His whole face lit up and those silver eyes practically twinkled. No wonder Pia fell for him.

Funny that he used the word *gem*. Did Pia tell him about the ruby? "What are you trying, very badly I might add, to say?"

He laughed and his whole demeanour changed. I found myself smiling.

"I don't even know. I feel like I am back in middle school. Telling her friend how much I like her."

I was relieved. This was nothing more than a fishing expedition.

"Pull yourself together, Detective. In this huge city, it's a crazy coincidence that we're assigned to the same task force and then you start seeing"—I looked up at him and he nodded, so I continued—"my best friend. What are the chances?"

"This city has fewer degrees of separation than most. I don't know why, but studies have been done. I agree that it's a coincidence, but then again, is it? Some people think there is no such thing as a coincidence. There are many factors at work to make things coincide."

I was at my subway station. I turned to him and said, as nicely as possible, "Look, Detective, we can debate and philosophize all night, but it doesn't change things. You are seeing Pia, my dearest friend, and realistically we may end up socializing together. Is there anything else before I go home to my husband?"

"Thanks for listening, Doc. I'm not even sure why I needed to talk to you. I apologize for taking up your time. Happy holidays. Get home safe."

He turned on his heel and walked past the entrance towards Broadway.

What the fuck was that? I asked myself as I tapped my phone on the metro reader. I couldn't wait to hear Kash's take on this. Jesus, what were we, twelve years old? If he thought I was going to give him insight into Pia's special abilities, he was mistaken. Most of the time I didn't even think about them, and when I did, my logical mind wanted to list reasons her abilities couldn't be real. *She cannot bring the dead back to life. Not in this sane world; magic is not real, time travel cannot happen, such things do not exist.* And yet, time after time, she had intervened or interfered or interrupted, and the person who had been dead was actually walking around alive. All except Joel.

Kash was waiting for me with open arms when I walked in the door. We downed a full bottle of wine while we discussed our respective days and we then exhausted all possibilities as to why the detective wanted the little chat with me. We fell gratefully into bed, both of us thinking our own thoughts, but both excited to be travelling to my family for the holidays. I kissed my husband and I kissed my beautiful ruby ring—not a materialistic thing, a gratitude thing. My best friend found it, my brother helped her locate a gemologist, and the love of my life presented it to me on our wedding day. Life had blessed me in more ways than I could express. I almost felt as if love would overwhelm me and swallow me whole. Would that be a bad thing? No, it would not.

California here we come!

Chapter 41

When Dream Becomes Reality

NARRATOR: PIA

The boarding announcement woke me from a vivid daydream of running beside Kevin. We were on the main path in Central Park and stopped for a breather at Turtle Lake. He had his arm draped on my shoulder and I was holding a small silver box. I was trying to rip open the wrapping paper but couldn't get it open. My fingers were glowing and tingling and I didn't want him to see them.

I kept tearing at the seams of the paper, but they were stuck like cement. My fingers were really glowing and seemed to elongate before my eyes. I looked at Kevin, to see if he'd noticed my fingers, but he was staring at the turtles going in and out of the water that was pitch black but glowing with bursts of bioluminescence.

I jerked upright, not sure where I was. I looked around the small waiting area and remembered. It had been a long day and the sun was setting now, making the last of the daylight all shadows. I shouldered my backpack and extended the roller handle as I made my way alone to the door. The flight attendant confirmed that I was to be the only passenger on the forty-five-minute flight to the lodge. I had spent the day flying, napping, napping, and flying. I felt like my body was not my own. I was disjointed and feared a migraine coming on. I hadn't had one in months. *Please, not today.* Usually coffee kept them at bay.

When I asked who was currently at the lodge, my mother had told me that Christmas week was blacked out for regular bookings. It would be just the three of us plus the full-time staff, who had their own quarters. My mother intimated that we would be having serious family time this year in honour of my very first visit to the frozen North. I had packed dominoes and Go to play, hoping that sitting by the fire playing games would be an acceptable family activity for my mother.

An airline employee wearing a heavy-duty parka with the hood up against the strong winds took my bags and directed me into the cabin of the small plane. The hinged door was tied to the fuselage with a rope. It still managed to clang and bang in the wind. There were wheels as well as large pontoons on the plane. I had never seen a plane like this up close and asked if we would be landing on water. I had seen small pontoon planes land in Esperanza Bay in Vieques and also on the Gowanus Canal in Brooklyn.

"There is no water, miss. Everything is frozen now." His breath was a white stream around his face and he shook his head at my apparently ridiculous question.

"Oh right. Of course." I zipped my parka up to my neck and pulled the gloves out of the pockets. I put the hood up and took the one seat on the plane. The other was for the pilot. I tried to control my shivering, but the more I thought about spending a week in sub-zero temperatures, the colder I felt. I closed my eyes and took deep breaths. This was the first day of seven. I needed to get a handle on this bone-chilling cold air.

"You all set?" a deep male voice said and I felt him squeeze past me and take the other seat. He too was wearing a parka and a fur cap.

His voice sounded familiar, and I tried to get a look at him as he flipped buttons, put on his headset, and handed me mine. As his eyes met mine, I almost screamed.

"Robert?" Was I seeing things? What the hell?

"Hello, Pia." He continued to stare at me and smile. His face was deeply tanned, very unlike his face when I saw him on the pier two months ago. When he was dead.

"What are you doing here?' I asked him and before he could answer I blurted out, "You died!"

"Died? I didn't die. If I died, would I be here?" He laughed as he continued to run through his pre-check and my mind went crazy trying to figure out what in the holy hell was happening. Was I dreaming? How is this possible? I saw him and his wife dead in Vieques. Now he was in Alaska.

"What are you doing here?" I said loudly, too loudly for this small plane.

"I am piloting the plane and taking you to your father's camp." He noticed me straining against my seatbelt and said, "Sit back and relax. We'll be there in less than an hour."

I couldn't relax. Was he crazy? Or was I? *What is going on here? How can this be happening?*

"Look, I know things didn't end well between us. I am so sorry about all that shit I put you through, but I can explain." He put his right hand on my knee. "If you let me."

I was steaming inside. I removed his hand and said, "Didn't end well? In one breath you said you loved me and in the next you disappeared. I expected you to show up for Thanksgiving! No call. No text, just poof, you vanished!" I took a deep breath to calm down. "Fly the plane, Robert. I don't really want to talk right now." That was completely not true. I had a million questions for him but needed to process this. I wished I could call Sam. She would flip. Kash would flip. I was flipping. He'd died. He drowned when his Cessna went down. I signed the death certificate, for Christ's sake. How was he here, alive and well and tanned and acting like we had just seen each other last week? *This is nuts!*

The plane took off and I kept my eyes closed. I could feel his eyes on me but I could not bear to look at him. I just kept repeating to myself, *He died, he died, he died. I chose not to save him, so he died.*

"Who told you I died?" His question cut off my internal dialogue and came through my headset loud and clear.

I could not answer. I did not know what to say. I couldn't tell him I'd seen him dead, that would make me sound crazy—except I had in fact seen him and his wife, very much dead on the pier.

I responded, "You were dead to me."

"Yeah, I guess I deserve that. But please let me explain…"

It sounded strange to hear the words I longed to hear last year. Words I never heard from him because we had stopped communicating. His choice, not mine. I waited for him to text. To call. To do anything to let me know what had happened.

I put my hand up to stop him and kept my eyes closed.

He concentrated on flying the plane, but I could feel he would rather be talking to me. Lying to me, more than likely.

The tension between us simmered as we flew north, and soon I could feel us descending into the vast white landscape. I was missing this beautiful view, but it was worth it to shut him out. He continued to point out lakes and structures, then the dark outline of the lodge from the air growing larger as we descended, and then smoke from two chimneys as we bumped onto the hard-packed surface of snow, sliding a little bit as we stopped. The frozen lake.

I felt the usual need to clap upon safe touchdown and resisted with all of my might. I didn't smile as I handed over the headset and started to stand.

He once again laid his hand on my leg.

"Pia, listen, could we talk? Please?" His voice was pleading, unsure.

"Talk about what, Robert? We were over a long time ago. Forget it." I had moved past him. I'd been really hurt when he disappeared from my life, but I was involved with Kevin now and telling myself that I had zero interest in Robert. I knew when he was lying dead on the pier that I'd closed off the part of me that loved him. And yet, if that was true, why was I so upset? Why did I feel as if I might faint? I could feel the heat from his hand through the denim of my jeans. God, I had loved this man. This prick. This asshole. This liar. And where was his wife? Was she alive too? Was that the next surprise for me here?

"Pia, wait." I moved past him and waited by the small door, uncertain how to get it open. Just as I was reaching for it, it whooshed open and I was hit with a blast of air colder than I had ever felt in my life.

My father, clothed in a knee-length parka and watch cap, stood smiling on the other side.

"Pia, surprise!" My father had his arms extended wide and was walking towards me. I staggered off the plane into those arms, all the while wondering what the surprise was. After all, my parents had known and planned for months for my visit.

He stepped back and held me at arms' length. "So, how was your flight? Were you surprised to see Robert?"

I stared at him, unable to form words, and then managed to squawk, "How is he here?"

Robert approached at that very moment and my father released me to shake hands with him.

"Join us for dinner?" my father asked Robert.

"Thanks, but no. I'm sure Pia wants some family time. See you tomorrow." He winked at me and turned to secure the plane's door. At one time, that sexy wink would have made my knees weak, but now it just incensed me. I watched him as he closed up the door and moved to the front of the plane, opening the hinged compartment.

I turned back to my father and saw he had my rolling suitcase and backpack and was heading to the lodge. I raced to keep up with him and saw the front door of the lodge open. My mother was backlit and almost jumping up and down with eagerness. As soon as I was a few feet away, she met me and enveloped me in a hug.

"Welcome, honey, I'm so glad you are here. Come inside, you must be exhausted. And hungry."

"Mom!" I hugged her tight, glad to see her looking healthy and happy. "I am exhausted and I guess a bit hungry." I wanted to ask how the fuck Robert was here, in Alaska, but I knew that was a conversation for my father, not for her.

She looked worried as she looked closely at my face. "Is everything okay?"

How could I explain that no, everything was definitely not okay? My world had just been sent into a spiral, and I felt as if I was losing my mind. *I have had a year of things happening that could not possibly happen, and could not be explained, but at least I had some control. And now Robert is alive when he should be dead, and I feel as if I am losing it. And to top it off, he is in friggin' Alaska. The exact opposite of Puerto Rico. What is happening?*

My mother continued, "Come in and have a drink. Let's get you warmed up. The intense cold is such a shock at first, but believe me, you do get used to it." She held her hand out for my jacket. I dutifully removed it and my hat and gloves and handed them over. She hung them on a peg on the wall and then led me into the great room. It was massive. Bigger than Kevin's cabin. She walked over to the full bar, a long, solid piece of four-inch-thick mahogany that gleamed, went behind it to the shelves, and brought down three mugs. She lifted a steaming pitcher off the bar and poured something very aromatic into one of the mugs. She handed it to me and began to fill the others.

"Mulled wine, honey. Drink it, you'll feel better."

Robotically I drank it down and it did taste wonderful. I walked over to a suede sofa that had to be twelve feet long and sat. I felt my insides loosen up and I realized I had been holding my breath, and so I exhaled. If I was going to spend a week in the frigid North, this drink would be a welcome addition.

"That's really delicious, Mom. Thanks."

She beamed and asked if I wanted another. My father joined us and offered up a toast to family, and we clinked our mugs and sat near the fire. They sat side by side on a loveseat across from me. The fire blazed and crackled and lit their clearly content, relaxed faces.

"Wait till you taste your father's special dinner," she said and took his hand. They smiled at each other and then at me. "He has been cooking all day."

"It's not beaver, is it?"

They both laughed, and I relaxed when they shook their heads.

I drank the wine and tamped down the questions boiling in my mind. I needed answers but tonight was clearly not the night to get them. It had been an incredibly long day. I felt completely drained, shocked, and confused. I would be rested and better able to solve this puzzle in the morning. This day felt as if it had been a week long, but I talked myself into enjoying my safe arrival, and with my mother's happiness so evident, I managed to enjoy the evening.

The next morning I woke to darkness. I checked my watch and it said 9:30. *Shouldn't it be light?* There was a knock on the door and my mother peeked in.

"How'd you sleep?" She walked over to the bed and sat down next to me.

"I slept amazingly. This weighted blanket is heaven." I patted the gray cotton spread, making a mental note to get one for my New York apartment the minute I was back. It cocooned me and I don't think I even rolled over in my sleep. I couldn't even remember dreaming, and that in itself was very unusual for me. Especially in the last year. My dreams had become so vivid and lifelike that there were times I couldn't distinguish between dream and reality. Last night my mind had blissfully taken a night off.

"Great, get dressed and I will take you on a tour of the camp."

"How about some coffee first, Mom?"

She smiled and I could see contentment written all over her face. She stood and hugged me, and said she would be downstairs getting breakfast ready and then we would have the tour.

"Take your time, honey. There's no rush. You need to fuel up here to ward off the cold."

I unpacked and showered in the en suite. The brown granite countertops, bronze enamel sinks, and flagstone floor were perfect for this setting. Outside the cedar-framed windows, with no blinds or curtains, all I could see was white extending for miles. If I looked on a diagonal I could just make out the wings of the beaver plane. I guessed Captain Robert wasn't flying today.

The vast landscape was too bright to look at. My eyes ached from the brightness and I considered putting on sunglasses inside the house. I decided not to and followed my nose to the amazing smells coming from the back of the lodge.

I sent a quick text to Sam asking her to call me later. California and Alaska are only one hour apart time wise. We would have an interesting conversation, and I fully expected her to tell me I'd blown her mind.

"Cassiopeia, would you like to eat or tour first?" My mother was pouring coffee into a mug for me.

I took it from her and had a sip. "It's delicious, Mom. How about I drink the coffee while we tour?"

"Perfect," she said, and picked up her mug to take with her.

The lodge was beyond massive. My mother took me around the ground floor, explaining the additions my father had done over the years. The new rooms blended seamlessly with the original log cabin structure. There was a massive great room, or centre room, from which six other rooms branched out. The upstairs rooms were reserved for family only and consisted of four large bedrooms with en suites. Their master bedroom also had a sitting room for my mother and an office space for her remote work.

The mess hall/kitchen was one of the additions, masterfully joined with the main structure by my father, who according to my mother had many talents. I let that one go.

The guest quarters were another addition. There were eight suites, four on either side of the central hallway. Each was identical. They looked comfy and roomy and very, very masculine.

The den, or "trophy room" as I called it in my mind, was the one I had seen in the brochure and I was positive I wouldn't be setting foot into it again. The glass eyes of the trophy animals were unworldly and creeped me out. Seeing the animal as it once was unnerved me. It seemed shameful to mount a defenseless animal as a trophy. That animal didn't stand a chance against the gun or longbow.

My mother seemed to take it in stride and moved us on to the next area, the library/office. Floor-to-ceiling shelves held every book, from bestsellers to antiquated encyclopedias. There were map books, wildlife coffee table books, and one of my personal favourites, *The View from Above*. A thousand-page pictorial tour of Earth from space. Sam had given it to me for Christmas one year.

In the far corner stood a photocopier, fax machine, and desktop computer. There was also a tall filing cabinet and a flat file setup that my mother explained held maps of the area.

Next we looked into the mud room that held all of the gear needed. Shelves and racks were piled high with camping gear, boots, outerwear, skiis and snowshoes. I could see that the gun racks and longbows were in a locked cabinet at the side of the office. Fishing poles and tackle took up one entire wall. It was amazing to see all of this equipment, lovingly cared for and respected. I was proud of what my father had accomplished.

I realized in that moment my feelings of abandonment had long since evaporated. Back then he had been unable to deal with what had happened to him, so he did the best he could. He was exactly my age when he fell into the bio bay, and now here we were together.

I had spent a year with this absolutely impossible gift of reversing time, and most of the time I felt like I did not even know who I was. He and I shared an unfathomable, completely impossible connection. And now we were together in the land of ice and snow, and we shared a secret.

Alaska. The last place I thought I would ever be. How strange this past year had been. Falling into the bio bay, working at the medical examiner's office, having an affair with Robert, meeting and saving my birth father, having two parents now together, my two best friends getting married, and being in a solid relationship with a wonderful new man. Everything sounded perfect except for the fact that my old, dead lover was alive and well and in Alaska.

My mind felt like it would explode. I drained the last of the coffee, hoping the caffeine would work its magic.

My mother had been talking the entire time I was caught up in my own thoughts.

"Wait until you see the glaciers, Pia."

"That sounds amazing, Mom." I was never one for geography in school. I was a science nerd, always doing experiments, and never spent any time thinking about travel or the vastness of the country. I never took an interest in glaciers, even in this last year, despite my mother going on about their beauty and the rate at which they were disappearing. Now I would get to see them up close, before they completely vanished.

We kept up a brisk pace as we headed to yet another wing.

"This place is huge, Mom. I feel like I have walked miles. No wonder you've stayed in great shape." She looked amazing. She had on navy stovepipe pants and a deep red turtleneck sweater. As usual her hair and makeup were perfect and her loafers had navy and red tassels. Her jewelry was minimal except for a ring on her left hand. A square cut diamond ring that sparkled every time she moved her hand. My fingers gravitated to my necklace and I slid the small sneaker on the chain.

She watched me finger the chain and raised one eyebrow. "You get used to it. It is like walking in the city. We are New Yorkers. We walk. The only difference being no pedestrians or traffic."

"Just polar bears and penguins," I quipped.

"That is ridiculous, Cassiopeia. I have seen neither in my time here. But your father's stories of the ferocity of polar bears are enough to keep me safely inside."

She led me to the final room. She turned and looked at me with a mischievous look on her face.

"What?" I asked, but she just turned to the door and with some effort, pushed it open.

She stepped aside, allowing me to enter before she did. It was a greenhouse. A massive, glass-enclosed, soaring greenhouse, not unlike the one at the Central Park Zoo. It was warm and moist, and greenery abounded, covering every table surface and soaring to the roof.

I was stunned. "This is breathtaking," I said, but that didn't do it justice.

"I know, right? I had some input about what we grow and this runs year round, providing vegetables and flowers. Some are hydroponic. I never gardened in my life and now look at me." She stood with her hands on her hips surveying this kingdom of hers.

The wind howled outside, and I could feel the pressure on the panes of glass causing them to rattle, which sounded almost like a moan. Snow blanketed the first four or five feet from the ground, making the large space feel almost cave-like. I followed the path that ran around the sides and straight up the middle. Nothing was planted close to the edge; there were at least three feet of distance so that nothing touched the exterior walls. Warm, humid air gushed up through vents around the side. I could feel perspiration on my forehead. I followed my mother as she walked and described and plucked the occasional petal or leaf.

I recognized peas climbing lattice and bean sprouts starting. I could smell tomatoes and good, earthy, dark soil.

I was impressed. This lodge could sustain the people within if a storm isolated them.

As if reading my mind, she went on. "We are self-sufficient here. We grow enough to feed ourselves, but of course when the weather permits we have supplies flown in."

"It is truly amazing, Mom. It's warm, almost tropical." I could strip down to a swimsuit here, it was that warm.

She preened and handed me a kirby. I took it and crunched the sweet cucumber. It was so incongruous I laughed out loud. She joined me and we stood side by side, munching on cucumbers in a greenhouse in Alaska.

I changed the subject. "Where is Juris?" He had been absent so far this morning.

"Oh, he's hauling in the tree we had cut. He said he'll tow it back with his new machine. He expects us to do all the decorating."

I had not even noticed the absence of a Christmas tree in this gigantic place. There were garlands of fresh greens, festive with plaid ribbon bows and bouquets of greens on the tables. The place already smelled like fresh-cut balsam and cedar.

"Let's go see if he has it up." She double checked that the door was shut tight and then took my hand.

We walked in comfortable silence across acres of barn board floors to the great room. He did have it up. All fifteen feet, possibly more, of fragrant fir. He stood beside the tree, dwarfed by its size. In New York City it would easily have cost over a thousand dollars. Here it was, with snow still clinging to its needles, in front of one of the equally massive windows.

"Well now, that's a project," my mother said as she walked over and stood next to my father.

"Speaking of projects," Juris said, "is anyone hungry?"

We went into the kitchen, and my parents cooked eggs Benedict to perfection. I had to admit, they worked well together. I kept circling back to the appearance of Robert. How had he appeared here when the last time I saw him, he was most definitely dead?

After breakfast, my mother left to sort through the Christmas lights and tree decorations and I took the opportunity to ask my father about Robert.

"Quite a surprise, huh?" he said as we moved into the great room and he shook tree branches, seemingly delighted at the water cascading off the branches. I looked at it pooling on the floor beneath the tree, mildly curious if he was going to leave it to evaporate on its own or mop it up.

When I didn't answer, he asked, "Good surprise?"

"Juris, how is he here?"

My father stopped shaking branches and sat down next to me.

"I did it." He reached for my hand. I let him hold it but looked at our hands with detachment. His strong, lean hands with long fingers, the same as mine.

"You did it?" I repeated.

"In Vieques, you seemed so upset about your boyfriend"—he corrected himself—"about the crash, that I took a shot. I have been wondering for twenty-five years, if I got the chance to do it again, could I save someone, not just myself?"

I nodded and he continued. "I went to the airport, thinking I was crazy, talked my way onto the flight with Carlos's help, and I unzipped the black bag, reached into the bag just to see if I felt anything at all, you know, magic, put my hand on his shoulder, and presto, we were back in time before the flight took off. It happened in a flash. One minute the plane was taking off in Vieques with me on it, and the next second I was in the airport parking lot and spotted him heading up the ramp to the terminal. I walked up to him, introduced myself, and bought him a couple of drinks at the airport cafe. His wife was inside, but at that point I knew it was his ex-wife. After those two drinks with me, he was too drunk to fly, so he didn't. It was all a matter of a few seconds. I imagine that wife was none too pleased when he told her he wasn't flying." He laughed loudly and continued, "And that is it. I saved him. Or them, if you count his ex-wife."

Everything he said made sense in my crazy, messed-up mind, because that is exactly what can happen in a split second, except the ex-wife part.

"*Ex*-wife?"

"Yes, he told me that she had finally decided to let him go and she was moving to San Juan."

I had nothing to say.

"So now, Pia, you have another chance. I feel vindicated, as if this makes up for my inability to save my shipmates all those years ago."

"So you played God?" He looked surprised at my tone.

"Pia, I have waited almost thirty years for a chance to prove to myself that what happened was not a hallucination. I did not play God. I took a chance to do something. This wasn't a random stranger. Your mother told me you love this man."

I just stared at him. He'd done this for him, not for me. So that he could feel good about himself, no matter how fucked up this was for me. "I did. I did love him. But this isn't another chance. Not with him. He was a liar. He lied to me and ghosted me. I thought we had a great thing going and he disappeared from my life. It hurt and frankly it still hurts." I was seething and I knew how petty and vengeful I sounded. I wanted to tell him right then and there that I'd had the chance to save Robert and chosen not to.

"If you didn't have strong feelings for him, you wouldn't be this angry. Love and hate are flip sides of the same coin, Pia."

"Not everything has a fairytale ending, Juris. I didn't like and still don't like being lied to. I am an adult and can handle the truth. If he had been honest from the start of our relationship, I could have decided for myself if I wanted it to continue." I took a calming breath before I continued.

We sat in silence for a few minutes and then I asked him, "So how did he end up here?"

"Oh well, when I was buying him the drinks, I told him I needed a pilot to ferry paying clients in and out. He said he would think about it. About a week later, he called just as your mother and I were landing here. Pia, let me tell you, he has been fantastic. He is a competent pilot."

"Except for his crash in Vieques," I said meanly.

"Yes, that was unfortunate, but it didn't actually happen, now, did it?"

My mother came into the room and broke the silence. "And who is going to mop up this mess?" She was looking pointedly at the melting snow pooling under the huge tree.

"I'm on it, Helena. The tree is just about thawed. How are those decorations coming along?" They walked out of the room together, his head bent low to hear her. He put his arm on her shoulders and she snaked hers around his waist. I watched them with longing. Did I even want to see Robert? No, I knew I did not.

I didn't have the energy to rehash what had happened. Once a liar, always a liar. And yet, I was a liar too. I lied to Sam and Kash about the reverse ripples that were still happening. I lied to my mother about the relationship with Robert. I told her we were crazy about each other briefly but ended by mutual agreement because of the distance issue. I lied to myself for years about my one-night stands.

But Robert's too many lies were unforgivable. I planned to avoid him. There was no way I wanted to see him except piloting the plane that would take me back to civilization and New York City and Kevin.

The next day I suited up, barely able to walk in long underwear, thermal pants, lined socks and boots, and the parka, and I went exploring with Juris. We rode on a snowmachine, his brand new toy and my first time on one. He bragged about the horsepower and pull and I just pretended to understand and care. I had to admit that the camp had a wonderful setup and I looked forward to sharing all the details with Sam and Kash. If it weren't so bone-chillingly cold, I could really have enjoyed myself.

We slowed as we pulled up to some ice-fishing huts, vacant at present. They were used by locals as well as camp clients. Juris showed me inside the huts; each came equipped with a heater, a long bench, tools, a lantern, and a shelf for provisions. I watched in amazement as he took a long corkscrew-shaped tool and drilled into the ice where the hole that had closed over was. I could see down through the blue ice, which had to be a foot thick. It was very interesting once I adjusted to the cold. Inside the hut, we were protected from the wind. Back on the snowmachine, the wind was biting despite the windshield diverting some off to the sides.

"Looks like we're in for some weather." He yelled to be heard over the roar of the engine.

"What will happen?" I yelled back, holding on to his waist and mashing my face into his back as the terrain got bumpy.

"Nothing. It's all good. The camp has generators and enough fuel to power things for a week. We have all the provisions we could possibly want. I even got your mother a cheesecake. You know how she loves cheesecake."

I was surprised at how thoughtful he was. My mother loved New York cheesecake. She would always order it for special occasions from Irene's in Soho. Irene's was now online and delivered to Alaska. Mom would be surprised.

"I have another surprise for her."

Oh boy, I thought. My mother wasn't big on surprises. Cheesecake, yes, but what else could he have in mind?

"What is it?" I asked.

"You will have to wait and see," he chuckled in a self-satisfied way.

I was certainly not going to beg him to tell me. But what could the surprise be? She already had his ring on her finger.

Chapter 42

California Christmas

Our Christmas was perfect except for Jarad sulking around. Kash was a trooper and did his best to cheer him up.

"I thought things were great," Jarad said for the umpteenth time to Kash.

Kash looked over at me and rolled his eyes.

"Yeah man, I get that. But if it's not mutual, then forget it. Move on." He turned on the PS5 and handed him a controller.

Jarad looked at it like it was from outer space. "I've been crazy about her since I first met her. Remember, Sam?" He looked at me, eyes pleading for me to wallow in his misery.

"Jarad, grow up," I said, not to be mean, just to let it go. I was stuck in between my best friend and my brother and secretly I was glad they weren't a couple. That would be too close for comfort.

"Real nice, sis," he moaned.

"Come on. Play with Kash. Pia is into her own thing right now. Let's just enjoy these next few days of relaxation. When we get back to New York, things are going to be crazy. My schedule is full right up to the end of January."

"Yes, and I have exams, so play now, I have to study later." Kash started the game.

"Thanks for letting us stay here, Jar," I said to my brother. "I'm going to make some falafel. You guys play."

"Put some meat in mine," Kash called over to me as I went into the kitchen. Jarad laughed out loud.

I gave him a dirty look and said, "I'll convert you one of these days!"

I could hear them getting into the competition of the game and decided it was a good time to call Pia. She picked up immediately and spilled all her news.

"He's actually alive?" I could not believe my ears.

"Oh yes he is, thanks to my father playing God," Pia answered.

"Pia, you can't say that. Be fair. It is no different than what you do. How did he look? Any different?"

"He looked the same. Gorgeous. Maybe a bit more gray in the hair. Same eyes and voice and everything. But he is a liar. It burns me up to think that I fell for his bullshit."

I could hear so many emotions in what she just said, anger, yes, but disappointment, love, hate, sadness, and a calmness that surprised me. I would be freaking out.

"Are you going to talk with him?" I hoped she would get some closure. That went out the window when he died. Now maybe she would get the answers she needed.

"Absolutely not." She sounded firm on that.

"What about Kevin? Have you guys talked?" The detective made me nervous. I felt as if he had an ulterior motive when it came to Pia, but that was just my opinion and I planned to keep that to myself.

"Yes, we talked last night and this morning. There is something very familiar, but also new about him." Her sentence drifted off and then she said, "I feel so comfortable around Kevin even though he has just come into my life. I love it. We are so in sync with each other. It is easy to be around him. And he is sexy and mature. I am starting to think maybe I do have a type." She laughed and I joined her.

"Yeah, you do have a type. Sexy older guy. It's his eyes. They are so intense." *Like a wolf,* I thought, and got a mental picture of him devouring Pia. I shook off that thought.

"His eyes are amazing," Pia said dreamily.

"You definitely know how to pick them." As soon as the words were out of my mouth, I regretted them. It had hurt Pia so much when Robert disappeared from her life. She covered well and hid the hurt from everyone but me. I was her sounding board, her shoulder to cry on, and her friend for the months that followed her breakup. I wanted to throttle him for what he put her through, but she had moved on, and although Kevin has so far been nothing but great for her, I had a strange feeling that he had an agenda that we did not know about. That would remain my thought only and I seriously hoped I was wrong.

"Haha. Look at your guy. He's no slouch."

"He is such a gift. I am forever in your debt, Pia, for finding him for me."

"Everything happens for a reason, Sam. Everything. I just wish I knew why this happened with Robert. My father should have let sleeping dogs lie."

Glad for the change in subject, I asked about her parents and got the long version of the tree decorating. Pia described the house and greenhouse and sent pics while we chatted. It looked amazing. Kash and I had an open invitation from Juris and Helena, but neither of us liked the cold.

Pia described everything so well I felt as if I was there with her, in the room, putting ornaments on the tree and drinking mulled wine. Her perceptiveness and recollection of details were absolutely amazing. Very handy in her line of work, but still astounding.

I told her about Kash's new ugly sweater he had yet to see and I was still laughing when we hung up. I went back into the living room where the boys were still gaming.

Kash looked over and said, "Falafel ready?"

I turned around and went back into the kitchen to start the falafel, looking forward to sharing Pia's revelation about Robert with my husband later.

Chapter 43

A Christmas Surprise

NARRATOR: PIA

Christmas Eve in Alaska. Dark skies practically the entire day. I had managed to avoid being alone with Robert. He had been busy and I had not been in a social mood. I begged off the night he came to dinner and much to my surprise and gratitude he left me alone.

My parents took me to see glaciers the previous day and I could not believe the beauty and majesty. The water was sapphire blue and the ice took on a bluish glow. Seeing orcas was icing on the already fantastic cake. These last few days had been so memorable and so much better than I could ever have imagined. I would definitely come back. I would love for Kevin to see this place and meet my parents. If we ended up staying together, and I hoped we would, he would have to meet them, and that would happen here. What a complete 180 my New York mother had made, moving up here to be with Juris. She didn't like Vieques because it was so rural, and now she was living in a place with no neighbours for a hundred miles. I didn't think I could do it.

I was getting ready for dinner when my reprieve ended. I heard a loud rap on the door.

"Come in," I responded.

The door opened and slowly he came inside, hesitating, but then walked over to me.

"Robert, what are you doing here?" I stood up as he walked towards me.

"I didn't want you to leave without a chance for me to explain what happened."

I said nothing.

"To explain what happened to us," he continued.

I answered, "There was no us, Robert; you saw to that. Why even bother to discuss it?"

"Look, it was the biggest mistake I've made in my life, doing that to you. I am sorry every day, Pia. I've changed. Believe me."

I said nothing, so he continued, "I tried to call you."

I cut him off, "Yeah, so you could lie some more."

"No, so I could apologize. Pia." He approached me and tried to take my hand, but I brushed him off. "Look, I was going through a messy divorce when I met you. My wife—I mean, my ex-wife— was crazy. She made things impossible for me. For us. I tried to call you many times, but you would just hang up."

"You didn't call me, Robert. My phone would have recognized your number."

"No, Sofia, my ex, threw my phone in the ocean. I had to get a new number, different carrier, different everything."

My mind jumped to the mysterious 787 calls I had gotten.

"So why lie? Why not tell me what was going on at the start?"

"I was too proud. It was my own problem and I thought I could handle it. She, her craziness, made me crazy. And I hurt you and ultimately ended up hurting myself. Did you get my card? I mailed it right before I came up here."

Big deal. Mailed a card. *Oh boo-hoo, asshole*, I thought to myself. All the hurt and confusion I'd felt at the time welled up inside me and came out.

"What an ass you are. We had such a good thing going. And you had to fuck it up with your lies. I didn't think you would hurt me. It was my own damn fault. I let myself believe we had something special." I was near tears but would not give him the satisfaction of seeing me cry. He was not worth it. But a tiny part of me wanted to take him in my arms and feel that amazing connection. This man made me feel alive like no other. I felt powerful and sexy and at my best with him. And he threw that away.

"We did have something special. We can again. Pia, give me another chance. Please."

I'd waited a year to hear him explain. I'd waited a year hoping against hope that he would come crawling back to me. Last year, I imagined what it would feel like to hear from him. And then when he was dead on the pier, I managed to let it all go. The pain, the hurt, the questions. I missed what we had and I'd loved every second of our relationship. But it was gone, and I had Kevin and could not get trapped in Robert's web of deceit again.

"No, Robert. It is way too late for us."

"How can that be, Pia? If we're here together, it's meant to be."

"It was meant to be a year ago, Robert. A year ago we had possibilities. I did not ask for a commitment from you. All I asked is that we be honest with one another. I was, you were not. I will not be made to look like a fool. Not again."

It took all of my strength to walk away from the man I had given my heart to when I was a teenager. For over a decade I'd dreamt and fantasized about being with him. When we found each other, purely by accident—but is there any such thing as an accident?—we'd fallen hard and then crashed and burned.

He turned and left the room.

My phone chirped and I looked at the Merry Christmas emoji Kevin had texted. He was still at work, on Christmas Eve. I sent him a screen full of heart-eyes emojis and went into the en suite to get dressed for dinner. My father hinted at it being formal before I left New York, so I donned my black velvet sheath dress and put in silver hoops. My silver pendant looked perfect. I slipped on black booties and went downstairs.

Robert was in the great room drinking champagne with my parents. He was wearing a black suit jacket and a very white dress shirt. He looked beautiful. I tore my eyes away from him and looked at my mother. She looked absolutely radiant. She was wearing an ivory knit dress that fell to the floor. It had long sleeves and a boat neck. Her only pieces of jewelry were diamond hoops that reflected the tree lights and her ring.

"What's going on?" I asked.

My mother cleared her throat and said, absolutely beaming, "Pia, your father and I are getting married this evening."

"Now?" I asked, but wasn't really surprised. It had been a long time coming and they were meant to be together. I was truly happy for them.

"He surprised me by planning this and I am thrilled that you will be our witness and my maid of honour. My first and only wedding." She looked ready to cry.

I rushed over to her and enveloped her in a hug. "Mom, I am so happy for you. For you both." Tears threatened to fall as we looked at each other. Mother and daughter. We had been through so much together.

All those years of being alone, raising me, working full time, navigating my schools and homework and friends and camps and activities. Now she had someone. The only man she'd ever truly wanted.

This week had been full of surprises, for both me and my mother. Mine was not a happy one, but looking at her beaming face restored my faith in the power of love. *Do I love Kevin like she loves my father?* I asked myself this as Juris walked over to stand next to my mother, who stood next to the beautiful Christmas tree.

The tree was fully decorated and stood majestically in the large room. The fire was blazing and the lights of the tree seemed to twinkle. This bucolic scene would have made a perfect Rockwell Christmas painting. It was a vast departure from lights on a palm branch the previous year in Vieques.

Juris cleared his throat and said, "Robert, looks like we are ready. Please get us married."

Robert was marrying them? My world was spinning and I could barely stand. But I did. And I held my mother's hand and her small bouquet of roses that I knew were from her greenhouse, as she and my father recited vows they each had written.

When Robert declared them husband and wife, they kissed and then they both kissed me. Robert congratulated each of them and looked at me expectantly. I had no intention of kissing him. Ever again.

"Thank you," I said formally. "That was well done. Very nice. Succinct." I met his eye.

"Your mother told me five minutes tops." He laughed self-consciously and my mother agreed. "That's what I told him. We have waited twenty-eight years, I don't want to wait one more minute than necessary."

First Sam and Kash, and now my mother and father. They say things happen in threes. Was I next? Would I spend the rest of my life with Kevin if he asked me? I thought so. But that was unlikely. We had only been dating for a short time.

I sure as hell never thought I would see Robert again. I had pushed his memory to the far recesses of my mind, and now here he was, pressuring me and dredging up all the crap I went through because of him.

Robert snapped some photos of the three of us, me between my parents, which was still an awkward and strange sensation for me, and I took multiple shots of the newlyweds. I sent the best ones off to Sam and Nona. I debated sending one to Kevin and in the end fired off a picture of the three of us making crazy faces as Robert said, *Say queso!*

My mother asked me to call Nona. My grandmother would be very happy for them both. She'd told me more than once that she always thought they were perfect for each other.

"My pleasure, Mom. You both look so happy. I am so glad you did this." I snapped a picture of the bride and groom, sent it off to Sam, and called my grandmother in Vieques, Puerto Rico. Both she and Carlos were ecstatic until I said, "You're next, Nona. When's your big day?"

"Now, you hush about that. We are too old for that nonsense," she said, but I heard Carlos in the background say, "Not necessarily."

"Nona, I wanted to ask Carlos a question. Can you ask him to call me tomorrow?" I wanted to find out about the morning Carlos took me to the pier where the bodies from the plane crash were. Did he remember doing that? He couldn't possibly have a memory of that event, because it did not happen.

Once my father and his reverse ripples brought Robert and his ex-wife back from the very, very dead, I could not have gone to that pier and seen their bodies. So why could I remember it? Why had Sam and Kash kept that memory too? Oh, my aching head. I just wanted confirmation from Carlos that he—we—never went that morning after Sam's wedding.

"Is everything okay, Cassiopeia?" She sounded concerned.

"Oh yes, you know. Just a Bermuda Triangle question for him."

She laughed and sounded relieved. "Oh, he will be more than happy to call you. Prepare yourself for a long conversation. His article was published and he is writing a book now."

I handed the phone to my mother and poured myself another drink.

My parents chatted with my grandmother and Carlos for what seemed like hours, but was probably thirty minutes. I heard my parents promise to spend next Christmas on the island and was happy to hear that. I would join them and imagined bringing Kevin there with all of us.

I was feeling a little tipsy as they disconnected the call and announced the formal dinner was ready.

We ate a full Christmas goose dinner, toasted the happy couple some more, ate wedding cake—also known as New York–style cheesecake—and I couldn't remember ever having eaten more in my life. I was stuffed. We all were. Despite Robert's and my friction, the meal was a wonderful event, with laughter, tears, toasts, joy, and hope buzzing in the air. I fantasized about Kevin being my significant other and him getting to know my parents.

Hell, I was still getting to know them as a couple. They complemented each other, seemed overjoyed to be together, and were grateful for this, their second chance.

Juris stood and declared this to be the best Christmas ever. We clinked glasses and drank more than we should have, and although I was happy, I missed Kevin. As I looked across at Robert, I felt a pang for what could have been. Water under the bridge. Next year we would all be together in Vieques, going to the beach Christmas Eve and having a bonfire instead of watching logs blazing in the fireplace. Maybe I could convince Sam and Kash to join us. I glanced at my phone and saw the heart emoji Sam had sent in response to the photos. Nothing from Kevin, but I did not let that worry me. He was probably busy or asleep.

Chapter 44

Leaving Robert and Alaska Behind

All too soon, my time in Alaska came to an end. I was packed and wearing as many layers as I could comfortably manage as I boarded the Beaver with Robert. I knew he would insist on talking about us on the flight and I dreaded it. My parents stood off to the side, waving and blowing kisses my way.

I envied them their complete happiness. Their fairytale had worked out. Mine had not. Now I was going back to New York, my job, my life, my reality and my new man.

I watched Robert do the flight check. He was sombre to the point of being morose. He handed me my headset and I thanked him politely.

"You know, Pia, I took this job because of you."

"Really? Well, enjoy it. Frankly it's the last place I ever expected to see you."

"Juris told me you were coming here for the holidays. I had hoped we would spend time together."

He left the thought hanging.

"What did you expect? I would say it's okay you lied, stood me up, and then ghosted me? All is forgiven because we're here together?"

"Kinda, yeah. I know that's stupid of me, but I can't change the past. I promise you I will make our future better. Come back.

Spend a week with me. Give me a chance. We were so good together."

I thought about the fact that he could not change the past. Yet, I could change the past and I could have saved him. But I hadn't. And here he was, completely unaware that he had crashed his precious little plane and drowned. I wonder where his plane was.

I still felt a jolt of electricity being near him. All those years of longing for him, and to have it realized…I was naive to think that just because we were great together, my fairytale would have a happy ending. My feelings had been stepped on. My pent-up helplessness and rage, and yes, my bruised ego, all reared up and said *No, not again.*

"There is no future for us, Robert." I said it slowly and in a monotone.

"Don't you believe in second chances, Pia? What can I do to make you believe in me?"

He had no idea his entire life now was his second chance. How would he react if he knew the truth?

"Robert, I appreciate your apology and I hear what you're saying. I am not going to start up with you again. Trust is huge to me. I do not trust you. That's it."

And that was it. I knew in my head and my heart that it was over. I knew I would never get over that hurt. It would lurk between us until he was late, or didn't call, or couldn't be reached. I did not want to live with uncertainty. We were done.

My trip back to New York was even longer than the one to Alaska, if that was even possible. Weather delayed the flight out of Chicago, and when we got to New York we had to circle for forty-five minutes while ground crews cleared the runway. I texted Kevin that I had landed. I was tired, cold and anxious to get back to my comfortable, homey place. It took all of my energy to order the rideshare, and I sank gratefully into the warm interior.

The traffic was horrendous; the Midtown tunnel was closed due to a snowplough breakdown, and when the rideshare finally pulled up outside my apartment, I practically fell out of the back seat. I was jetlagged and shivering, and the four-hour time difference didn't help.

When Sam called to welcome me back and suggested dinner, I begged off. I called in sick to work for the first time in my career, but let my office know I would be on call on the weekend as usual. I turned off my phone, pulled the blankets up to my neck, sipped a warm cup of chamomile tea, and still couldn't shake the unwell feeling. I realized that I should do a rapid test, but opted instead to sleep.

A pounding on the door woke me, and looking at the clock, I saw that it was noon the next day. I had been asleep for over sixteen hours.

I grabbed my robe and staggered to the door, opened it, and Kevin rushed in.

He put his arms around me, "Pia, thank god. I have been calling since last night. I just came from your office and you weren't there. Jesus, I thought something had happened to you! I was ready to break down this door." Kevin was breathless. He reached for me and pulled me into his embrace.

I closed the door behind him, still groggy. "Didn't you get my text last night?" He let me go but kept his hands on my shoulders.

"No, I didn't get your text but I knew your flight had landed. You're shaking. Are you all right?"

"I'm shaking because you're freezing. Yes, I'm okay. I'm just jetlagged." I led him into the bedroom and climbed back into bed. He sat on the edge, still wearing his winter jacket and heavy boots. His leather holster was visible over his left rib cage when his jacket gaped open. I found that very sexy, even though I was not a gun person. He looked good. To be honest, he always looked good. He was wearing a gray cashmere pullover that matched his eyes. His leather jacket was butter-soft kid leather and molded to his shoulders.

He made eye contact with me and slowly took off his jacket, holster, and clothes and climbed into bed beside me. "Can I warm you up?"

Welcome back to New York, I thought to myself, and lost myself in the strong arms of my man.

Chapter 45

New Year's News

We spent New Year's watching the ball drop from the comfy L-shaped sectional in Kevin's tenth-floor apartment. We could just see the lights of Times Square through his living room windows. He had stocked champagne and ordered in mini egg rolls and dumplings as well as an assortment of ice creams for no other reason than that we both liked salted-caramel-cone flavour and all plain vanilla with any crunchy chocolate bits. We were being wickedly decadent as we said goodbye to the old year and welcomed a brand new year in. Our year. The year we would spend getting to know one another even more. A year full of hope and promise.

When I returned from Alaska, I described in detail my parents' wedding ceremony, leaving out the part about Robert being in attendance. Kevin looked at me with those amazing crystal eyes and asked if marriage was important to me. That threw me, because I had never really thought about it. I answered honestly that I was not religious, but to spend the rest of my life with someone, I would like the piece of paper. He smiled and hugged me and then the moment was over.

Kash and Sam were due to stop in before midnight after spending the day with Trez and Juan, and all felt right in my world. I hadn't completely recovered from my exhausting trip and my unwell feeling, but I was content and maybe a little bit drunk.

I had already texted *Happy New Year!* to my grandmother and Carlos, as it was an hour later in Puerto Rico, already midnight, and I was expecting my parents to text or call at any moment. They had no plans for New Year's other than to sit by the fire and toast their own newlywed happiness.

Kash and Sam arrived with more champagne, and we sat around on the sectional playing cards until 11:59 p.m. Kash put the cards away and got another bottle of prosecco out of the mini fridge in the living room, also known as the man cave, by me.

"This is it. Say goodbye to this year," Kash said, sounding more than a little bit drunk. Sam and Kevin lifted their glasses. We all clinked and I set mine down and made a dash for the bathroom saying, "I'll be back before the ball drops!"

A wave of nausea had hit me. In fact, I realized I had felt unwell since Christmas, but refused to give in to the feeling. I was functioning on autopilot, but there was definitely something off. My hands were tingling and I could discern a faint blue glow between them. It was probably only visible to me, but it was there. It signified death, and I didn't want to deal with that on this last day of the year. My parents were married, my best friends were happy in their marriage, and I was dating a wonderful man. I had hopes and aspirations for the next year and none of them involved someone I knew dying. What was going on with me?

"Pia, come on," I heard Sam call from the living room. I splashed water on my face, dried it, and squared my shoulders to face them. They all turned and looked at me, expressing concern that I looked so pale, but I pretended that everything was fine, I was still coping with jet lag. Sam didn't look convinced, but she smiled and patted the sofa between her and Kevin. Kevin stood to let me squeeze in next to Sam and he sat down next to me.

I nestled into Kevin's body, and although he felt warm, I felt a chill run through me so strong I thought my insides would freeze. As if he sensed my thoughts, he pulled me in closer and wrapped his arms around me. Normally that would feel too stifling, but right now it felt good.

The ball dropped, the confetti flew all over hundreds of thousands of people in Times Square, we all kissed and drank more champagne, and then Kash and Sam left to rideshare back to their place.

My mother still hadn't called or texted, and it was bothering me.

Kevin saw me looking at my phone and said, "Call her. You won't relax until you do." He was very aware of my closeness to my mother; however, since learning about his parents' deaths, I'd tried to minimize how much time I spent on the phone with her in his presence.

"I'll get the dishes. Call her, Pia." He started to scoop up plates and glasses and bring them into the kitchen. I sank down in an armchair and dialled Alaska. My mother's phone went right to voicemail. I tried my father's. Same thing. *Weird*, I thought. *Maybe they both have them turned off.*

Kevin was drying his hands as he walked towards me. "Success?"

"No, both of their phones went straight to voicemail," I said, and as I put my phone down on the side table, I could see the bluish glow from my fingers. *Oh please, no, please don't let anything happen tonight.* Saying that to myself made the certainty that something terrible had happened take root inside me. It was building and I was starting to panic.

Kevin pulled me up and said, "It's been a long day. Come on, let's go to bed."

As much as I loved being with him, I didn't feel like being here in his apartment and made the excuse that I should get home.

"Why? Are you that worried?" He looked into my eyes and could see that clearly I was. "Try them again." So I did, with the same result.

"You have to know my mother," I explained. "She is never forgetful. She is organized to a fault. She would not forget to wish me Happy New Year. Something is wrong."

My head was pounding and I was sweating. I could taste vomit at the back of my throat. I wanted to run screaming from the apartment just to be doing something. My parents were over four thousand miles away; what could I do?

"Is there a main number for the lodge?" Kevin, so levelheaded, asked.

"Yes, yes there is." *Yes, that makes sense,* I thought. "I have it in my wallet. Let me get it." I felt brief relief at the action of actually doing something. I pulled out the card, and with shaky fingers called the number. It seemed to ring for a year, then the answering machine clicked on. I left a message and hung up. "No answer."

"Let me make a call." He said. He held his hand out for the card I was holding with the address of the lodge and the landline.

He spoke into his phone, nodded, hung up, and then dialled another number. He spoke briefly and then turned to me.

"Okay, I got the number of the closest detachment up there. I called and gave them your parents' address and info. It's not close, but they will do a wellness check, just in case. Professional courtesy."

"Thank you." I threw myself against him.

"It could be a while, it's over fifty miles away, but they'll send a helicopter out there. Go and lie down and I will let you know if I hear anything."

"No, I can't lie down not knowing anything." I could feel adrenaline revving me up and I was now fully sober. "I'll just wait here until either my parents call or you hear back."

I lay down on the sectional. Kevin turned off the TV and sat beside me.

We dozed, and when we woke two hours later, neither of us had gotten a call. I tried both the cells and landline again. Still no answer.

Kevin was dialling the number he had called before when his phone rang. The sound was loud and jarring and he dropped the phone. He scrambled to pick it up and answer.

He listened for a long time, briefly interjecting with an *I see,* or a *yes,* or *no.*

I craned to hear what was being said and did not like the look on Kevin's face as he listened.

"Yes. Yes, I see, thank you, I will. Yes, thank you so much. I appreciate it."

He hung up and turned to face me. He said nothing but I could see emotions rolling over his face. Fear, sadness, despair.

"What is it? What did they say? Is everything all right?" As I asked, I knew damn well everything was not all right. His face spoke volumes.

"Pia, there's been an accident."

"No!" I shot up off the sofa. "No, no, no." I started sobbing. He took my hand and sat me back down. "Your father fell through the ice, Pia. He drowned. Your mother was there, and she tried to get him out, but she couldn't. She was taken to the hospital with hypothermia."

"Is she…" I couldn't finish.

"No, she's going to be okay."

"No, she is never going to be okay again." I sobbed until there were no tears left. I drank a bottle of water and we both went into the bedroom and lay down on the covers, fully clothed. I wanted to run through the streets screaming, but it was the middle of the night and anything I needed to do, I would do in the morning.

I slept in Kevin's arms until the sun shone through the blinds welcoming in a bright sunny first day of January. My dreams were of my biological father lying dead on my table in the morgue. How amazing it had been in the dream to feel the power of the reverse ripples and we became a family. Deep inside me I knew that there were no second times. I did not have the power to save him again and I felt my heart break.

Chapter 46

Back to the Top of the World

I composed a text to Sam and Kash, then Kevin and I went back to my place across town. Kevin waited with me until Sam arrived, and then he went downtown to his precinct to make some calls and arrange some time off.

Sam arrived armed with bagels and the works, made coffee, and brought it all on a tray into the bedroom.

"Oh my god, Pia. I can't believe it. I just can't. Poor Helena." She sat down and handed me a cup. I took it robotically and drank the hot brew.

I was dazed. I was in denial and still had not spoken to my mother. I could think of nothing to say. This tragedy was beyond anything I could have imagined. I wanted to wake up and be told it was a nightmare. That didn't happen.

We moved into the living room and I tried my mother's cell.

"Hello," a shaky voice answered.

"Mom?" I practically screamed.

"Yes, Pia. It's me. Oh my god, Pia, your father, your father." She started sobbing and so did I.

Sam took the phone. "Helena, it's Sam here. What do you need? Do you want us to come up there?" I marvelled at how levelheaded she sounded.

"Oh Sam, I don't know. I don't know what to do." Sam looked shaken, not used to my no-nonsense mother being so rattled.

"Helena, Pia and I are on our way. Call if you need anything, but we will see you as soon as possible." She hung up.

"We will?" I asked her.

"Yes, of course we will. Now get your shit together. I'll call your office and Kash to let them know."

"Okay, I'll let Kevin know." I sent a text off to Kevin and just stood leaning against the doorway of the living room. I felt unwell. And scared, and mostly I felt grief that I couldn't save him.

Sam was busy on her phone and looked up at me. "What is it, Pia?"

"I have no idea what to do." I started sobbing all over again and she took me in her arms.

Sam gathered all of my clothing from my trip to Alaska a few days ago, bundled me into my parka, and ordered a rideshare to take us to her place. She watered the plants, grabbed my charger and passport, turned off the lights, and locked the apartment.

"Let's go." She led me down the front steps to the waiting car. She handed the bag to the driver and said to me, "We are booked out of Newark in ninety minutes."

Once we were airborne the reality hit me. My father was gone and my mother was alone. Sam handed me a pill and a bottle of water. "Take this, you will feel better."

"What is it?" I dutifully popped the small yellow pill and gulped a mouthful of water.

"A mild anti-anxiety med. So you can relax. You've had a terrible shock."

"Sam, how can you do this? Don't you have patients?" I was concerned we had overlooked something.

"Jessie will clear my calendar for the week. Family emergency. Everyone will understand."

Family emergency. It was a family emergency, for sure.

"Rest, Pia. I will wake you when we are close to Chicago."

I closed my eyes and opened them to the wheels hitting the ground. As the plane slowed, the tragic events came flooding back and I felt my lungs tighten. How could this have happened?

I sleepwalked through the terminal to the next gate, and as we took off I felt Sam reach for my hand. Her fear of takeoffs and landings was something I had always made fun of. Now she was the strong one and I was barely conscious. I squeezed her hand to let her know I was doing all right, and also to let her know that she was doing amazing. I have never had a better friend than Sam.

"Wow, talk about exhausting." Sam sat beside me in Alaska, waiting for our puddle jumper. "I thought you were exaggerating when you described getting here. It's amazing we haven't had any delays."

"No exaggeration needed. Getting here is a drag. Twice in one week is too much." As soon as I said it, I remembered that this was not a pleasure trip. This was me racing to be with my widowed mother. She had been married less than a week. It was beyond comprehension.

"Your poor mother. Waiting and hoping for all of those years to reunite with your father and now this."

"I still can't believe it. My father can swim and is fit and careful. What was he doing on the ice? And how could he have drowned? The ice was well over a foot thick. I saw it. I was on that ice too. It doesn't make sense."

I got up and started pacing the small waiting area.

"We'll find out what happened. Right now Helena must be a complete basket case. The police said she was there when it happened?"

"That's what they told Kevin. The info was sketchy to say the least. I just thought of something."

"What?" Sam asked.

I stopped in front of her and said, "Robert will be our pilot."

"Ah, yes, Captain Robert in the flesh." She said it with a smirk. "I feel like giving him a piece of my mind." Sam sounded furious.

"No, don't. That just gives it too much weight. It is over and will stay over."

I looked at the snowflakes falling outside the terminal window. There was nothing to see but the runway straight ahead. I craned my neck to look towards the left and could see a large open hangar. There was a plane just inside the door that looked like Robert's Beaver plane. I told myself that this type of plane, outfitted with pontoons, was probably common up here in the North. It most likely wasn't Robert's. I scanned the skies and saw nothing, so I sat down next to Sam and closed my eyes.

We waited for what seemed like forever, and finally, after four or five attempts to call the lodge to see where he was, and checking with the attendant, who told us private flights were not arranged through the airport, we concluded he would not be picking us up.

In my haze, I remembered that my father was the one who set Robert's schedule, based on clients coming to the lodge. Either there were no clients, or he was off elsewhere, and now we had to find another way to the lodge.

I called Kevin and luckily he answered. I explained what had happened and that we had no way to get to the lodge. He very rationally reminded me that my mother had been airlifted to the hospital and we should head there, not the camp.

"I am so glad you called him," Sam said. "Imagine if we had arrived at your father's place and then realized your mother was here." It was funny, but not laugh-out-loud funny. Neither one of us was thinking clearly, and the long day of travel had us feeling punchy. There was a taxi line of three cars outside the small terminal. We rolled our bags over to the first one, a Chevy Malibu.

I remembered my childhood friend Richie from Vieques getting a used Malibu as his first car when he turned sixteen. He was so proud to drive me around the island in that car he nicknamed the Purple Pig, because we had painted it purple using spray paint he lifted from his father's art studio. That car was my taste of summer freedom. He taught me to drive, and although I had no license, I drove almost every day. My grandmother no longer had to ferry me up to the North Shore surfing beach, or to a bonfire at Playa Caracas. Heady times on a tropical island for this New York City girl.

We buckled up in the ancient car and I leaned back to rest my eyes.

Sam whispered, "Pia, can I ask you something?"

I nodded without opening my eyes.

"Are you going to…" She hesitated and I opened my eyes to look at her. "Are you going to see, to touch your father?"

I looked into my best friend's eyes and tried to explain that I knew I could not. And then we cried together.

Chapter 47

Helena

Helena looked so tiny in the hospital bed. Her dark hair was loose on the pillow and she had dark circles that almost appeared to be bruises under both eyes.

I rushed to her bedside. "Mom!" I gripped her pale hand in both of mine and squeezed gently.

She opened her eyes and saw both me and Sam leaning down over the bed.

She broke into tears, unable to stop the flood as Sam went around to the other side of the bed and took her other hand.

When the tears abated, she accepted a tissue from Sam and indicated for me to put the head of the bed up. I found the remote clipped to the bed rail and did as she asked. She looked more in control of her emotions when she sat up. She looked from me to Sam and back to me.

"Oh girls, thank you for coming. This has been my worst nightmare." She started sobbing again.

"Helena, what happened?" Sam used a soothing voice, the kind she reserved for coaxing patients. I had laughed out loud the first time I heard her drop her voice an octave and slow her speech, but I had to admit, her voice was very soothing, and my mother seemed to respond.

"It was a freak accident. He shouldn't even have been out there, but we saw a light and Juris, well, you know your father, he went to investigate."

She looked at me to acknowledge, but in reality, I didn't know my father. Our times together in the last year had been very limited and at most I had secondhand knowledge of how he did things from my mother's observations.

She continued, "He went out to investigate and when he didn't return, I went out to see what was going on."

Sam asked, "What was going on? It was New Year's Eve, right?"

My mother appeared exhausted. She had closed her eyes, and I felt her hand relax in my grip.

"I think she's asleep," I said to Sam, stating the obvious.

"Jesus, Pia. Now it's more of a mystery than before. He saw a light? And then he fell through the ice? You told me the ice was a foot thick. How could he fall through that?"

She wasn't asking me, just stating the questions we both wanted answered. We sat with my mother until it was obvious she was out for the night. The nurse confirmed it and agreed to pass on my phone number to the attending doctor.

We made our way to the front desk to ask about a hotel.

The only motel open in town was a short distance from the hospital, and we decided to walk it, dragging our rolling bags behind us. The crunch of our boots on the hard-packed snow was the only sound we heard in the small town. The streetlights cast long shadows, and no cars passed on the ten-minute walk.

We checked into a tiny but cozy hunting-themed room with two twin beds, a small desk, a mini fridge, and an oversized television mounted to the wall opposite the beds.

"Wow, Kash would love this television," Sam said, and then instantly clamped her hand over her mouth. "Oh Pia, I am so sorry, talking about a TV at a time like this." She walked over to me and put her hands on my upper arms. "What do you want to do? Eat? Sleep? Drink?"

I slept like the dead was the first thought that entered my mind when I woke and had to rub crusty sleep out of my eyes. The room was dim and quiet, and all I could hear was my own breathing. I looked over at the other bed; it was made and empty. *Where is Sam?*

Just then the door opened and a cold wind blew into the room, howling and whipping Sam's hair around her face.

"Jesus H. Christ, it is so frickin' cold." She said this laughing as she came in carrying a paper bag and a tray with two disposable cups. She handed me one. "You sure slept. I asked you if you wanted anything, and there was no answer. This is strong coffee and I have breakfast for each of us."

I gratefully sipped at the coffee, cooled enough for me to take a big sip. "Thanks, Sam. I needed this." I removed the lidded container for breakfast and was pleased to see a bacon, egg, and cheese sandwich on a kaiser roll. It smelled delicious and tasted even better. "I can't believe you found us breakfast up here." I meant in the far North.

"It is Alaska, part of the United States. But yes, I was lucky. The motel owner made it in her own kitchen."

"Really?"

"Yes, there's no restaurant within walking distance, so she took pity on us."

Sam opened her container and took out her toasted roll. As a vegan, her food choices would be severely limited on this trip. She looked content to be eating the roll with red berry jam.

I devoured my sandwich in five bites. It was as good as at Oskar's deli. The food buoyed my body and mind. As I sipped my coffee I said, "I still cannot believe this freak accident. To die by drowning, it seems so wrong."

"I know what you mean; it doesn't seem possible. Everything up here is frozen. Including me." She got under the covers of the once-tidy bed and sipped her tea.

"What are you drinking?" I asked as I finished my coffee and placed the empty cup on the nightstand between the two small beds.

"I brought tea bags with me. This one is chamomile."

Of course she did, I mused. *Sam is always prepared.*

"I guess we should head back to the hospital," I said, dreading it.

"Of course," Sam replied. "I just want to take a hot shower and then I will get us a cab."

"Yeah, I need to shower off yesterday," I said, with no conviction. I felt drained and empty and like I might start crying at any second.

Sam looked at me, got out of bed, and sat next to me. "You don't have to be strong. This is a horrible situation and there is no right way to feel. Cry, scream, vent, or if all else fails, drink. Just kidding, but you know what I mean." She leaned in close to me, my best friend, my rock.

"I want to make this all go away, but I don't feel any premonitions, or tingling, or the headache that precedes an episode. Right now I feel only emptiness."

"Pia, follow your heart. You can't make the magic happen just by wishing for it. You said it yourself, you don't know when you can do it. And if you don't have the tingle or whatever you call it, you just don't have it."

"It will sound weird when I say this, but I feel like I knew this was coming. I knew something was going to happen to him. Ever since he first came back into our lives, I've felt as though I was waiting for the axe to fall. So to speak."

Sam was quiet for a minute and then said, "Your priority now is your mother. She is shocked and devastated, but she has you and you will be there for her."

"Yes, my mom. What is she going to do now? Stay here alone or come back to New York and…do what? Live with me?" I put my head in my hands. "I can't handle that. I love her, but I don't want to live with her."

"Pia, you are getting way ahead of yourself. She isn't going to make decisions like that right away. She needs time to figure things out."

Sam got up and paced, the way I usually do.

"Do you even know my mother?" I got up as well and dropped my food container into the trash can. "She is the most organized person I know. She has a plan for everything and is always two steps ahead of everyone else. She is already planning, trust me on this." I went over to my suitcase and carried it to my twin bed.

"I am going to shower and then call Kash." Sam went into the small bathroom and I could hear the water running.

"Yay, it's hot!" She yelled over the din.

"Save me some!" I yelled back and thought I heard her laughing.

Chapter 48

An Empty Hospital

The hospital was eerily quiet as we made our way down the hall, past the nurses' station to my mother's room. We whispered to each other almost as if we were in a library.

"Where is everybody?" Sam looked around at the emptiness.

"It's like a Stephen King novel. Everyone has disappeared and we're the only two people left alive." I was joking, but at the same time, it was strange. I had been working in busy New York City hospitals for years.

We arrived at her room, number 107 on the quiet, empty corridor.

My mother's door was ajar and she was sitting up in bed. A man in uniform sat in the only chair next to her bed and was taking notes. My mother's voice was hushed as if she, too, felt the need to whisper in this place.

"Hi, Mom," I said brightly.

"Oh Pia, I wasn't sure you were really here. I thought I dreamt it. Sam, you are here too." She patted the bed and made the introductions.

Sergeant Murphy extended his hand and offered me his condolences. He turned to Sam and did the same. Then he said to her, "We have the same name." She looked puzzled and he continued, "My first name is Sam."

"Oh, right," Sam responded and shook his hand.

He spoke briefly to my mother and then turned to me. "If there is anything you need, here's my card."

He bade us goodbye and left. Sam and I sat down, me on the end of the bed and Sam in the visitor's chair the cop had occupied.

"How are you feeling, Helena?" Sam picked up a pitcher on the table and poured some water into a plastic cup. She offered it to my mother, who nodded and took a long sip.

"I am reeling. Physically there is nothing wrong with me now. The doctor told me I can leave today. But where will I go? Back to the camp without Juris?" She started to cry.

I looked over at Sam, who signalled for me to just let her cry. To let her get it all out. So I sat and waited. I looked around the room. I realized I had seldom ever seen my mother cry. I could feel my phone vibrating in my pocket and got up to answer in the hall.

"Hello?" I said to my detective.

"How are things there?" Right to the point.

"I'm at the hospital now with my mother. She can be released. I guess we'll head to the lodge." I leaned against the wall, feeling my energy sapping away. I wished he was by my side, for his strength and calmness.

"How are you?" Care in his voice that made tears well up in my eyes.

"I'm fine. Tired, but okay. It's surreal. I was just with them a week ago. I can't believe this is happening." I gave in to the urge to sink to the floor. I sat with my back up against the wall. From my vantage point, I could see that the nurses' station was still unoccupied.

"Hang in there. Your mother needs you now. Where is Sam?"

"She's with my mother too. She has been my rock. Honestly, I don't know what I would have done without her."

"You would have done what you needed to do, but nothing beats a best friend." I knew he had a partner, and his partner had been his best friend for years. They were a dynamic duo.

"Yeah, well, the big question is what do we do now? Do we go back to the camp or head back to New York? Mom isn't making any decisions, and when I brought it up, she just cried." I felt so exhausted, holding the phone was making my arm ache.

"Give her time, Pia. You just got there. She has some tough decisions to make."

He sounded so sensible, much like Sam.

"You're right. I need to just be here for her. Sam and I will do whatever she wants. It is all so sudden and shocking."

"Imagine how she feels. Married one week." He said he would check in with me later and we said our goodbyes.

My mom was a bride and now a widow within a week.

Chapter 49

Juris's Lodge

The police pilot ferried us back to my father's camp the next day. He was the same one who brought my mother to the hospital and my father's body to the morgue. Sergeant Murphy had arranged the transport and asked if I wanted to see my father. I declined. Sam raised her eyebrows at this, but said nothing.

To say she was impressed with the camp is an understatement. She tried her best to keep her tone neutral, but I could hear excitement in her voice and knew she would be calling Kash with all the details.

I ushered Mom into the great room and set about making a fire. I had watched my father at Christmas and knew the basics. I managed to get it going after a few false starts.

"What can I get you, Mom?" She was sitting on the sofa, frozen like a statue. Not moving. Not speaking. Her eyes were glazed and her posture defeated. This was not the strong, take-charge woman I was used to.

"This can't be happening. It can't be. We were planning our lives together. He can't be gone."

She looked at me and our eyes met. She saw the truth in my eyes and began to cry.

I didn't know what to do to make this better. It would never be better. Sam went over to the bar and took the stopper out of one of the bottles. She poured two fingers of amber liquid into a glass, added some water, and handed it to my mother. My mother took it and drank it.

The fire crackled, we were silent and time stretched as the sun disappeared. I turned on the lights in the room and hallway and went into the kitchen to see if the fridge was as stocked as it had been the previous week.

I turned on the electric kettle and called Kevin to thank him for his help. I was pretty certain he had pulled some strings to arrange the pilot, since he was in touch with the local precinct.

I made tomato-and-watercress sandwiches and heated some vegetable soup. We ate in the living room, slurping, chewing, and swallowing, but not tasting the food. We were all silent, lost in the profound sadness that had brought us together. I kept asking myself if I'd made the right decision to not see my father. It seemed like lately all I did was second guess myself. I chose not to save Robert in Vieques; however, thirteen months ago I had reversed time and saved my father from death. If he had died, we would never have known him. My mother would have gone the rest of her life pining for a man, a John Doe in my morgue, who had died on the way to reunite with her. Was that what the fates had had in store until I intervened? Had I messed with destiny?

And now, in the comedy of the universe, I was involved with a man who knew something was going on with me, something to do with the incidents we'd both witnessed, but despite his curiosity had managed to set that inquiry aside to be with me. Or had he? Was he just biding his time?

And now I refused the police offer to view Juris's body, afraid to intervene and afraid to not intervene. I didn't have the feeling that I would be able to save him this time. Was this fate? How could he drown on his own property? He was a cautious man who knew the risks of being on the ice. The ice was a foot thick, for fuck's sake. None of this made sense. I had to ask Kevin to look into it. Had he been pushed?

My head was starting to pound, and my body was screaming for caffeine. "I'm having coffee, anyone else?" I had made Mom a cup of tea earlier; it sat untouched on the coffee table. "Mom, can I make you a fresh cup of tea or coffee? A hot toddy?"

"I'll do it," said Sam, and she scooped up the plates and went into the kitchen.

"Pia, I don't want to stay here alone," my mother said robotically, and I thought she meant she wanted me to stay with her. I couldn't do that. I had a job and a life in New York City. And I had Kevin. She can't seriously expect me to stay in Alaska.

"I understand that, Mom, but there is no need to make rash decisions." She seemed to be coming out of her trance. She sat up straighter on the big sofa.

"I don't mean here. I'm going to Vieques to stay with my mother for now, until I figure out what to do."

"Mom, that's perfect." It was the best solution, and I was glad she didn't want to stay with me in New York. I knew it was a selfish reaction, but I was being honest with myself. My mother would always be a priority and a very important person in my life, but right now, with my hectic job and my relationship with Kevin just beginning, I didn't think moving back in with me in her apartment was the best idea. My grandmother was the perfect person to be with at a time like this. Not only was she familiar with loss, she was a perfect sounding board if my mother wanted to rant or vent or cry. Nona would take care of her only child.

"Let's figure it out in the morning. It's been a long day," I said, and reached for her hand. It was ice cold. "You are freezing. Drink some tea and then maybe a hot bath."

Sam returned with a tray and three cups. She handed tea to Mom and coffee to me. The aroma perked me right up and I drank it gratefully.

"Thank you, Sam. For everything." I was grateful beyond words for Sam stepping in and taking control.

"De nada," she replied smugly, and when I looked at her, she winked. "Kash is rubbing off on me." Double entendre intended. "Drink the tea, Helena," Sam said in her doctor voice and my mother complied.

The fire was ebbing and we were all drowsy despite the dose of caffeine. The day had been too long, too sad, and with no end in sight to the pain, we were all drained.

I turned off the outside porch lights and saw that snow was falling in blankets. It was eerie looking in the amber glow of the sodium lamps that illuminated the front parking area. I watched, mesmerized by the snow falling, until Sam said quietly, "Let's get your Mom settled. I was going to give her one of the sedatives she came from the hospital with, but she seems so tired she probably doesn't need one."

We both escorted my mother to her room and settled her into the king-sized bed. She looked so small and almost childlike as she lay down fully clothed. She was an extraordinarily beautiful woman, made even more so by the paleness of her face as her dark hair spread out on the white pillowcase. We covered her, and pulled down the window shades.

She reached her arm over to where my father had slept, curled on her side, and closed her eyes. I wasn't certain, but it sounded like she was crying softly when we exited the room.

"Goodnight, Mom. I love you," I whispered as I retreated.

"Goodnight, Helena. Call out if you need anything. We are right down the hall." Sam left her door ajar.

Once we were out in the hallway, Sam asked, "My god, Pia. What is she going to do here alone in this place?"

"She wants to go to Vieques. To her mother's."

Sam sounded relieved. "That is perfect. Vieques will heal her. Nona is the best person right now for her, and it is such a magical place."

I felt the weight of the world and the weight of death on me. First Robert and now my father. What was happening? I dealt with death every day at work. Now my life and job were melding into a looping movie of death and what ifs. The what ifs were driving me crazy.

Sam and I made our way to the corridor of guest rooms, and as we opened two random side-by-side doors to rooms, Sam said, "I know you sent pictures of this place, but they don't do it justice. This is freaking amazing."

"You haven't even seen the best part." I meant the greenhouse. Sam would lose her mind.

"Tour me in the morning, but I don't want Helena to think I am being nosy," Sam replied.

"No, she wouldn't think that. She is proud of her marks on this place. It was to be her forever home, before…" I paused, gulped. "Before this."

Sam hugged me, and said, "We will get through this. We are family."

I started to sob. "Yeah, but now what will happen to it?" We stood in our respective doorways, both lost in thought, tears on both of our faces.

"Does your father have any other family? Brothers or sisters?" She rubbed the tears away with her hand and then rolled her bag inside the door and reached for a light switch.

"I have no idea. I will have to ask Mom. He must have some family somewhere. Come to think of it, I don't even know where he is originally from. I hope there is someone out there who would like to run this place." I let my tears stay on my face. It felt good to let out some emotion. I was crying for my mother, for my father, for their lost future together, and for myself that I was not the hero this time.

I pushed my bag into my room with my foot and reached in to flick the light on, then stood still, looking at the beautiful room in this enormous lodge. I tried to picture it closed up and knew it would fall into disrepair in a short time. Harsh weather conditions existed much of the year. The need for full-time maintenance was daunting. *Who is going to look after all of this? Surely not my mother.*

Sam pulled her phone out of her pocket and said, "I am going to update Kash. Goodnight, Pia." She hugged me. "Try to get some sleep. See you in the morning."

I went over to the bed and sat down. I pulled the throw over my legs and got my phone out. I sent a text off to Kevin asking him to call. If anyone could find out if my father had a family, it was Kevin.

Chapter 50

Where is Robert?

Freezing rain or hail woke me as it pounded the windows of the room. It was cold and I could almost see my breath. I realized I should have checked the furnace before going to bed. So much for me taking care of things. I had no idea on how to look after a house. I had lived in an apartment all of my life. The super took care of the heat and any other problems that arose.

This house was well insulated, but there was a definite drop in the temperature inside. I dressed quickly in multiple layers and went downstairs to light a fire. From there I would find the furnace controls and then go check on my mother.

I made the fire and waited as it caught. I felt proud that this city girl was doing all right in the fire-making department, but although it crackled and blazed, it would not heat the house, so I went into my father's office to see if the furnace thermostat was there. It was, on the far wall next to the temperature controls for individual rooms and a floor map like in hotels showing the fire route out. I pushed buttons for the bank of rooms Sam and I were occupying, and then the master suite. I cranked the temp up to a balmy 74 degrees from the 59 degrees the system was showing and went to my mother's room, proud that I could at least keep us from freezing.

I knocked softly on her door, not wanting to wake her, and was surprised she answered right away.

"Come in, Pia." She was sitting at the corner desk looking at her laptop, fully dressed in fresh clothes, not the ones she had been wearing when she went to bed.

"How are you feeling, Mom?" I sat on the corner of the already made bed, closest to her. I could see that she looked almost like her old self. Put together and in charge.

"Well, I am still in shock, to say the least, but there are decisions to be made." She closed the laptop and turned to face me, sounding more like the mother I know. "Have you seen or heard from Robert?" she asked.

"What?" I asked her.

"Robert, the pilot. Your Robert. Have you seen him?"

I was so surprised she was even thinking about him. "No, I haven't seen him. When did you last see him?" She didn't answer. "Mom, what's going on?"

"Your father and he had a big blowout argument after you left. Robert stormed out and your father was worried about him. That's why he went out that night. He thought Robert was on the ice. Then he fell through while I stood in the doorway watching." She put her head in her hands.

"Oh no! Mom, that's awful." I went over to her and knelt beside her chair. I put my head on her lap like I had when I was a child and she was working on her editorials. She absently stroked my hair. It was comforting, but I should have been the one comforting her.

"Do you think Robert did something to Juris?" I asked cautiously as I sat back on the floor.

"God no, Pia! Honestly, your imagination really runs away with you. I simply meant that Robert was talking about going back to Puerto Rico, and your father reminded him of the contract he signed and the fact that guests were arriving next week. They argued about it, loudly with some door slamming, but nothing else. They were both distraught." She started to get up and then sat down heavily. "Oh god, we have guests arriving in a few days' time."

She sat with that sentence heavy in the air.

We heard a knock and both turned to look at the door. I half expected Robert, but of course it was Sam.

"Good morning, ladies. Helena, you look rested." She walked over to the desk and embraced my mother. Sam put her hands on my mother's shoulders and said, "Kash sends his love to you."

At that my mother's façade crumbled and she began to cry. Sam held her tight and when the tears subsided, my mother said, "Let's get some breakfast. You need to eat heartily up here to keep the cold away. And speaking of cold, it seems like you found the thermostats." She smiled at me and I nodded.

She pointed to the control on the wall by the door of the room. "The rooms each have their own setting."

They did? Of course they did. Now I remembered Juris telling me that guests could set their room temperature separately from the rest of the lodge.

"Well duh," I said, and they both laughed.

"It's all good," my mother said and stood up. Sam and I both got up off the floor, and we headed to the kitchen to rustle up some breakfast. My mother suggested I give Sam a tour while she made coffee. Sam readily agreed.

Chapter 51

What Will We Do Now?

"Where is Robert's plane?" I asked my mother as we ate in the kitchen. The two walls of windows barely let in light with snow coating them and still falling. I stared out at the whiteness in this surreal landscape. Sam was looking out also.

She said, "It is so beautiful. The only snow I have ever seen is the few snowstorms New York has had. There the snow is nice when it first falls, but soon turns dirty and disgusting when plows clear the streets. This is so clean and so white."

"Oh, that's right, you grew up in California." My mother had barely touched her breakfast despite telling us repeatedly to eat. She pushed her fruit around and hadn't touched her toast.

"Yes, and we had snow only once in the eighteen years I lived there. That was crazy. At first we actually thought a volcano had erupted and it was ash falling, but it melted on our skin and we realized it was snow." She was lost in the memory.

"Mom grew up in Puerto Rico. I never thought she would live in Alaska."

"Me neither." She laughed, but the sound was hollow, sad. "And now, well, I can't stay here alone."

"We will figure it out," I said, but I didn't sound convincing. What could we do with the place? What would Juris want? And where was Robert?

"Did Robert leave?"

She stood up and went to the window. She looked over to the right and said, "His plane is gone. He keeps it tethered over there by the maintenance shed, out of the wind."

"I think I saw it in a hangar at the airport." I was now certain that it was his Beaver plane I had seen.

"I don't have Robert's number, and Juris's cell is gone. Your father has a standby pilot and if need be, he could fly up and get us. And he will need to be scheduled for the guest pickup." My mother picked up a piece of toast and took a bite.

I was glad to see her eat something.

"Not in this weather," Sam said, still gazing out at the whiteness.

"No, not today, but planes can still fly in snow." I remembered my first flight up here and the extreme cold. Even the inside of the plane was cold and never really warmed up during the flight.

"Are you girls okay if I go upstairs and call Nona?"

"Of course, Mom. We are fine."

She refilled her coffee cup and left the room.

I turned to Sam and said quietly, "I asked Kevin to look into Juris to see if he has any other family. Maybe he has been in touch with them all along. Someone might want to come and help out here until we decide, or rather Mom decides, what to do with the place." I finished my third cup of coffee and could feel my nerves jangling.

"Good idea. Do you think your father has a will?"

"I have no idea. I will have to ask Mom that also. I know there is a full staff with a caretaker. Max, I think his name was. I met him and he seems great. He should be able to handle things until we sort out what will happen with the place. He took care of everything while Juris was in Vieques and New York. The staff is all off now until the seventh, when guests are due to arrive."

Sam seemed lost in deep thought. "There are so many loose ends here. Where is Robert? Who can take over? What is your mother going to do with your dad's body? We are kind of stuck up here in the middle of nowhere. In a snowstorm." She laughed nervously.

"Sam, it's not *The Shining*. Jack Nicholson isn't going to come in through the door and kill us." I turned to the windows. "Plus, it looks like the snow has stopped. For now."

"Come on, let's do something." I picked up my dishes and my mother's uneaten food and brought them over to the sink. I put the food in the portable composter that sat next to the sink, making soil that my mother swore was the reason her plants did so well. She bought it as a crowdfunding project and said it was her favourite appliance.

Sam brought her plate and cup over and agreed. "Let's go back to the greenhouse. I am mesmerized. Plus the plants look like they could use watering."

"There's a sprinkler set on a timer. I'll check it. Maybe it didn't get turned on because my parents hadn't expected to leave." We made our way to the greenhouse, and while Sam watered the plants, I found the sprinkler system control panel and turned it on to water once every forty-eight hours.

"I'll have to check with Mom about this timer, but for now it should be okay." We closed the heavy door and went into the living room. I stoked the fire and then we went to see what my mother was up to.

Chapter 52

The Will

I couldn't find her anywhere, and after I calmed my initial panic, I located her sitting in my father's desk chair, going through the filing cabinet.

She heard me enter but didn't turn around. "Your father was so organized. These files are dated, labelled and completely up to date. And his will is here."

"What does it say?" I walked over to the desk and perched on the corner closest to her.

"I don't know." She held up the yellow envelope and I could see that it had been sealed and taped.

"Are you going to open it?" I had to admit, I was very curious.

"Not right now. I need to get ahold of Robert, and I'm not sure how. His contract is here, but there's no cell phone listed because he lived on site." She closed the open drawer and turned around.

Suddenly I remembered those missed calls from the 787 number. I never bothered clearing my call logs. "I have his number. I'll call him. Do you want me to have him call you or should I ask him to fly back up here? We need to go to town, right?"

"Yes, Pia, please ask him to come back. For now. I need to make arrangements in town for the cremation." She stopped speaking and looked as if she would start to cry again.

I leaned in and hugged her. "It will be okay, Mom. Eventually."

"Oh honey, I know. I am so grateful he came back into our lives, but now I cannot imagine the rest of my life without him." She took my hand and laid it against her wet cheek.

My father was the only man she had ever really wanted. Over the many years in New York, she had dated plenty, but I knew without her having to tell me that she had given her heart away to my father a long time ago. She was a fierce, determined woman, and when I looked back on her life, I could now see that she had just been biding her time. Waiting and hoping.

"I will grab my phone and call Robert." I started towards the door.

"Cassiopeia, we can look at the will later." She held up the envelope and carried it with her, walking behind me.

Sam was in the kitchen speaking with Kash, and I went into the living room to stoke the fire and attempt to reach Robert.

I hit redial on the 787 number and he picked up after the first ring. "Pia?"

"Yes. Robert?"

"Yeah, it's me. What's going on?" He sounded out of breath and surprised to hear from me.

"Robert, Juris drowned, and I am here at Lost Lake."

"What?" he yelled into the phone.

I moved the blasting voice away from my ear. Then I returned it to my ear and I spoke slowly and articulated, "My father drowned three days ago. I am with my mother at the lodge."

"Jesus! Did you say he drowned? How?"

"In the lake, for chrissakes!" I was yelling back, angry with him, angry at life, and angry at myself for getting angry. I need to calm down.

"Holy shit. The lake was frozen. Solid. That doesn't make sense." He sounded perplexed.

"That may be true, but it happened."

"What are you going to do?"

"I don't know. But right now we need to fly to town to deal with some things. Where are you?"

"Shit, I'm in Fairbanks. Okay, I will head to the airport. I will be there this afternoon and can fly you to town in the morning. And Helena. My god, she must be freaking out."

"She is. I'm here with my friend Sam and we are doing our best to support her right now. See you soon, and Robert, thanks."

"No problem, Pia. Your father was a good man. I really respected him."

"Thank you for saying that. One more thing." I paused to phrase my question. "Why did you leave?"

"Let's talk when I get there, okay? I'll see you soon."

I had no choice. He obviously didn't want to talk over the phone. "Sure," I agreed reluctantly.

I rehashed the conversation over and over in my head and came to the conclusion that Robert wasn't hiding anything or hiding from us. He'd sounded legitimately shocked when I told him what had happened. I was not looking forward to seeing him and having the conversation I needed to have. I wanted to know about their supposed argument, and where Robert was when my father drowned.

I went to tell Sam about the conversation and then I planned to let my mother know that Robert was flying back and he would take us to town in the morning.

"So he will be back today?" Sam was sitting at the kitchen table drinking tea. She pointed to the full coffee maker and I poured myself a cup. My mother joined us and we sat silent, each lost in thought after I told them that Robert was shocked about what had happened and that he would be back later.

"Did he say anything else?" my mother asked me.

"No, I asked him why he left and he said we would talk later. A real man of mystery." I snorted.

"Pia, he is a good pilot. Your father wouldn't have hired him if he wasn't. I know you two had a breakup, but that doesn't have anything to do with what's going on here." She sipped her coffee and closed her eyes.

"We didn't have a break up, Mom. He lied to me and ghosted me."

She opened her eyes and looked as if she was going to roll them at me.

"There's a difference," I said stubbornly and knew it was a juvenile reaction.

Sam interjected. "We get it, Pia. He bruised your ego, but your mom is right. If your dad saw something in him, then let's just be adults and give him the benefit of the doubt."

They didn't get it. They did not understand what I barely wanted to acknowledge. I still loved him, and he was alive, and we could have maybe been together. But instead, he was living in Alaska and I was involved with someone new. It was my ego that was bruised, but also my heart.

"Do you want privacy?" Sam asked when my mother set the sealed envelope with my father's will in it down on the kitchen table.

"No, Sam, you stay. You are family." My mother used the letter opener she was carrying to slice through the seal and flip open the yellow manila envelope.

I felt as if I could hear my heart beat and could see my mother holding back tears as she started to read.

Sam reached for my hand as we listened.

When my mother finished, she put down the document and said, "Well, that's that."

Sam and I looked at each other and then at my mother, who was now the co-owner of the lodge and other properties my father had amassed.

She looked at me, the other co-owner, and asked, "Any questions?"

I was too stunned to think straight, but Sam asked, "This must be a fairly recent will?"

"Yes, it is dated this past November. I suppose Juris saw his lawyers when we came back from New York. The fact that he included a lump sum for Robert proves that it is new. I am glad he made provisions for all of the staff."

We sat in silence until my mother spoke. "Your father was very clear that he wanted to be cremated and his ashes scattered where we chose."

"I will see to that," Sam said. "The police officer gave me a number to call."

"Thank you Sam, for everything. We will arrange to get back to New York as soon as possible and then I will stay in Vieques until I figure things out.

"What about the lodge, Mom?"

She looked at me and replied, "I am going to ask Robert to stay on for now and oversee things."

"Robert?" I burst out. "He doesn't know anything about this business."

"Your father had great trust and faith in him. There is enough staff here, and if Robert agrees, that will be the best solution for us for now."

Sam and I went upstairs to make our separate calls. Sam said as she went into her room, "I guess you're stuck with Robert for a while longer, since he is going to be running your family business."

Chapter 53

The Truth Will Set You Free

Robert came back and agreed to run the lodge until spring. I asked him again why he'd left, and he claimed he had personal things to take care of. It sounded so sketchy and I sensed he was lying, but I let it drop. My priority was my mother and getting her back to New York.

He flew us to Fairbanks and we travelled via Los Angeles to Newark. Our flights were uneventful but exhausting. I did note that Sam had become a better traveller. She seemed to take takeoffs and landings in stride, paying more attention to my mother's needs than her own. She would probably call it deflection, but it worked.

Both Kash and Kevin met us at the airport, for which I was extremely grateful. I felt as if I was made of lead and wasn't much help to my mother.

I introduced her to Kevin and she gave me the look that meant she approved.

"Your mother seems to be holding up well," Kevin said to me as he put the suitcases in the trunk of his car.

"She is. She's a rock. Sam thinks she is in shock or denial, but I know my mother has processed and is coping. She will have a tough time ahead of her, because she has spent her entire life waiting for him, but Vieques will be good for her."

"How are you holding up?" He put his arms around me and I just sobbed.

"I'm heartbroken for her. Just heartbroken."

Sam called over to us, "Pia, let's talk tomorrow. Kash said his mother is at our place now, making food." She rolled her eyes as she got in their car.

I waved to her and blew a kiss and nodded.

"I wish I could have met your father," Kevin said, as he opened the passenger side door for me.

"I do too. You would have liked him. He was very charming and very interesting. Like you."

I looked up at him as I said this and was pleased to see him blush. He closed my door, went around to his side, and drove us expertly to the Upper West Side.

I went in with my mother, to my apartment, her apartment, our apartment. I wasn't even sure where to put her things.

"Mom, you take my room, I'll sleep on the sofa." I pointed for Kevin to put her bags in my room.

"No, Pia, absolutely not. I am not taking your bed."

"My office only has a sofa. Come on, you take the bedroom." Again I pointed for Kevin to move the bags, but my mother's stubbornness kicked in and she started towards the office.

It was a losing battle and we gave in.

Kevin asked, "Should I stay or go?"

My mother answered from the office, "You should stay."

We both laughed and I ordered takeout while he carried the suitcases into our rooms.

The apartment was quiet, and other than the occasional horn honking outside, the streets were silent. Kevin and I lay side by side in the dark bedroom. I was exhausted, maybe so exhausted that I couldn't sleep, and he was quiet, but I could tell he wasn't sleeping either.

"I feel as if I have been gone a month, but it's been less than a week," I whispered.

"I missed you. I should have gone with you." He reached for my hand in the dark.

"Kevin, thank you. I would have loved that, but let me tell you, Sam was fantastic. She really took charge. She was amazing."

"So the lodge is yours now?"

"Well, mine and my mother's, but to tell you the truth, I can't imagine ever going there again. Not without my father there." That was true. I especially was not going back there with Robert at the helm. My mother may have trusted him, but I did not.

"Pia, can I ask you something?" He sounded so serious, it frightened me a little bit. I hesitated and he quickly said, "Never mind. You are tired; it can wait."

I knew I would never go to sleep wondering what he needed to ask permission to ask. "No, go ahead and ask." I could not imagine what he would ask me. It was too soon for a marriage proposal…or was it?

"Pia, please don't be upset with what I am about to ask."

Oh boy, I thought, *this can't possibly be good.* I braced myself.

"Could you have saved him?"

"Saved who?" I blurted out.

"Your father. Saved your father."

"You mean, if I was there?" I asked him, sitting up now. No sleep for me tonight.

"No, Pia, I mean when you got there. I know there is something going on with you. I know I haven't brought it up, but I think about it a lot. I saw the woman on the pier, and I know that boy shot me. I felt the bullets rip into me. But it didn't happen, technically. I don't understand what happened, but I know what I saw. What I felt."

Oh my good god. How am I going to answer this? How can I make him forget? How come he saw these things and remembers?

"Kevin," I paused while I tried frantically to think of a response.

"Do you trust me, Pia?"

I didn't hesitate. "Yes, I do trust you." And it was true.

"Then trust me now and tell me what is going on with you."

And so I told him. I told him everything from the beginning at the bio bay and he let me speak, without interrupting me once. When I finished, he said simply, "Your father too?"

"Yes, he experienced the same from the bio bay before I was born. He found out when the boat he was on sank in Alaska."

"Drowning then and now. That's interesting."

I hadn't made that connection, but it was interesting. Water at every turn. "Water is usually involved," I said absently, thinking back to when time had first shifted for mc.

"And you couldn't save him again?" he asked kindly, not in a judgmental way.

I shook my head and then realized he could not see me in the dark. "No, I couldn't save him. I didn't see his body and I didn't feel the glow while I was there. It wasn't meant to be." I started to cry, unleashing all of my pent-up fears, impossibilities, and energy spent covering up what was happening to me. I cried on his shoulder and he gently rubbed my back.

When the tears stopped he said simply, "You are powerful, Pia. This is such a gift."

Kash's words exactly.

"How many have you saved?" His voice was barely a whisper.

I whispered back, "Twenty three so far."

He let out a long quiet whistle. "Wow."

We slept and then woke to the smell of coffee and the sound of the doorbell. Sam, Kash, Trez, and Juan had arrived.

Chapter 54

Pia's New Normal

I felt lighter. The burden of secrecy had been weighing me down, and now my closest friends and Kevin knowing the truth lightened my load immensely. I went back to work the day my mother left for Vieques, and although I grieved my father's death, I focused on work and my relationship.

Kevin and I were closer than I had ever been with anyone.

We talked about moving in together. I went to his young cousin's fourteenth birthday party and got to meet three of his first cousins and their families.

I now knew how Sam felt at her family gatherings, with food tables piled high, small kids racing around, the older people in the corner gossiping and pointing fingers at people, and the smokers in the bunch gathered near the doorways.

Kevin's niece Sophia had just gotten into the High School of Math, Science and Engineering, and Kevin teased her mercifully about being a brainiac.

"I bet you were a brainiac too, Pia. Am I right?" he teased me as his young cousins gathered around us.

"No, I was smart, but in school I was really into parkour."

"Wow, that's so cool," one of them said. "I always wanted to do parkour, like they do in the movies."

"Can you still do it?" another one asked me.

"You bet she can. She can do it all. But now I am taking my parkour lady home." We left amidst catcalls and more ribbing. It felt amazing to be accepted by this loud bunch of Irishmen and their wives and kids. His family had indeed circled their wagons around him and were his source of strength.

"I love them all," I gushed when we were back at his apartment.

"They are very special. I couldn't have gotten through everything without them. Sophia is my goddaughter. I call her my niece, but she is really my second cousin."

"I don't have any cousins." That fact was never more glaring to me than tonight.

"You do now. They're all yours too. They loved you, and I love you." He realized what he'd said and looked at me to gauge my reaction. It was not something that we said to each other since the first time he said it and I whispered it back.

I met his gaze and said in a serious voice, "I love you with all of my heart."

"So, what do you think? Move in with me or marry me or both?"

I was so stunned by the question I just stood there for a full minute. Finally I answered, "Both."

Chapter 55

Secrets

Our news was big, but we decided to keep it from my mother for the time being. My mother was adjusting to being back in Vieques; she had resigned from the newspaper and was considering writing short stories. She kept busy helping Carlos out with the book he was working on. Nona was busy as always with her art, and for now, I was able to focus on my work and my relationship.

Sam and I spoke daily, double dating on weekends, usually to eat at Pep's on Grand. Kash and Kevin hung out sometimes, and Kevin and I started to formulate plans to live together. We decided to rent out his place, because it was smaller than my West End apartment, and live in mine for now.

Sam was floored when I told her we were moving in together. We were having a late dinner at Teacher's while our men worked.

"You are certainly moving fast," she said in a teasing way.

"No faster than you and Kash. Engaged after two months," I replied.

"You know, I forgot about that. It seems like Kash and I have been together forever. I can't even believe it has been just over a year. I really feel like I knew him as a teenager and sometimes I can picture him as a little kid. Is that creepy?"

"It's only creepy if he is a kid and you're an adult!"

"No, I'm not a pervert. You know what I mean."

"I do. You guys were destined to meet and be together," I said seriously.

"Yoga is starting soon. You game?"

"Yes, I am definitely in need of some exercise. I was thinking about doing parkour again."

"Really?" Sam looked like she was about to laugh. "Isn't that a young person's game?" She arched her eyebrow.

"I'm not exactly a senior citizen," I replied, trying to keep a stern face and failing. I added, "Kevin's young cousins are interested in learning. The basics I think I can still handle."

"I'll never forget when I tried it. I hurt for days. Make sure you stretch first. But are you going to take the outdoor class with me? Randall's Island starts up soon."

"Saturdays?" I asked.

"Yes, noon class. Same teacher as before. She just opened an amazing studio in that gorgeous piano building in Astoria. But I love being outdoors and spring is springing now. I think I want a baby."

I spat out my drink. "What?" I gulped and wiped my face. "A baby?"

"I know it's not the time. My practice is new, my husband is in school, I have that task force every couple weeks, life is crazy expensive right now paying the two rents, but I kinda feel like this *is* the time."

"What does Kash think?"

"Oh, yeah, Kash. I haven't mentioned it to him yet." She looked up at me and quickly added, "But I will. I'm not going to do anything without him knowing."

"What brought this on? The last I heard from you, there was a three-year hold in place while you got your patient list up and he finished school."

"I admit, one of my patients got to me. She lost her only daughter in that school shooting, you remember, in Connecticut, and she talks about how she always begged her husband for more than one child. I shouldn't have told you that, but it kills me thinking about it."

"Yeah, I can't imagine her absolute sadness." My mind drifted to the little girl I'd saved right before Christmas.

Sam sighed and drank the last of her martini.

"On a different note, how is the task force?"

Sam seemed to be thinking hard about how to answer. "Good change of subject. At first I thought it was a waste of my time, but now I am not so sure. We have that principal, Vincent, I told you about and he has ideas. Good ideas."

"Is the mayor listening?"

"The problem is too many entities are involved. The board of ed, the mayor's office, the NYPD, the school faculties, the buildings department, and the unions."

"Wow, red tape and no inter-department communication."

"Exactly," Sam replied. "But we have some things planned. We're attempting to set up a hotline as well as an early warning system. To manage lockdowns and alerts. The best plan is to identify a potential shooter before there is a crisis, but once there is a crisis, we need to have plans in place. Teaching kids to dive under desks only does so much."

I never could have imagined having to teach small children how to dive for cover from gunshots. The new reality was that it was happening across the country. No school or school system was safe.

"Kevin doesn't talk about it?"

"We don't discuss his job. Like mine. We talk about family and our future and things like that."

"Your future?" she asked. "Your future together?"

"Yeah, sure. You know." I answered vaguely. But Sam didn't let it drop.

"Your future together? You discuss it?" She was like a dog with a bone.

"Of course we do. I told you we are moving in together."

"Pia, I have known you for a long time and I have never heard you discuss your future with anyone. How serious are these plans?"

"Serious."

She jumped up and pulled me up with her. "Serious, serious?"

"Yes," I replied and she whooped and signalled for two more martinis.

"Cheers, chica." She clinked her goblet with mine. "I was worried about you for a few years, and then the whole Robert fiasco had me doubly worried, and now a cop? You fell for a cop?" She didn't wait for an answer, just carried on. "Are you sure this is what you want? It won't be easy."

"He is everything I want." I said seriously.

She looked intently at me, studying my expression. "He proposed, didn't he? And you didn't tell me?" She swatted my arm.

"Jesus, Sam, are you psychic? We haven't told anyone because of my father. My mother should be the first to know and we can't tell her yet."

"Of course not. Oh my god, Pia, you and Kevin. Wolf eyes. Congratulations to you, my best friend in the world getting married. Wait, you said yes?"

"Of course I said yes. But we have no immediate plans."

CHAPTER 56

Double Date

Spring brought crocuses out of the ground and forsythia blooms along the streets, creating a feeling of hope in the city. The death rate dropped from the peak in the dreary, dark months of January and February. Overdoses outnumbered the amount of murders and gun fatalities combined by 400 percent. A horrible statistic that was ever increasing; however, my office was always busy seven days a week. There was no end to death, whether accidental or intentional.

My assistant Olivia had exams and announced she had decided to major in pathology. She was capable and enthusiastic and I was glad to have her on staff. She made things much easier for me. I was still getting used to meeting with families who had lost loved ones, but I was getting better at managing it.

Kevin met me for lunch a few days a week, and we attended Sophia's volleyball game at her school in Tribeca last night. Afterwards we met Sam and Kash at Pep's.

"What's new with you two?" Kash asked casually while clinking beers with Kevin.

Kevin looked like the cat that swallowed the canary when he replied, "Your buddy Trez is joining the Academy."

Kash almost choked on his beer.

"What? Trez?" We all looked at Kevin.

"Yes, he didn't tell you he applied?" Kevin asked Kash.

"Hell no, he didn't. Isn't he too old?"

"Well, he's older than most applicants, but I heard he got in. He should hear this week. Act surprised when he tells you." He nonchalantly lifted his glass.

I asked him, "How do you know, then?"

"He asked me for a recommendation."

We were all silent as we thought about that, and how small the world of 11 million people was in New York City.

"Wow," Sam said. "Trez, a cop. Yes, I can see that."

Kash said, "So can I. He always dreamt of being a cop; he had real cruiser envy."

Kevin's phone rang and he stood to answer it. We watched him walk out of the restaurant and stand on Grand Street, talking and gesturing into the phone.

He came back in and put cash down on the table. "Sorry, gotta go." He looked at me, "You okay to get home?"

Kash answered, "We'll drop her. Go, man, do what you gotta do."

I stood up and kissed him and he left.

Sam said, "You'll have to get used to that, I guess."

Yes, I will, I thought to myself.

Chapter 57

Second Time Around

The doorbell rang just as I zipped up my overnight bag. I looked at my phone and saw that it was Kevin, right on time, picking me up to drive to the conference, rescheduled from the fall.

"You set?" he asked into the phone.

"Yes, be right down."

He took my bag and put it in the backseat with his.

"Whose car is this?" I asked when I slid into the sexy two-door vehicle.

"Mine. The other one is my work car."

That made sense. The other sedan looked like a cop car, an undercover ghost car.

"This is sexy," I said as I ran my hand along the smooth leather of the console. I could see hand stitching and burled wood accents. "I have never owned a car," I said.

"You don't need one in the city," he replied, strong hands steady on the smallish steering wheel.

"Can you drive?" he asked.

"Oh yes, I can. Even manual. I drive in Puerto Rico."

"Oh wow, impressive. Not too many can drive a stick these days." He reached over and took my hand. "You nervous?"

"About what?"

"The conference. You're giving a presentation, aren't you?"

"Yes, just like you are. No, I'm not nervous. I know my stats and I know that education is important for everyone if we are ever going to stop this epidemic. The number of casualties last year alone was more than the previous five years." I took a deep breath and exhaled loudly.

"Calm down, relax. We have a two-hour drive to Albany."

Kevin had seventies rock playing quietly on the car speakers and I must have dozed, despite having slept a full eight hours the night before. He, on the other hand, had worked late and grabbed three hours' sleep at his apartment before picking me up.

"Wake up, Pia, we are almost there."

I roused and sat up straighter. I had an overwhelming sense of déjà vu when I looked at the town we were passing. Low brick buildings spread out next to empty fields that would be planted soon. Scattered shops, fast food restaurants, independent corner stores, empty lots, and an occasional gas station.

"Where are we?" I gulped a mouthful of water from my travel mug.

"Ravena. Just south of Albany. My cousin owns that pizza shop over there." He pointed to a small white building on the next corner. "Let's grab a bite and then head to the hotel."

The hotel was a motel right next to the Thruway, noisy but convenient. We were presenting at the convention centre. The decision was made to keep the conference out of schools, after what had almost happened at the last one. This conference was more low key, but some big names in law enforcement and education were presenting.

Kevin was giving a summation of the task force's ideas, and I was scheduled to do a two-hour presentation about the Office of the Coroner of New York City's statistics and numbers. Cut and dry. I was excited to meet with other professionals in my field. Although I had no new information or solutions, this was better than doing nothing and then complaining that nothing was being done. As Sam said, if we couldn't *get the guns*, we couldn't expect change. But I felt hopeful that this was a start.

We checked in and found we could walk to the convention centre, which was about an eighth of a mile down the road behind the motel. Kevin had his presentation at two o'clock, and we walked together, talking about everything except what had happened the last time he presented.

He went straight to the room he was assigned to and I mingled out in the lobby with the people gathered there. I recognized Mrs. Paisley, the principal from Binghamton, just as she came over to me.

She took my hand and greeted me like family. "Dr. Barnes, it is so good to see you again. I saw you are presenting."

I felt a warmth come over me and I relaxed. "You as well. How is he?" We both knew who I was talking about. The shooter.

"Well, he is an angry young man. He is being treated. His family has not been to see him once. They act like he doesn't exist. His younger brother told me that he is forbidden to even say his name at home. All traces of him in the home have been removed, like he never existed. So sad."

"It's interesting that they have disowned him. We still don't know what triggered him?"

"Not that I have heard, or will hear. He was always a loner, and angry. But to bring the guns to school with intent to shoot? That is so tragic. Luckily, thanks to your quick actions, averted."

She was referring to me telling her to lock the doors, having no idea that my reverse ripples that day saved not only Kevin, but also the students he had shot.

I ran into a couple of fellow pathologists with whom I attended school, and Kevin introduced me to countless colleagues and friends of his from the various crime labs and police departments.

The two days were a whirlwind of meetings, panels, and talks, and on the drive back to the city Sunday night, it was all I could do to keep my eyes open. I felt guilty for dozing off, as I had slept the entire ride up.

"Are you going to your place, or mine?" Kevin asked quietly.

I opened my eyes to see the familiar Bronx River Parkway signs and knew we were almost home.

"Let's go to yours. I have extra clothes in my bag for work tomorrow." I tried to keep my eyes open.

"Good answer," he said, smiling, and he added, "Next month, we will be going to *our* place." He made a smooth turn heading south.

"Yes," I murmured, "I can't wait." It would be wonderful to live full time with this amazing man.

Chapter 58

Full Circle

K evin's phone was ringing on the bedside table and I could hear the shower running.

"Kevin!" I yelled. "Your phone."

I sat up and saw that it was his personal phone, not his work one.

I reached over and hit accept. "Hello, it's Pia on Kevin's phone," I said, trying to sound awake.

I listened and heard nothing and then just a whisper: "Kevin, help."

I could see Kevin coming in from the bathroom, towel wrapped around his middle.

He looked at me holding his phone and a question appeared on his face.

I held the phone out to him, mouthing "I don't know?"

For a brief second it registered that it was a woman's voice on the other end of the line. *Please let him not be a cheater like Robert*, I silently prayed in the seconds he took to put the phone on speaker on the bed between us.

"Hello, who is this?"

"Uncle Kevin?" came the whispered answer.

"Sophia, is that you? What's wrong?"

We both simultaneously got off the bed. He dropped the towel and started dressing. I grabbed my bag and pulled out my work clothes.

"Sophia, is everything all right?"

Bang!

"Was that a gunshot?" I said to him and he nodded, fastening his holster and grabbing his jacket.

"Are you at school?" He was holding the phone while we gathered what we needed and were racing to the door.

Bang!

"Oh my god, Kevin. It's an active shooter."

We did not speak as we rode down the elevator and ran to his cruiser parked out front. He ripped the orange ticket off the windshield and shoved it into his pocket as he unlocked and we got in.

He was still holding the phone and handed it to me.

I said into it, "Hang in there, Sophia, we are coming." I held the phone and could see that it was still an active call. Wherever she was, she still had not disconnected. I thought that was a good sign.

"If something happens to her…" He let his sentence trail off, but I knew what he was thinking. His goddaughter. He loved her so much, and after losing his parents, he couldn't take any more loss.

I whispered into the phone, "Sophia, if you can hear me, tell us where you are." We were holding our breath waiting for her reply, but it never came. I called 911 from my cell, giving Kevin's badge number and details and, held on for dear life as he raced down the West Side Highway, light on the dash flashing and our hearts in our throats as he turned onto Chambers Street. He pulled up to the front of the school and we raced inside.

The school was eerily quiet. It was early. The school security person was not at the desk yet.

I tried again. "Sophia, we are in the school. Where are you?"

I didn't expect an answer, so when the phone crackled, I almost didn't make out what she said.

"Theatre?" I repeated.

"Got it. Follow me. He took off running down the long corridor and up the flight of steps.

The theatre was at the end of the second-floor hallway. The small glass window on the door was illuminated and partially open.

"Bitch!" came the voice from within.

Kevin shoved the door wide open and burst into the room.

I watched this thinking that he did not have his vest on. What if he was shot? Again. I looked down at my hands and saw the blue glow, meaning someone was already, or soon would be dead. Oh my god, what a nightmare. We were in bed asleep thirty minutes ago.

"You bitch! What did you do? Where are you?"

I could see a young man silhouetted in the dim light and he turned to the door, to Kevin. He lifted his gun to shoot and Sophia screamed. In a split second of the young man's hesitation, Kevin charged at him and knocked the gun out of his hands.

"Sophia, run, get out of here!" he yelled while he subdued the teenager.

"I can't. He shot Claire." She was sobbing as she stood.

"Where is Claire?" I asked her as I led her out into the hall.

Sophia slumped to the floor. I could hear sirens outside and knew the troops had arrived.

"On the stage. He shot her. He shot her." Tears flowed down her cheeks as she sobbed. I wiped them away and was going to dry my hands on my jacket but saw the blue glow on my fingers and left them wet.

"Stay here. The police are coming. I will check on Claire."

I walked past Kevin, who had the boy cuffed on the floor, and down to the stage, where Claire lay face down in a pool of blood. I knelt beside her, my heart racing, my forehead sweating, and my head clanging like a drum. The light was dim on the stage and the blue glow radiated out of me. I touched her hand, watching the bioluminescence work its magic. It would never stop feeling like magic.

A brief flash, and Kevin and I were outside the theatre, standing together, waiting. We both knew who was coming and what was going to happen. It was unspoken, but somehow, in some way, we both knew.

Sophia and Claire were on the stage practicing their lines. We could hear them laughing at their mistakes through the open door.

We looked down the hall at the teenager approaching us. He was muttering to himself and barely glanced our way.

There was no eye contact as he passed us, a bulky puffer jacket hiding what we knew he carried hidden, and then suddenly Kevin grabbed him from behind as the police came up the stairs.

There was a brief scuffle, but the kid was no match for Kevin's size and experience.

Kevin handed over the weapon and the teen was escorted out. He spoke with one of the officers as I waited by the doors.

Sophia and Claire came out of the theatre looking around at the activity and Sophia asked us, "Uncle Kevin and Pia, what are you both doing here?" She looked at the boy being led away and asked, "What's going on?"

"Everything is fine, Sophia. Go back in with your friend," Kevin said, as he put his hand gently on her shoulder.

She seemed uncertain and looked at me for confirmation. I nodded.

"It's all good." And I smiled. My hands were back to normal colour, my breathing had slowed, and I felt euphoric. I had no idea how Kevin was part of these reverse ripples with me.

Kevin looked over at me and agreed, "Yes, it is. It's all good."

Epilogue

"To Pia!"

"Happy Birthday!"

"Cheers, honey!" We all touched glasses of champagne and sparkling apple cider for the younger girls and me.

Trez, Juan, Carol, Olivia, Sophia, Claire, Kevin, Kash, Manny, Jessie, and Sam all gathered at our place, our West End Avenue apartment, for my birthday celebration. Kevin had other plans and presented me with a beautiful engagement ring made by none other than my grandmother, who was branching out to gemstone rings. *Luckily my birthstone is diamond*, I thought as I watched the light glimmer off the ring and reflect on the smiling faces gathered around.

"Congratulations are in order!" Kash refilled everyone's glasses.

I tapped my glass to get everyone's attention. "Thanks, everyone. This is a new chapter for us. For sure. I really appreciate you all being here with us tonight. I guess I am officially engaged." I held up my hand to clapping from everyone.

"You guess?" Kevin said and everyone laughed.

Kevin and I had spent Easter weekend in Vieques, which turned out to be magical. He secretly schemed with my grandmother to make the ring. My mother was healing and becoming active in horse rescue on the island. Something near and dear to everyone's heart.

Kevin and I went to the bio bay and experienced the magic together. He could not get over the experience, slipping into the water with me, mesmerized by the glow and splashing the surface with the kayak paddles to startle the fish below. We talked freely about my powers, or my gift as he called it, and his openness brought us even closer together.

My mother was planning to go back to Alaska for the summer, with Carlos and Nona, just to touch base there. We planned to keep the lodge for now, and surprisingly, Robert had risen to the occasion and was doing a very good job running things. He was there with his ex-wife Sofia, which was probably the reason he was cagey with me. I wished them happiness—well, mostly I did. I still stung a bit from his deception, but had moved on from holding a grudge.

"Kash and I have decided we are ready to try for a baby." Sam broke the silence in the room as we all ate paella and tostones, made by Kash's mother. Manny jumped up and proclaimed that he couldn't wait to be an uncle. There were more cheers and more toasts, and as I looked around this room, I knew I couldn't ask for or imagine better friends, a better life, or for anything to be different.

I had one last piece of news as the evening drew to a close, something that even my fiancé didn't know. I hoped after Sam's announcement that she would be okay with what I was about to say.

I stood up as the crowd was starting to gather their belongings to head to their respective homes. "We want to thank you all for coming. It has been a busy and sad few months for my family, but better times are coming. I really appreciate celebrating with you tonight. We have so much to be grateful for." I felt the overwhelming urge to cry.

Seeing this, Sam asked, "So, Pia. When's the wedding?"

I let silence fill the room. I looked over at Kevin and met his eye and answered, "I am thinking the wedding will be before our baby"—I put my hand on my stomach and looked over to Kevin's surprised face—"is born."

About the Author

M.E. Strautmanis, a native of Cape Breton, Nova Scotia, has come full circle—returning to the tranquil shores of the Bras d'Or Lakes after three decades immersed in the energy of New York City. She finds inspiration in the ebb and flow of water, a powerful and recurring theme in her *Reverse Ripples* series. Though Cape Breton is home, the spirit of New York City and the vibrant beauty of Vieques, Puerto Rico, continue to shape her storytelling.

A passionate writer and lifelong reader, M.E. is currently expanding her literary repertoire with a children's book while continuing her work in fiction. When she's not crafting stories, she's exploring the rugged beauty of Cape Breton Island, tending to her garden, and giving back to her community through volunteer work. She also channels her creativity into sea glass and driftwood art, transforming nature's remnants into meaningful, one-of-a-kind pieces.

Connect with M.E.

Website: mestrautmanis.com
TikTok: sohomama6
Instagram: sohomama6
Threads: sohomama6
Facebook: maryellen.strautmanis
LinkedIn: linkedin.com/in/maryellen-strautmanis-7b9a88104

Author's Note

Thank you so much for reading *Visible Ripples*, the second book in the *Reverse Ripples* series! I truly hope you enjoyed the journey as much as I loved writing it.

Your feedback means the world to me. If *Visible Ripples* resonated with you, the best way to share your thoughts is by leaving a review on Amazon, Indigo, Barnes & Noble, or Goodreads. Reviews help other readers discover the book, and I would be incredibly grateful for your support. Feel free to spread the word on social media too!

I would love for more readers to experience the magic of bioluminescence through this series. If you haven't yet witnessed it in person, I hope you get the chance someday. Having visited the Bioluminescent Bay in Vieques dozens of times, I'm still in awe every time. It's a sight that defies belief—yet it's absolutely real, and truly worth seeing.

Thank you again for being part of this adventure. Your support keeps the ripples going!

Warmest regards,
M.E.